THE GOMBEEN MAN

THE GOMBEEN MAN

A Novel

Randy Lee Eickhoff

Walker and Company
New York

Hollywood
3511 9807

All the characters and events portrayed in this work are fictitious
except those of historical note.

First published in the United States of America in 1992 by
Walker Publishing Company, Inc.

Published simultaneously in Canada by Thomas Allen & Son
Canada, Limited, Markham, Ontario.

Library of Congress Cataloging-in-Publication Data
Eickhoff, Randy Lee.
The Gombeen man / by Randy Lee Eickhoff.
p.   cm.
ISBN 0-8027-1197-9
I. Title.
PS3555.I23G66   1992
813'.54—dc20   91-35704
CIP

The verse on page 154 is from the old country ballad *"Spailpiin
Faanach"* ("The Roving Worker"), written by an anonymous poet in
perhaps the eighteenth century. The translation is the author's.

Printed in the United States of America

2   4   6   8   10   9   7   5   3   1

TO THE PARENTS:
RAYMOND AND ELDINA EICKHOFF
AND
STANLEY AND KATHRYN PEHRSON

Il n'y ague le dernier amour d'une femme qui satisfasse le premier d'un homme.
   —from *La Duchesse de Langeais,* by Honoré de Balzac

The ceremony of innocence is drowned.
   —from "The Second Coming," by William Butler Yeats

PART ONE

1979

The white-capped, gunmetal waves of the Irish Sea scudded toward the craggy English shore where I stood shivering in the bitter November wind. Behind me, the sexton's breath exploded from his lungs as he tried to force his spade through the half-frozen earth of the graveyard. The lead gray sky, swollen with promised snow, lent a certain quixotic irony to the season. Like most Irish poets, Conor Larkin had been touched with a black humor that accommodated a comedic love for the theatrical. He would have been delighted with the day.

The sexton cursed as his spade struck a stone and skewed in his hands. I turned away and gazed at the small church of St. Brigid-On-The-Hill at the far side of a graveyard filled with Celtic crosses and winged angels. The large granite blocks of the church hinted at its ancestry: a large, Norman pile erected on what had once been Druid land, now the repository for expatriate Irish bones. The church itself sat on the crown of a hill the locals in the distant town of Belmont called Cairn Cloumcille while the graveyard fell down the side of the hill seaward, offering the dead an eternal view west toward their homeland: Ireland.

I supposed at the time I should have appreciated the gesture made by some forgotten expatriate Irish priest who first began to lay out the graves in solemn rank and file reminiscent of an Irish Republican Army (IRA) brigade marching toward the tide, but I didn't. I felt uneasy, surrounded by a ghostly host of embittered warriors fallen short of their objective.

The sexton politely coughed. I turned back to him. He stood respectfully beside the freshly opened grave, scully cap in gnarled fingers, thick-nailed and dirt-encrusted. "Beg pa-don, sor," he said, the vowels broad in his Lancashire dialect. "I'm finished. If yer reddy, I'll fetch Father."

My eyes strayed to the black coffin resting at his feet, the deep lacquer gleaming coldly in the afternoon's gray light. I nodded and he hurried off. It would be a short service and with luck he would still be able to catch opening time at The Cock and Bull in town.

"Well," I said softly, mimicking the lilting rhythm of Conor's speech, " 'tis ourselves alone again, my friend."

A stone clicked against a stone. I turned to the sound. A man and a woman stood five feet away, their faces mirroring their apprehension of my greeting. She gave me a wan smile. The muscles knotted along my jaw. She wasn't unexpected, but I still felt the surprise in my stomach. For a moment, I thought she would even be receptive to an embrace, but I knew it would be the type of embrace exchanged by old friends and that I did not want.

"Hello, Con," she said, her words lilting softly like butterflies dancing among the flowers. Her triangular face had high cheekbones framed by soft, auburn hair falling in waves on either side of a patrician neck. Her almond-shaped eyes had a slight slant to them, the irises emerald green and vulnerable, nose long and thin above a full, generous mouth. Her skin was almost translucent. She had a peasant's body beneath the long raincoat she wore, wide-shouldered, pear-shaped breasts; the type of woman that men remember. A beryl ring flashed on her left hand as she clutched the collar of her coat tightly about her neck. Conor's wedding ring to her.

"Maeve," I managed, nodding.

Strangely, I felt more warmth toward the man. We had been through a lot together. Eight years ago, it had been Liam who had rescued me from an angry mob demonstrating against the return of internment in Northern Ireland, and Liam again who had taken me to my first Provisional IRA interview. We had formed a bond unique to those who hold secrets together. He held out his hand, and I shook it warmly.

"Liam. It's been a long time."

"That it has, Con," he said quietly. "Eight years since Castlereagh. Sorry it has to be like this." I nodded. Impulsively, I reached out and touched his lapels.

"This looks better than I remember last," I said. "Newspaper business must have picked up in Belfast."

He reddened slightly, but I could tell he was pleased. His suit had the subtle cut of Bond Street tailoring, shoes pigskin moccasins bearing a small silver *R* inlaid on the overstrap beneath the tassels, the famous mark of a Scottish *souter*. He smoothed his lapel and a heavy, twisted gold signet ring flashed from his left pinky. He wore a matching banded watch on his wrist, but I knew he hadn't earned his tie: the blue and maroon of the First Dragoons. "Well, I'm moving up in the world now and away from all that race. I'm beginning with TRANCO, now. You know: the Porcupine Banks Project?"

I nodded. The Porcupine Banks Project would pump new funds into an economically weakened Ireland and go a long way toward uniting the North and the Republic. A recent geologic survey had found geo-domes on the Porcupine Bank 120 miles off the coast of Galway that indicated the possibility of a new oil field with twice the capacity of the North Sea stations. The problem was that the Porcupine Bank lies at fourteen hundred–plus feet—twice the depth of the North Sea fields. Last I had heard, however, the project was still in the planning stages.

"I didn't think that was rolling," I said. He shook his head.

"It isn't really. But we are getting the groundwork done now. How have you been?"

"Oh, the usual," I said, shrugging my shoulders. I released his hand. "Trying to forget." I glanced involuntarily at Maeve. Color rode high in her cheeks. She ignored my words and stared at the coffin.

"I am sorry, Con," she said. "But he needed me more than you."

"Perhaps. Or is it that you needed him more?" I asked, my words tight in my throat.

She sighed and looked away from the coffin out to the sea. "If it's any consolation, we'd been separated for six months."

"It isn't. Had you realized the mistake you made?" The words were out before I could stop them. Liam shook his head admonishingly.

"Con," he said. "This isn't the time."

"You're right," I said. I tried to smile but failed. "I'm sorry, Maeve." Surprisingly, I was sorry. And, I suppose, a bit ashamed, too. Conor deserved more than the airing of petty grievances at his graveside. "Forgive me?"

She smiled and nodded. "Forgiven. You know, I really didn't expect to find you here. But that was rather silly of me, wasn't it? Always the faithful."

"*Sinn Fein*," I said. "That's me."

"But not them, I'm thinking," Drumm said. We looked at him. He nodded toward the gate of the cemetery. Two men dressed in twin trench coats with wide lapels and epaulets

[5]

stood patiently watching from beneath a twisted cypress tree. I felt a grim laughter bubbling up inside. If they were waiting for additional mourners, they were in for a long wait.

"Do they really think the boys would be so stupid as to show up today?" he asked, his voice dripping contempt. He shook his head. "And they wonder why they make no progress against the Provos."

"There is the question of his death," I said. "It's not everybody who gets gunned down on the Manchester docks." I looked at Maeve. "Do you have any idea what he was doing in Manchester?" She shook her head.

"I told you: we had been separated for the past six months." She shook her head and stared soberly at the coffin. "He had started working with the Provos again. Did you know that?"

I was surprised. Conor belonged to the days when the IRA had a romantic image before a splinter group calling itself "Provisional" made wholesale murder the standard for rebellion.

"Why?"

She shook her head. "I don't know. That's what caused the argument between us: his secrecy. I moved out, hoping that he would come to his senses." She looked up at the two men at the top of the hill. "'Why do you suppose they are here?"

"They probably remember the old days," I suggested. "Bad habits are hard to break." She nodded and stuffed her hands deep into the pockets of her coat.

"Yes. Well, things seem to stand still in bureaucracy," Liam interjected. "People don't want to change because that's the way they've always done things and to try something different is to appear original in a place where conformity is highly valued. Sorry." He gave a sheepish grin as Maeve and I stared at him. "I see them and I get irritated. Christ! Why can't they just let us bury him in peace?" Maeve placed a hand upon his arm, patting it.

"It's all right, Liam," she said. "We all have a sense of what is right."

"A rare commodity in this world," I murmured. They gave me a questioning look. "The IRA thinks it knows what is right; the Provos are positive they have the inside track on right; and the UDA believes they are the anointed ones." I nodded up the hill at the pair beneath the cypress tree. "And they're caught in the middle." I glanced back at the coffin. "You know, I think Conor would get quite a laugh out of that, don't you?"

Maeve gave me a startled look, then a slow smile spread over her face, and she nodded. "Yes, I think he would."

We stood alone for a long moment, each remembering the enigma of the man we had known as Conor Larkin—poet, professor, philosopher, and at one time the most feared IRA gunman in Ireland. And husband of the woman I loved.

A door slammed high up the hill, and I turned to watch the priest appear at the top of the graveyard followed by the sexton. He moved purposefully toward the grave with long, angry strides pushing tautly against the front of his cassock. He had not wanted Conor Larkin buried in his cemetery since there was some question as to just how good a Catholic Conor had been. But one does not argue with one's bishop. I could almost hear Conor chuckling with glee at the problems his death had caused, and my lips twitched in response to memory as I watched the priest's approach, chasuble and pallium fervently flapping behind him in the frigid wind. Anger made him look ludicrous, a grandiloquent grandee from a play by Cosgrove. I turned away lest he see my smile and forced myself to look somberly at the grave, wishing Conor in death could have had the recognition due a poet-soldier, as had Byron. But, then, Conor had written a refutation of that:

> Do not steal my death, Passer-by!
> Do not stop to grieve
> over these dusty bones.
> Leave me to the dry,
> musty memories of those not alive
> who live their lives
> by making my life theirs
> like the devil a mortgaged soul.
> Only the death matters
> and should be forgotten,
> not carved into stone

for pigeons to rest upon.
Do not steal my death, Passer-by!

"*In nomine Patris, et Filii, et Spiritus sancti* . . ." the priest intoned, and a last thought flickered through my mind: the death did matter if it was "unnatural," and Conor's death was most definitely unnatural. He had recognized that many people did not want the "troubles" to end, for they had developed, over the years, a type of siege mentality. They took a false comfort in the familiarity of a constant state of war in Northern Ireland. Conor refused to continue as part of such a world and retired to Trinity College in Dublin to teach and bury himself in the academic world.

"*Dominus vobiscum*," the priest intoned, shaking me from my memory. For a brief moment, the response echoed as part of the *Rituale Romanum* used in exorcisms, but the absurdity of the thought quickly disappeared with his abrupt "Amen." He curtly nodded at Maeve and Liam, glanced at me, and without another word, marched back up the hill.

"Well, that was quick," Liam murmured. Maeve bent and picked up a couple of frozen clods and dropped them on the coffin lid. The sound echoed hollowly, and I shivered. She turned without a word and began walking up the hill to the gate. Liam fell in beside her. The men at the top of the graveyard were gone. Apparently, they had realized the futility of watching us and sacrificed diligence for comfort. I collected a handful of frozen earth to drop on Conor's coffin, then hurried after Liam and Maeve. I caught them at the gate.

"Thank you for coming, Con," Maeve said, holding out her hand. I automatically took it, my fingers closing familiarly over it like a long-lost friend. Suddenly, I knew I didn't want the day to end with a casual good-bye at the cemetery gate.

"How about a drink?" I suggested. "After all, wouldn't it be appropriate in the circumstances?" I looked at Liam. He grinned.

"And therapeutic," he added. We looked at Maeve. She nodded and gestured down the lane to where a black Volvo stood parked on the road leading past the church.

"We can drive," she said. "That is, if you don't mind?" I shook my head.

"I was going to have to call for a lift," I said. "Frankly, I'd just as soon not go back in the church office."

"I know what you mean," Liam said. " 'Tis not the good graces he was offering us, and that's for sure."

"Have you heard anything from Richard O'Bannion?" I asked as we fell in beside each other. He shrugged his shoulders.

"A bit now and then, but Dickie's got nothing to say. Surely, you didn't expect him here," he said, throwing a backward glance at the cemetery.

"No, but I did expect some sort of gesture."

"Like what?"

"I don't know. Flowers, maybe. Or a message of some sort. Lesser men than Conor have been sent off with remembrances of some sort."

"Conor was from the old school," Maeve said. "He wasn't, you remember, all that popular with the new people."

We reached the Volvo, and Liam opened the door and swung it wide. "There you are. I know just the place in Belmont not far from Back High Street."

As we drove away from the church, I watched Maeve as she automatically touched her hair, adjusting it with familiar gestures, and remembered. . . .

PART TWO

1971

ONE

Belfast in 1971 was a whore suffering from a severe beating by a terrible brute: gaping holes where teeth had been, nose smeared across scarred cheeks, smelling of filth and fear and vomit. At night along the Shankill Road, down Northumberland Street and the Falls Road, rats, some of them the size of small terriers, appeared in packs. Their red eyes glowed as they watched the prostitutes work the streets. The people said they could tell when the British or "the Prods" were going to raid a sector because the rats would suddenly disappear. No one knew why this happened. Maybe they could hear the approaching lorries and Saracens long before they appeared. The mountebanks among the residents suggested a kinship between the rats and Prods and composed little ditties that earned them pints in their locals.

I was in Belfast to do a series of stories on the conflict between the Protestants and Catholics. Friends had suggested that in Dublin I visit Conor Larkin, who might provide me with a "contact" in Belfast to help me with the more difficult "unofficial" perspectives. Conor had sent me to Maeve Nolan, a strong civil rights worker who had bitterly opposed the Protestant prejudice against Catholic workers at several rallies across Ulster over the past couple of years. As we walked toward Stormont, I was vividly conscious of her striding by my side, wearing a rose heather sweater and matching skirt, her face glowing with health. I made a mental note to send Conor a bottle of Black Bush in thanks.

The Northern Ireland Parliament building at Stormont in East Belfast reminded me of the United States Capitol in Washington, D.C., minus its dome. It sat on the far side of a large green reached by a wide, concrete walk flanked by lovely old coach lanterns. Behind the Parliament stretched a windbreak of trees, while in front a steadily growing crowd milled like an angry sea of molten lava ready to erupt at any moment.

A few scully-capped, tweed-coated men standing together in casual groups respectfully nodded to Maeve Nolan and watched me with veiled eyes as I trailed her through the crowd. Others, wearing slouch hats and jean or khaki jackets adorned with patches and mock medals identifying them as members of the Ulster Defense Association, glared murderously at us as we passed. Maeve ignored their muttered comments of "quean" and "chip-py" and "slut." None, however, attempted to stop us. I was surprised; the manner of the mob was growing mean and ugly as random insults, borderline provocations, began to fly back and forth from one group to the other.

When we reached the steps leading up to the portico, we had to step carefully over thick cables housing leads to lights, microphones, and cameras belonging to Telefis Eireann, the southern Ireland television network. Maeve did not stop but simply stepped over the cables and climbed to the entrance.

"Whatever the announcement, it must be important," I puffed beside her, feeling the climb in the backs of my calves.

She grinned bleakly. "So it would seem."

The guard near the door closely checked my credentials, then consulted a master list. Satisfied, he returned my credentials and motioned me to enter. His eyes flicked over Maeve.

"She's with me," I said quickly.

"That may be. But 'tis here she'll wait for you," he answered, the vowels long in his Ulster brogue.

"Now, see here," I began, feeling my temper beginning to fray at his officiousness. "I'm a representative of the *Times*, here from the United States at Mr. Faulkner's express invitation."

He shrugged. "Sorry. But there's no mention of any but yourself on the roster."

"What seems to be the problem?" a richly polished voice asked from behind me. I turned. The speaker was tall and broad-shouldered. His deep chest was covered in black below a clerical collar. He wore a well-tailored, dark, Aran Island suit. His well-oiled hair, liberally silver-streaked, swept back from a high forehead away from heavy-lidded, saurian eyes. Thick, brutal lips clenched tightly together as he stared disapprovingly at my companion. I could picture the face with little trouble above the white robes of the Grand Dragon of the Ku Klux Klan. Undaunted, Maeve nodded slightly in greeting.

"Hello, Ian," she said coolly, her eyes narrowing fractionally. "Are you here for the blessing?"

He smiled thinly. "How are you, Maeve?" His voice had a singsong lilt obviously homiletically practiced to make it appealing to the listener. But he had not quite been able to rid it of a slight nasal twang that made it grate on the ears.

"Fine, till now," she answered. "It must be the fish. Perhaps a bit tainted."

A dull, burnished red began to glow across his wide jowls. His eyes shrewdly sized me up. "Will you be introducing us, Maeve?" he asked. He stretched out thick fingers toward me, the nails manicured and polished.

"This is the Reverend Ian Paisley," she said to me. I remembered the name from talks with Conor Larkin and considered him with interest. At first glance, he didn't seem to be the rabble-rousing bigot and segregationist Conor had painted.

"Con Edwards. *Times*," I said.

"Ah, yes. I've read some of your work. A bit inflammatory in some cases."

I shrugged. "When the occasion warrants."

He raised his eyes to include the guard. "Are you having difficulties?"

"Only himself is cleared, Reverend," the guard said before I could speak. He defensively held the master list out for Paisley's perusal.

Paisley said smoothly, "I am sure that Miss Nolan may be added to the list with little difficulty."

"Well," the guard said doubtfully.

"You may mark Maeve Nolan as one of my party," he said, his voice tightening just enough to provide a warning.

"Yes, sir," the guard said. He took a pen from an inside pocket of his coat and carefully printed her name in tiny block letters next to Paisley's.

[15]

"Good. Then it's settled. There, you see. No harm done, Mr. Edwards." He beamed at me.

"Thank you," I murmured uncertainly. I had a funny feeling I was supposed to remember his generosity against the day when a like favor would be asked. Or, more likely, demanded. Paisley did not strike me as the type to ask. His followers had made him powerful enough that even Faulkner had to be tactfully cautious about excluding him from his office.

"Think nothing of it," he said magnanimously. He nodded at both of us and stepped through the door. His entourage immediately followed, carefully flanking him. Their suits were not cut right to completely hide noticeable bulges beneath their arms.

"And that," Maeve said with distaste, "is Black Ian himself. What did you think of him?"

"I wouldn't buy a used car from him," I said. She turned puzzled eyes toward me. "Forget it," I said. "An American aphorism. Let's go in."

We followed the trail of television coils, twisting like giant anacondas, to Brian Faulkner's office, dark-paneled with an oversized desk. In front of the desk stood a podium festooned with microphones. Paisley and his followers disappeared through a closed door at the far end of the room. The *sanctum sanctorum*, I thought, and glanced around. Several reporters waited patiently in a corner of the room. A small, wiry man stood on the outskirts of the group furiously scribbling in a notebook. His blue pin-striped suit was stained, red and blue tie askew and splattered with fallen ash. An unruly mop of dark-red hair fell over his forehead to bushy black eyebrows. His cheeks were heavily scarred from an adolescent bout with acne. Maeve smiled and tugged my arm in his direction.

"Liam," she said as we approached. His head snapped up, blue eyes wary, then his face broke into a wide smile.

"Maeve, my beauty," he said with delight. "How did you ever slip past the *gombeen* men for this affair?" He jammed the notepad into a side pocket of his sport jacket and, in the same motion, removed a cigarette and thrust it into his mouth, lighting it.

"I didn't. It was himself that did it." She nodded at the closed door.

"Black Ian?" He shook his head and mockingly crossed himself. "There must be witchcraft afoot if the two of you are doing each other favors. Have you been in communion with Dame Alice?" He looked pointedly at me.

"Actually, it was Mr. Edwards here who managed the favor. Con Edwards, Liam Drumm."

"Of the *Times*?" he asked, stretching forth his hand. I nodded. "I'm impressed, Maeve. And how, if one were to ask, did you manage to make the acquaintance of so estimable a reporter as Con Edwards?"

"From friends in the south," she said vaguely. Liam's eyes darted quickly back and forth between us. He exhaled cigarette smoke in rapid little puffs.

"Mutual friends?" he asked guardedly, his voice noticeably lower. She didn't answer but gave him a lazy look from beneath half-lidded eyes, knowing and aloof.

"Oh, come on, Maeve!" he exclaimed, exasperation tingeing his words. "You can't leave it like that!" She looked away. I spoke hastily to dispel the awkward silence beginning to build.

"Actually, I was drawn to her mind."

"What?" Brief confusion flitted across his face. "What was that?"

"Her mind," I said patiently. "Far across a crowded room, I saw her legs and was immediately drawn to her mind."

"Don't be paying any attention to him," she said to Liam, archly looking at me. " 'Tis just his silly American humor."

"I see," he slowly answered, but it was apparent that he did not. His face cleared suddenly and the excitement returned to his eyes. "Conor Larkin! You saw Conor Larkin at Trinity College in Dublin!"

"Liam has a very romantic nature," Maeve said, giving Drumm a warning look. "He likes to think the worst of everybody. Of course, he's often right. But at times, his enthusiasm gets the better of his good intentions."

Liam sheepishly ducked his head. "Sorry, Maeve," he mumbled.

"But," she continued, a fond note creeping into her voice,

"for all of that, his exuberance makes him the only Catholic reporter on the *Belfast Telegraph*. And not a bad one at that."

"Sure, and isn't that because I'm telling my editors I'm an agnostic?" he said. He rubbed his nose with the palm of his hand, ignoring the ash that dribbled off the end of his cigarette and fell on his tie. "Anyway, what brings you to Belfast, Mr. Edwards? Last I heard, you were in Germany."

"Con," I said automatically. "And you're right. I'm sort of filling in at the moment. My editor got word about a major announcement to be made and here I am."

The door to the room off the one in which we waited opened and Brian Faulkner, followed by Paisley and his cohorts, strode purposefully to the podium. Their visages were grim as if they had been arguing about what was forthcoming. They were followed by the new British General Commanding in Northern Ireland, General Sir Harry Tuzo. The reporters immediately broke away from their cliques and fanned out around the front of the podium. Liam nudged me with his elbow and nodded toward Paisley.

"Looks like ol' Black Ian is none too pleased with what is about to transpire. His face looks like a little nudge would cause it to rain."

"Why do you suppose that is?" I whispered back.

"He's used to being obeyed, that one," Liam said softly. "The Prods go to their churches and pray to the peacemaker to give them the strength to destroy the Catholics; profoundly sacerdotal, that, a communion with bullets as the host and Molotov cocktails for the wine, and being the pious God-fearing, commandment-keeping churchman that he is, Black Ian makes sure they keep the sacraments. I would bet that he tried to push Faulkner into something more advantageous for the Prods and Faulkner balked."

"Why did he think he could influence Faulkner? He's just a minister, isn't he?"

Liam flashed a wry look at me to see if I was joking. "*I dtír na ndall is rí fear na leathshúile.*"

"Translate. I'm just a poor, ignorant American, remember? Bring me to light," I demanded.

"In the land of the blind the one-eyed man is king," he said. "Old Irish proverb."

"Which means?"

"Black Ian just found out he's only a pawn who thought himself king and doesn't like it. Shh. Faulkner's about to speak."

I turned my attention to the podium. Faulkner, his square jaw grimly clenched, silver hair flashing under the sudden glare of quartz lights, faced the phalanx of reporters. He cleared his throat and without preamble swung into his announcement.

"It is with deep regret that I spoke this morning with British Prime Minister Edward Heath in regards to the recent destruction of the *Daily Mirror* printing plant at Dunmurry. This, coupled with the February death of Gunnar Robert Curtis and the recent murders of other soldiers attributed to and claimed by a terrorist organization calling itself the Irish Republican Army (Provisional), forced me to recommend that the time for the return of internment has arrived. He acquiesced."

A buzz like the droning of a large bee went rapidly around the room, accompanied by sudden demands from reporters present that Faulkner give them his attention. He ignored them and raised his hand for silence.

"I wish to further emphasize that this policy is not directed to any one faction but will be enforced regardless of religious affiliation." He turned his head to stare bleakly at Paisley, whose saurian eyes glittered unflinchingly into Faulkner's own. "Whether," he continued, his voice a fine rasp of steel on steel, "the detainee is Catholic or Protestant." He turned back to the television cameras. "I will be visiting London in two weeks to meet with Mr. Heath. At that time, I fully expect the policy of internment will be in force. In the meantime, I am reviving the Special Powers Act to give General Tuzo the means necessary to halt the bloodshed upon our streets and establish peace. I deeply regret the necessity of this action, but steps must be taken to ensure the peace and safety of our citizens. Thank you."

Abruptly, he stepped back from the podium, ignoring the shouts of the reporters and, followed by his entourage, marched quickly from the room. I became aware of a dull booming sound as of distant surf crashing on the shore and suddenly realized the sound was coming from the crowd outside.

"That does it," Liam said from beside me. "He has just

given the Prods and the British carte blanche to do whatever the hell they want to control the Catholics."

"But he said 'regardless of religious affiliation,' " I protested. Liam smiled humorlessly.

"And which sect will be doing the enforcing?" he asked softly. "There will be no Protestant interned, for all of their terrorism will be done in the name of the Special Powers Act. They will be the enforcers and thus immune. Here, what's he up to now?"

I swiveled my attention back to the podium. Paisley had seized one of the microphones from its stand and was shouting into it. "Internment for Catholic *and* Protestant! Again, we are being forced to suffer for being the victims of Catholic aggression! Hear me, Protestants! This is yet another attempt being made to subjugate our authority in our homeland!" he cried. "Traitors in our government are coddling papal insurgents by stooping to their demands for equality. I say there can be no equality for terrorists! No equality! What we have seen here today brings us down yet another step closer to their barbaric papal order!"

"Oh, sweet mother of Christ protect us," Liam muttered. "He's off again. Let's get out of here while we can."

"What?" I said indignantly. "This is news, this—"

"—is the time to run," he finished, interrupting me in the process. He seized one arm and Maeve the other. Together, they determinedly hauled me protesting from the room. The last I saw of Paisley that day he had drawn himself up to his full six foot four inches and, lips drawn in a wolfish snarl, was punctuating his words with a clenched fist raised high overhead.

"I say unto you there will be many martyrs to our holy cause, but we will never surrender! Never!" We hurried down the long hall to the portico of Stormont with Paisley's voice echoing around us: "Destroy, O Lord, and divide their tongues: for I have seen violence and strife in the city. . . ."

We broke into the sunlight and paused on the steps outside. Police armed with spring-loaded batons had formed a cordon around the bottom of the steps. An angry mob surged back and forth, reluctant to crash against the plastic shields of the Spartans in front. Vaguely, I wondered how the police could have formed so swiftly dressed in riot gear. We slipped down the side of the steps and ducked under the arms of the police. Immediately, we were swallowed up by the mob. Maeve and Liam stepped tightly next to me, each gripping an arm against the press of the mob. I smelled onions, stale porter and stronger drink, and the sweaty mixture of anger and fear. Suddenly, a large, florid-faced man recognized Maeve and pushed his way toward us.

"Catholic whore! To me! To me!" He tried to grab her. I caught a flash of white thigh as she pulled up her skirt and rammed a knee hard into his crotch. Blood rushed from his face, leaving it pasty white. A flood of vomit spewed from his mouth. She hastily stepped back away from it and instantly disappeared behind a phalanx of men who angrily stepped around her to face her attacker.

"Maeve!" I yelled. I tried to force my way to her, but Liam tugged me in the opposite direction.

"This way!" he shouted.

"But Maeve—"

"She'll be all right! Come on! We've got to get away!"

Reluctantly, I allowed myself to be led across the green. Behind us, we could hear the roar of riot steadily building and then the sudden shrill blast of whistles.

"Oh, shit!" Liam moaned and scampered up a flight of stairs, across a street, then down a narrow, twisting alley. We ran for a couple of blocks, then stopped, leaning against a wall for breath.

"Close. Close," he muttered, fumbling for a cigarette in his pocket. A spurt of flame flashed in the dim light of the alley. I choked as a cloud of blue-gray smoke rolled around my head. "Sorry," he said and stepped across the alley away from me.

"What about the story?" I asked, trying to bring my panting under control.

"Plenty of time for filing when things calm down," he said, exhaling. "In the meantime, it's here and there we'll be flitting to get a few quotes from the right people. The television and radio boy-os will have the initial story, of course, as well you know. Beautiful spontaneity, wouldn't you say?"

"Yes. Almost as if it had been planned," I said, the pounding in my temples beginning to ease.

"My thoughts exactly," he said, flashing a grin. "The question is, however, whose plan was it: Faulkner's or Paisley's?"

"The question," I said, "is what has happened to Maeve?"

He gave a low, grim chuckle and drew deeply upon his cigarette. "I wouldn't be worrying myself about that one," he said somberly. "If anything, I'd worry about the poor bastard who gets in her way. Besides, she had plenty of friends there. They'll be looking after her."

"I don't know," I said doubtfully.

He shrugged. "What else can you do? Be reasonable, man." He waved the cigarette in my direction. "Give yourself a good look. What do you know about Belfast? Who would you believe? Who would believe you?"

He was right. There was absolutely nothing I could do except make a fool of myself by rushing back into the melee. I was a middle-aged man with the beginnings of a paunch, the occasional twinges in the joints that foreshadow the coming retardation of flexibility, and a marked tendency toward dyspnea. I had no business trying to behave like a hero. I tried to comfort myself by remembering what I had once written: There is no honor in war, only the posturing of fools.

TWO

A brimstone yellow fog crept after us as we detoured around Divis Street barricades and down the Shankill Road. Protestant patrols led by the Royal Ulster Constabulary (RUC) swaggering around Clonard forced us into back alleys. We cut through Beechmount to the Falls Road and followed its twistings and turnings into the southeastern section of Whiterock.

We passed small groups of women hurrying home, their arms laden with tea, cheese, apples, bread, and packets of dried soup. Some nodded at us, others ignored us as they struggled past on swollen feet, their shoulders hunched beneath their burdens, faces grim. None stopped.

"Christ," he said, a touch of awe in his voice. "You'd think they were getting ready for bloody Christmas."

We pulled up short in front of what appeared to be a railroad flat. Liam glanced around then rang the bell, paused, then rapidly twisted the bell twice more: long, short, short, the international *D*. The door opened to reveal a thin, short, elderly lady neatly dressed in black. She wore a crisp, starched, white apron over the front of her dress. Lively gray eyes sparkled behind wire-rimmed glasses beneath a crown of white hair pulled back into a tight bun. She reminded me of a character by Norman Rockwell.

"Yes?" she asked, then recognized Liam. "Well, isn't this nice that you'd be coming to see me on such a day as this." She beamed, dimples glowing from the happiness of her smile. "Step in! Step in! And bring your friend. I'll be puttin' on the kettle."

"Hello, Gran," Liam said, and bent to kiss her cheek. "Is himself at home?"

"Now, now, now. There'll be none of that," she scolded. She caught him by the arm and with surprising strength drew him in through the door. I stepped after, barely missing being nipped by the door closing hard behind me. I turned back to Liam and Gran and found myself staring into the large bore of a Webley.

"Have you lost the little sense you were born with, Liam Drumm, bringing a stranger here on this of all days without so much as a by-your-leave?" She formed an incongruous picture with the large revolver clutched in her tiny fist. From barrel end to grip it was as long as her forearm, and the steadiness with which she gripped it, the hammer lying back at full-cock, made it no laughing matter.

"Easy, now," Liam said. "It couldn't be helped. He's all right. 'Tis the one Maeve Nolan was with; the one sent by Conor Larkin."

She blinked for a minute, shrewdly eyeing me, then reluctantly lowered the Webley, carefully easing down the hammer. "Humph," she snorted, placing the pistol beneath a towel on a small table beside the door. "If that's by way of making things right, you've got another think coming." She eyed me closely again. "But being as how *he* sent you and remembering what *he* was once, I'll be asking what's to be done with you. Wait here," she commanded, and disappeared through a curtained doorway at the far end of the room.

"Whew," I said, unable to keep the surprise out of my voice. "Your grandmother must have been a terror in her younger days."

"That one's no relation of mine," Liam said firmly. "She's the devil's own. She fought with Eamon de Valera at Boland's Mill during the 1916 Easter Rising in Dublin. Over the years, she's said to have killed thirty-two men and hasn't there been a price on her head since '23 when she assassinated Declan Brandon, the Cork MP? Although not many remember that now." He smiled faintly at my look of incredulity. "She would have killed you. Make no mistake about that. Your body would probably have been found in Ballymacarret, if ever it was. Like you said, she was a terror. Now she guards Seamus MacCauley and Richard O'Bannion—the Provo leaders in this area."

"Should you be telling me all this?" I asked nervously. "I mean, I appreciate your help and all, but I don't exactly feel welcome. Know what I mean?"

He shrugged. "I'm thinking you'll be all right." His face brightened. "And, if you're not, well then, no sense worrying about it, is there? We're here now. Besides, you've got Conor Larkin's blessing, haven't you?"

"Maybe it would be better if we made this meeting some other time? After they've had a chance to verify us? That blessing seems less impressive to her than you."

"Well, it's a strange situation," he said, ignoring my urgings. He stepped to the edge of a window beside the door and eased back the starched balbriggan curtains for a look into the street. It seemed strangely silent, ominously silent. Liam, however, appeared almost relaxed, as if he had brought home a friend for dinner. "Conor is one of the very few who was allowed to retire from the IRA. That's practically unheard of. Some of the old ones are a bit affronted that anyone should be given that privilege. But Conor was there when the Provisional IRA was formed. You see, he did not agree with the bombing campaign, and the new leaders discreetly allowed him to retire to Dublin for past services to the cause. In actuality," he continued wryly, letting the curtain drop and turning to face me, "I think they were a bit afraid the cost to remove him, ah, permanently, would have been prohibitive. That one bears a charmed life. Some claim it's because he made a pact with the devil. He may well have."

The curtains shielding the doorway parted, and Gran returned followed by a thin, ascetic youth clad in black leather. He carried frost with him. I shivered.

"Tomas," Liam said politely, respect obvious in his voice. The youth nodded and stood in front of me, black eyes probing mine.

" 'Tis unhappy he is with you," Gran said admonishingly to Liam. "But he'll see you." She looked at me. "And him," she grudgingly added.

The youth touched my arms and gestured upward. I raised my hands shoulder level. Rapidly, but thoroughly, he patted me down, then stepped back and to his right. The position allowed him to keep both Liam and me in view. I revised my initial thought: he had far too much experience to be that young. Years, I thought, mean nothing in Northern Ireland.

"Thanks, Gran," Liam said. He darted a quick, nervous look at the youth before stepping through the curtains. I hesitated. The youth smiled faintly and stepped to the curtains, politely parting them for me.

"Thank you," I murmured, and entered a small hallway. Two doors on my right were shut along with one on my left. At the far end, a door stood slightly ajar. The youth gently nudged me toward the opened door. Dutifully, I stepped inside. The room, obviously once a master bedroom but now an operations room, had two cots pushed against the far wall beneath a large street map of the city of Belfast. A 7.62 mm FN FAL and a 5.56 mm Armalite AR leaned in a corner in the middle of a jumbled pile of cartridge clips. A desk stood in the center of the room with four chairs arranged in front. Behind the desk sat a burly man, square-jawed and unsmiling, a shock of black hair falling over a wide forehead. He held a cigarette in his left hand. His right casually rested on the desk near a .38 caliber Smith & Wesson. Behind him stood a tall man of medium build, thinning blond hair combed straight back from a high widow's peak, blue eyes curiously regarding us. Liam stood against the wall to my left beneath a Sacred Heart.

"My name is Seamus MacCauley," the man at the desk said. He jabbed a thumb over his shoulder. "This is Richard O'Bannion. Behind you, Tomas Fallon. Mr. Drumm speaks highly of you and suggests that we cooperate with you in light of what happened earlier at Stormont. Won't you have a seat?" He courteously gestured at the chairs across from him.

"When you're fighting the type of war we are, friendly press is of the utmost importance. Otherwise, the world only hears the 'official' news from the Brits and the Prods courtesy of Black Ian."

I said slowly, "And that's why I am here? To give you favorable press?"

"We hope so. At least, we will have made the effort. It's my understanding that is one of the reasons you came to Belfast: to interview the Provos."

"You are in charge? Of the area, I mean."

"I am the assistant chief of staff to Sean MacStiofain and Mr. O'Bannion is the Third Brigade commander directly in charge of Belfast operations of the Provisionals," he emphasized, watching to see if I was aware of the animus between the two. "Mr. Drumm is our press liaison."

"And Mr. Fallon?" I asked, turning my head to look at him. He smiled faintly.

"Is Mr. Fallon," MacCauley said pointedly. "Now, as we are a bit pressed for time, I hope you forgive my rudeness when I ask if we may get on with your interview?"

"In a moment," I said, leaning forward, my hands upon my knees. "Would you by any chance know what happened to my friend, Maeve Nolan?" MacCauley looked at O'Bannion, who shook his head and directed his attention to Liam. O'Bannion spoke for the first time since I had entered the room.

"Liam? Now then, what is this about Maeve? 'Tis sure I am that you never mentioned her before," he said, his voice soft with lilting vowels. Liam shrugged.

"We were separated in the crowd. She'll be all right. Plenty of the lads were on-and-about."

O'Bannion's brow furrowed. "I would have thought such a cavalier attitude to be far from you, Liam. Considering you and she and all before."

Liam's eyes flashed with anger, then he forced a lopsided grin that did not reach his eyes. "And what, Major O'Bannion, would you be after meaning by that?"

"Ah, and you know my meaning, Liam Drumm," he said calmly, ignoring the undercurrent of threat in Liam's voice. "Was it not with Maeve you were doing your walking and your talking two years ago before she went south to university? And was it not with Maeve that you posted the first banns before she broke them?"

"You son of a bitch," Liam said thickly. His body hunched forward away from the wall, hands curled into fists.

"Perhaps," O'Bannion said mildly. "But why did you not look to Maeve? This is unlike you, Liam, trusting others in the case of Maeve." I began to feel uneasy. Liam gave a short, ugly bark of laughter, then leaned back against the wall.

[27]

"That which once we were is over. What made you think it was still on between us?"

O'Bannion cast a swift glance at me as if suddenly aware of my presence. *"Is milis fíon, ach is searbh a íoc,"* he said. Liam laughed, but there was still no humor in the sound.

"An old aphorism, my friend, and not entirely appropriate." He drew a deep breath and moved away from the wall and crossed to O'Bannion. He placed his hands upon O'Bannion's shoulders. "It is over, I tell you," he said softly, earnestly. "We were simply not meant to be."

O'Bannion looked in his eyes for a long moment, then nodded. "Aye, that I can see. But, still, I would think that you would watch for her. We cannot depend on others, you know."

"Dickie," MacCauley said quietly, impatience putting a snap to his words, "let it drop."

O'Bannion looked at his superior, amazed that he might have done something remiss. "Aye." He looked apologetically at Liam. "Sorry, Liam. I did not mean to be suggesting anything."

Liam smiled and clapped him on the shoulder in forced esprit de corps. "Think nothing of it. 'Tis nothing but a sign of the times."

"Aye. That it is," O'Bannion said. He looked toward MacCauley, then nodded at me and left the room. MacCauley's eyes lingered for a moment on Liam, then switched to me.

"Forgive the housecleaning and dirty laundry, Mr. Edwards. Rest assured that we will find out what happened to Maeve. She is—and this is off-the-record, as your president is prone to say—most valuable to us. While we are waiting, however, I would suggest that you put forward the questions you mean to ask."

Obediently, I opened my notebook. A vague uneasiness crept over me as I tried to collect my thoughts. The more we talked, the more I began to develop a sense of *fait accompli* concerning the unrest in Northern Ireland. War was inevitable, needing only a formal declaration to be so labeled. But that, I also knew, was an impossibility. Britain would never declare war, for that would officially acknowledge the Provisionals as a revolutionary government instead of terrorists; an acknowledgment that would never be forthcoming, as witnessed by the recent internment decision. The play had been running for almost sixty years. MacCauley was a victim of events set in motion long before his birth, and such events dictated their own endings.

We were halfway through the interview when O'Bannion burst through the door. "Prods!" he snapped. His eyes blazed with fury. "The RUC! Saracens are coming down the street now!" MacCauley leaped to his feet, his chair slamming back against the wall.

"How?" he asked. He didn't wait for an answer but began throwing papers into a rucksack. Fallon, followed by three nervous youths, slipped through the door behind O'Bannion. They quickly gathered the guns and ammunition and disappeared back through the door. "This was supposed to be a safe house!" O'Bannion shook his head.

"I don't know!" he said. "Hurry! We have to get out of here!" MacCauley glanced at Drumm.

"We'll be better off splitting up. Liam, you come with me. Dickie, you take Mr. Edwards. That way at least one of us should get away. We'll meet at Magheny in three days. Take care, Dickie! We can't afford to lose you!"

"You take care," O'Bannion said. "Better me lost than you. Now, off with you!" MacCauley gave me a brief nod, touched O'Bannion on the arm, then disappeared through the door. O'Bannion jerked his head toward the door. "Unless you want to meet some Prods who'd be more than happy to meet you, we'd best be off." I flinched as a loud, furious banging of metal against stone suddenly erupted from the street. O'Bannion grimly smiled. "Hear that? The ladies are warning us. 'Tis ash can lids they're banging on the stones."

"Where to?" I asked. He shrugged.

"Wherever we can. A man can't be planning something like this. We'll go where they're not." He led the way out of the room and down the narrow hall to the back door. We stepped out into the darkness of an alley. The banging had become a din. I smelled boiled cabbage and flinched as O'Bannion gripped my elbow, pulling me deeper into the alley between high brick walls. "Come on, man! Time's a-wasting!" he said cheerfully.

We broke into a jog, zigzagging our way through a maze of

brick and garbage and broken glass. At last we slowed, pausing to catch our breath in a small courtyard. Dull thumps sounded nearby, followed by the harsh chatter of automatic weapons fire. The slate roofs above us glowed red from fires burning. At the far side of the courtyard, a small band of young boys and girls mixed gasoline and liquid detergent together in empty wine bottles to set homemade napalm. A young girl, her tongue clenched in concentration between her teeth, soberly stuffed cotton wadding into the necks of the bottles. I pulled my camera from my pocket and prepared to take their picture. One of the kids spied me, frowned, and shouted threateningly, "Take my foackin' picture and I'll slit yer foackin' throat!" He thrust his jaw out and stood defiantly in front of the others, hands on hips, eyes hostile. O'Bannion chuckled beside me.

"Well, now," he said. "What have we here?" The boy insolently spat on the ground between us.

"None of yer foackin' business," he said. "Go yer way."

"And that we will," O'Bannion said, lips twitching hard to keep from smiling. "But there's a bit of a problem here. A few of the Prods are after keeping us from our homes. You wouldn't be having a place we could lay up for a bit, would you? Just an hour or two?"

The girl's eyes suddenly widened as she recognized O'Bannion. The bottle slipped from her fingers as she gestured at us. " 'Tis himself," she said in awe. "The Major. He came to my house once with my da."

O'Bannion grinned. "And, how are you, little Jen? And your da?" She stood respectfully.

"He's in Long Kesh. His fourteenth month now. They caught him with a pistol."

"It's sorry I am to hear that," O'Bannion said. The explosions seemed closer. He grinned and jerked his thumb over his shoulder. "Do you think you could be helping us?"

The boy puffed up with importance, glancing over to see if the others were duly impressed with his new standing as an equal among two bandits.

"Follow me," he said offhandedly, voice trembling with excitement. "Me da's away, but me mam will be after making you welcome for an hour or two." He led the way down a narrow alley shooting off at an angle from a corner of the courtyard. We came to a street crossing and paused while he casually stepped out to scout the street. Satisfied, he motioned to us, and we hurried across the street to a narrow row house.

We stepped into a small hallway. A stained curtain covered a doorway to our left, stairs running up to the second floor. He led us through the curtained doorway and a sitting room filled with tattered furniture to the kitchen. A woman stood over the stove frying bacon. The entire house smelled of old bacon fat. She looked up at us with dead eyes, a nervous twitch starting in her cheek.

"I've brought two home," the boy said. " 'Tis them the Prods are looking for." She turned from the stove, covering her cheek with a thin, blue-veined hand. Her slip hung two inches beneath the hem of her dress. Bony elbows showed through holes in the sleeves of her sweater. O'Bannion smiled and stepped toward her.

"We're sorry to be bothering you."

She said in a reedy voice, "Would you be having a cup of tae?"

O'Bannion nodded. "That would be nice. My American friend here looks fair famished." The boy looked wonderingly at me.

"American?"

"Con Edwards," I answered. "Of the *Times*." A disgusted look spread over the boy's face.

"Another bleedin' newsman. Sure, and what lies will yuh be printin' about us, now?"

"Danny, mind your manners," the woman said. "Welcome," she said to me. "And I'll be apologizing for his bad manners. I'm sorry my husband isn't home to be wishing you welcome. Will you have a cup of tae and a bite?"

"Tea would be fine," I said. "Is your husband at work?"

"He's in Long Kesh," the boy said, pride showing in his voice. "With Jen's da. They say he had a pistol, too."

"Did he?" O'Bannion asked. The boy shook his head.

"Nah. The Prods picked him up on the way home from the pub an' he flattened one of 'em, being in his cups the way he were."

"Hush," the woman said, and motioned us to the table. " 'Tis not seemly to be telling others our problems."

[31]

"No," I said, taking a chair at the table. "I'm interested. What do you think of the day's happenings?" She shrugged her shoulders, turning to the stove to put the kettle on.

"They tell us this is a religious war, the priests and the reverends and such, but it's not. Me sister and two cousins are married to Prods, and when we first moved here from Donegal our neighbors around us were all Protestants. Many's the fine picnic we had together in Devil's Glen. But when the troubles started three, four years ago, all the Protestants living around here left. That was right after the Derry riots. I remember watching them on the telly. Back then, we had three council members from this area, but when the Protestants left, that Ian Paisley seen us as a threat to the Prod vote. The Loyalists like to keep their own communities together for the voting. So, when the Protestants moved out and Paisley saw how the voting was going to go in this area, he had the district lines redrawn to take two of the representatives away from us."

"Black bastard," the boy said from between gritted teeth.

"Hush," his mother automatically said. "It's politics, all politics." She brought the tea to the table and poured. "It's about them, too," she continued, nodding at the boy. "There ain't nothin' here for them anymore 'cept the streets."

"What about school?" I asked. She shook her head and went back to the stove, taking the bacon from the pan and putting it on newspaper to drain.

"Can't afford to send them to school. And that's Paisley, too. He knows what education will do for the Catholics, so the money for public education goes to the districts where the Prods live."

"What work do you do?" I asked the boy. He gave me a mystified look.

"You just plain stoopid, mister, or you workin' at it?" He shook his head in disgust. I started to reply, but O'Bannion nudged me under the table.

"We'd better go," he said. He drained his cup and looked at the boy. "Would you be doing us a favor and check the street?" The boy shrugged and left. "We'll be thanking you for the tea, and hopin' your man's soon at home."

"You are welcome to what we have," she said, her face

puzzled at O'Bannion's sudden urgency. "But there's surely no rush?"

O'Bannion smiled. "Sure, and wouldn't we like to remain with you for a while. But, as your husband's in prison, 'tis here they'll come looking for us. You know that."

She nodded, half-convinced by his explanation. "There is that," she admitted. "But, there are others they'll check first."

"And that," O'Bannion said easily, "is what will give us a head start. Now, when they ask, tell them you saw us, but didn't let us in."

"I'll tell them nothing," she said, pride creeping into her voice.

"All clear," the boy called from the doorway. O'Bannion nodded and clasped her hand.

"You're a good woman," he said. She blushed. He jerked his head at me, and I followed him to the street. We hurried away from the house, moving through a labyrinth that left me directionless.

"What was the hurry?" I puffed, trying to keep up with him.

"The boy," he said. "And your questions of a fool."

"Fool?"

"Where there's no work for men what work would there be for a boy?"

"Stealing?" I asked.

"What else?"

"Does his mother know?"

"Of course she does. But the family honor is saved as long as no one brings it to her attention. You know what I'm saying?" he asked.

"Yes, I do," I said. "And I'm sorry."

"No harm for now," he said. We rounded a corner and nearly walked into a patrol coming toward us a half-block down the street.

"Halt!" someone shouted. Heads swiveled toward us as the patrol spread out, seeking shelter in doorways. My stomach lurched. Suddenly, I had to go to the bathroom.

"Jaysus!" groaned O'Bannion. He seized my arm, propelling me across the street toward the dark mouth of an alley.

"Halt!" the voice rang out again. O'Bannion began to swear

under his breath. "Halt! Or we'll fire!" A bullet sang by over-head, ricocheting off the building in front of us. Another bullet fired as a warning struck the building. Then we were in the alley, running fast into its black depths.

"Down!" O'Bannion shouted, flinging me to the side. I found myself falling into a stairwell. I landed painfully on an ash can. The breath wooshed from my lungs as O'Bannion crashed on top of me. A fusillade of bullets buzzed angrily past where we had been into the depths of the alley.

"Now!" O'Bannion breathed fiercely, and yanked me to my feet. Clumsily, I followed him from the stairwell and staggered after him as he ran deeper into the alley. We ran for what seemed hours through the twisting, turning streets. My lungs burned, and I knew I would have blisters on the heels of both feet if I ever lived long enough to remove my shoes.

At last, we pulled up beside an old building. We leaned against a doorway, gasping for breath. "Tell me," I whispered hoarsely. "How did you know they wouldn't shoot again into the alley?"

"Because they were moving into it," he said. "They wouldn't risk hitting their own men."

"But how did you *know* that?" I persisted.

"They always work that way. It's part of their manual."

"Somehow, that doesn't reassure me. Someone may not have read the manual." I took a deep breath and forced myself to slowly let it out. I couldn't remember when last I had been so tired. "I'm afraid I won't last much longer."

"You won't have to," he said. "We're here."

"Where?" I asked.

"Marta's house," he said. He reached for the door and gave a coded knock: three, two, two, one. The top half of the door cautiously opened. A beam of light shined through onto the bricks. A cat's eyes glowed greenly for a brief moment, then disappeared.

"Who's there?" a woman's voice suspiciously demanded.

"Ourselves alone," O'Bannion answered. The door imme-diately swung open to reveal a young woman dressed in a thin wrapper, her body clearly outlined by the light behind her. A mass of reddish gold curls framed a pixieish face with wide, china blue eyes green-lined above a full, generous mouth. She gave us a quick glance, then swung open the lower half of the door.

"Quick!" she said. O'Bannion shoved me inside. I winced as he stepped on my heels. The door slammed to behind us. I blinked in the dim light, staring in disbelief at three scantily clad women sitting on an old couch covered in a garish floral pattern. "Well, Dickie O'Bannion, and if I wasn't wondering when you'd be around!" the woman saucily said behind me. The women on the couch giggled. One, a young, black-eyed woman with long, black hair falling in waves over her large, creamy bosom, slowly crossed her legs, giving me a calculating smile.

"I'll be damned!" I blurted in surprise. "A whorehouse!" The black-haired woman giggled as the others laughed.

"Home," O'Bannion sighed from beside me. The black-haired woman grinned widely and rose, slowly crossing to me.

THREE

I woke to the sound of church bells, feeling a moment's panic as I failed to recognize my hotel room in the gray light filtering through a small window in the opposite wall. Then I felt the warmth of a body next to mine and remembered the black-haired woman from the night before. I rolled to my side to face her. A sudden shock jolted me awake as I realized the tousled black mane belonged to a young girl not yet out of her teens. I sat up abruptly, wildly looking around the room for my clothes. My movement woke her. She stretched, lazily grinning.

"Good morning," she said. She yawned, then smacked her lips. A smear of bright-red lipstick lay across one cheek. Mascara smudges made her eyes look hollow. "Is it a fine day?"

"Uh, I think so," I answered, primly pushing the bedclothes between us. She looked at me quizzically.

"What's wrong?" she asked. She sat up, using both hands to smooth back her hair. The bedclothes fell to her waist, baring her breasts. I swallowed, looking away. She laughed lowly. "A morning touch of the guilts?"

"You could say that," I said. My clothes were piled in a jumbled heap over a ladder-back chair at the end of the room. A basin and ewer stood on top of a cracked, unvarnished bureau next to the bed. A black, filmy teddy carelessly draped over the foot of the iron bedstead.

"And why would the friend of O'Bannion be feeling that way?" she teased.

"Well." Suddenly I felt embarrassed. "You're a lot younger in the morning light. Last night, you were . . . different."

"And this morning you feel like a dirty old man. Is that it?" she asked dryly. Her eyes mocked me.

"Something like that," I admitted, feeling flustered by her directness. "I'm old enough to be your father. How old are you?"

"Does it matter?" She leaned back against her pillow, leaving her breasts bare.

"I guess not. Look, do you have to do that?"

"Seventeen," she said, but she pulled the covers up over her breasts and primly folded her arms across them. "Why should it bother you?"

"Good God!" I took a deep breath and danced across the room, using the chair as a shield. I began to dress hurriedly. "I'm sorry!"

"For what?" she asked, puzzlement showing in her eyes. "For enjoying yourself?" I paused in my dressing to stare at her. Her eyes met mine with a frankness beyond her years.

"How long have you been doing this?" I asked.

"Three years," she said. Stunned, I moved around the chair, dropping onto it.

"Why?" I blurted. The smile slipped from her face. A hurt look replaced the hardness, making her vulnerable.

"It's a living," she defensively said.

"What about your parents? How . . ." I stopped myself as I became aware of the hypocritical foolishness I was about to spout. "I'm sorry. I didn't mean to sound so . . . so self-righteous."

"That's all right," she said. A smile fluttered around the corners of her lips. She primly tucked the bedclothes around her. "In a way, it's rather nice. Usually the men don't say anything in the morning. Just grate their teeth an' grab their pants an' leave. Rather refreshin' to have a man polite enough to stick around a bit."

"Okay," I said. "What's your name?"

The smile appeared fully. "Deirdre. Like of the sorrows. You know Yeats?" I nodded. "We studied him in school." She sighed longingly. "I wish I could have stayed in school."

"Why didn't you?" I curiously asked. The moment of embarrassment had passed. I was beginning to think of her and not myself.

"Da was killed by the Prods down at the docks five years ago. Mum turned tricks to feed us—I have two sisters and a brother, all younger—until a drunk used a razor on her one night." She shrugged. "That left me to go behind the half-door. Things could have been worse." She fell silent for a minute, then gave a thin, resigned laugh. "One of my girlfriends was killed in a Clonard Street bombing and another died when the boys bombed a Prod club with nail bombs. My cousin was pinned under the rubble of a pub bombed by some of Paisley's boys and today tosses down Valium like Dolly Mixtures. At least here I'm fairly safe at night."

"What about clerking?"

"I'm Catholic," she simply said. "At least I'm working."

"And the future? What are you going to do when you get older?" She shrugged.

"Die, I suppose. Not much else left to do," she said matter-of-factly without a trace of irony or pity. "Would you like to see my collection?" she suddenly asked, her eyes shining with excitement. Heedless of her nudity, she bounded out of bed, awkward like a colt, to the bureau.

"Uh, collection?" I asked. "What collection?"

"These," she said, darting back beneath the covers. She held an old cigar box in her hand. She opened the box and carefully pulled out pieces of colored glass wrapped in cotton balls. "This," she said, holding up a shard of green-stained glass, "came from The Eagle and the Lion, a pub the Provos bombed. This," a piece of yellow glass like topaz, "came from The Knight and Cross, a pub the Prods bombed in retaliation." Slowly, she lined up the pieces on the blanket between us like potsherd from a dead Sumerian civilization, each a remnant, a memory of something past. At the bottom of the box, covered with three layers of cotton, rested her pride: a wide, flawless, blue eye against a red-stained background on a three-by-four piece of glass from the Clonard Monastery, the result of concussion from a nearby blast that shattered the stained-glass-window representation of the Virgin Mary.

"When I was a little girl I used to sneak into the grounds and sit for hours just looking at her," she said in a little voice wistful with memory. "She was so beautiful. I used to make wishes on her eyes. When the sun struck them just right, they looked like sapphires. So beautiful." A lone tear trickled down her cheek. I put my arm around her, and she snuggled deep into my shoulder, crying softly for lost youth.

Maeve found O'Bannion and me later that afternoon in the coffee shop. We were celebrating the finish of the story on the MacCauley interview, and the story of the children I had just dispatched to the *Times* from the cable office. The first story had almost written itself. The other story, "In Darkest Belfast: The Lost Generation," had been much harder to write. I was rather proud of my effort. O'Bannion had been equally pleased.

"Well," Maeve said as she approached my chair. "I am happy to see that you came to no harm in the donnybrook."

O'Bannion waved his knife at her before slathering a gob of butter across half a heated roll. " 'Lo, Maeve," he mumbled around the other half of the roll.

I hastily rose and pulled back a chair for her to join me. She wore a green linen skirt that matched the emerald of her eyes and a white blouse heavy with fine lace around the high neck and cuffs of her sleeves. Her cheeks glowed from the bite of the cold outside.

"Did you have any trouble? I tried to get back to you, but Liam said you'd be all right and I believed him and . . ." I caught myself as an impish smile curved her lips.

"Sorry," I said sheepishly. "I didn't mean to babble."

"It's touching. I appreciate it." She reached over the table to pat my hand. "Did you get your story?"

"Uh, yes. Two." I felt a weakness I hadn't felt for a long time. I quickly reached for an amenity to cover my confusion. "Would you care for some coffee? A roll?" She eyed the rapidly diminishing plate of rolls in front of O'Bannion and shook her head.

"Coffee would be fine," she said and brought her hands together to form a cup for her chin, elbows resting on the table. I signaled to a waiter for another cup. Her eyes considered me for a moment, then she spoke. "So. Now what will be next for you?"

"Maybe I'll try to get an interview with Ian Paisley," I said. "Do you think I'll have much trouble getting to see him?"

O'Bannion made a rude noise and again waved his knife back and forth, this time like a saber.

"That one." He swallowed and growled. "His name is in our book with a pen ready to scratch a line through it, too. But the time is na' right for all of that. I was telling himself just the other day how easy it would be to catch a few of the boys and nip him away from his bully-boys." He sighed and carefully selected another roll from the plate. It didn't take long; only three were left. "And wasn't Seamus telling me, too, that the time for the bastard's deliverance was coming but not yet. Too many people still think him St. Patrick's brother." He shook his head disgustedly. "Aye. He'll talk, that one. Right, Maeve? Talk the blasted ear off a cow, he will."

She made a face and waited until the waiter had left, then reached for the pot of coffee on the table, pouring while she spoke.

"If it's Paisley you're after you'll find him a willing participant. He likes to see his name in print. And he doesn't care if the publicity is good or bad. Either way, he'll use his pulpit to make himself appear either saint or martyr. Rest assured of that, Con, before you interview him. It's a no-win proposition because he owns the final forum, and the thin-lipped, pinched, Protestant women who flock to his services, temperance leaders all, have the same thought of him that the eighteenth-century Catholic housewife had of her priest."

"What's that?" I asked as she took a sip of her coffee and added a dollop of cream to correct the taste.

"Now, Maeve," O'Bannion said, rolling his eyes nervously. He glanced around to see if we were being overheard. "Be kind, be kind. No sense bringing the eye down upon us."

"What's this?" she said. "Dickie the bandit going religious?" He flushed and wiped a big hand across his mouth to clean it of crumbs.

"It's not like that," he said defensively. "But why tempt what you don't have to? Play the dozens, girl, play the dozens!"

"The priest," I prodded.

"The priest," she explained, "held awesome power, for he had priestly infallibility and ownership of the Irish man or woman's private thoughts. His house was held in the same high esteem as an ancient chieftain's castle: remote, aloof, and autocratic, yet comforting at the same time, for it also gave the man or woman a visible conduit to the mystical beyond he couldn't understand but had to accept on faith alone. And the bloody priests were quick to realize the power they held over their people. The Protestant landlords quickly realized that they had to keep peace with the priests if they wanted to keep control of the Catholics who outnumbered them four or five to one." She paused to take another sip of coffee. "Yes, the Church had much to do with the plight of the Irishman, for it always reaped its fields with British scythes. Paisley goes on about the inadequacies of the British—most notably the prime minister—but when a suggestion ripples its way across the waters that perhaps it would be best if Britain would pull out of Northern Ireland and let the Irish solve their own problems, he is quick to offer fiery rhetoric damning the officials for abandoning their people in their 'darkest hour.' "

"Sounds a bit inconsistent," I said. She shook her head in disagreement.

"No. He's very consistent: pro-Paisley, anti–everyone else. But since he's a minister, a man of God, he can get away with pretty much anything he wishes. He's the biggest liability toward a peaceful negotiation there is, for the minute peace is attained, he'll lose the power he enjoys."

"Who's that?" We jumped. I looked up. Liam stood over us, a tiny grin working across his thin lips. "Sorry. Mind if I join you?"

"Not at all," I said, waving at the last chair at our table. "I'll get another cup." I looked for a waiter.

"My guess is you've been talking about Black Ian," he said, grinning across at Maeve. "You've got that delightful blush across your cheeks you get whenever his name's mentioned. Mornin', Dickie."

"Ah, Liam! We could have used you last night, they being so many and . . ." He gulped, his face turning dull red. He gave me a quick look, then picked up his cup and made a great show of blowing on its contents. My ears burned. Maeve gave a quiet chuckle.

Liam grinned. "Marta's house. I never thought to look there for you. Oh, don't bother," he said, as the waiter made to place a cup and saucer in front of him. "I really do not have any time for coffee. Nor do you if you wish to go with me," he added, including both of us in his glance.

"Where to?" I asked, my journalistic senses beginning to prickle. O'Bannion replaced his cup on its saucer and sat back in his chair, regarding Liam.

"Londonderry." He smiled bleakly at Maeve. "It looks like 1969 all over again." O'Bannion muttered an imprecation under his voice. Maeve's face whitened.

"Dear God," she whispered. "What have you heard?"

He shrugged. "Not much. Just that several people were killed and some streets fired early this morning."

"*Whole* streets?" I asked incredulously.

"We don't do things halfway here," he said acidly. "Well, what do you say, my beauty? Yes or no. I'm off."

"We'll go part of the way," Maeve said. She glanced at me; I nodded. "Dickie? Any ideas about MacCauley?"

"A few," he said, furrowing his brow in thought. "But you know how it is when they break a safe house. You gotta find the toe to get the foot. We'll try O'Rourke at The Wild Duck," he said, mentioning a pub below Shankill. She nodded.

"At least, we may get an idea as to what we can expect in the next couple of days if this is a planned rising. Are you about ready?" she impatiently asked.

"Yes," I said, hurriedly swallowing the last of my coffee. "What's first?"

"I think we'll try Paisley first before the others get to him—if they already haven't—and before he gets a chance to prepare something. Sometimes spontaneity causes him a bit of a problem. Then we'll try The Wild Duck." She glanced at O'Bannion questioningly. He nodded. "Sound right to you? You're the journalist, after all."

"But a fledgling when it comes to this. Let's give your plan a try," I answered. She grinned.

"Right. I'll get the car and meet you outside," Liam said, rising. Maeve handed him the keys to the Morris Minor, and he hurried away.

We paused at the door only long enough for me to pay the check, Maeve drumming her hands impatiently on the door.

Outside, the early rain I encountered during my trip to the cable office had eased, leaving the street damp and rainbowed with oil streaks. The virga aftermath left me clammy and chilled. Maeve glanced up and down the street, frowning. "Now where do you suppose Liam went?" she asked, puzzled.

A figure wearing a tan trench coat approached us from the recessed doorway of a men's clothier. Two soldiers followed him, each holding Liam by an arm. O'Bannion warily stepped away from us, his eyes darting left and right down the street. Three other soldiers approached from opposite points of the compass. A Saracen armored personnel carrier moved slowly up the street toward us, a squad of soldiers forming out behind it. Alarmed, I tried to shout a warning, but a thick arm clad in mufti wrapped around my throat simultaneous with a savage jab just beneath my ribs, leaving me gasping with pain.

"Well, now, me Catholic bastard, you'll be a nice boy-o, wot?" hissed a voice in my ear accompanied by several sharp digs beneath my ribs with what I now recognized as a pistol.

O'Bannion leaped forward to help, but three soldiers immediately seized him and carried him kicking and fighting to the ground. He shouted in rage and sunk his teeth into the ear of one of the soldiers. The soldier screamed and reeled away, clutching the side of his head where O'Bannion's teeth had torn away a piece of his ear. One of the soldiers holding Liam let go of his arm and pulled a flat blackjack from a side pocket. He stepped forward and rapped O'Bannion behind the ear. He slumped forward, dazed from the blow.

Liam spun and threw a knee into the groin of the soldier holding his arm. The soldier whimpered and fell to the ground. Liam dashed into an alley across the street. Two soldiers started to give chase but pulled up short as the man from the doorway stopped them.

"Let him go," he ordered. "He's nobody." Obediently, they returned to his side.

Maeve's eyes widened in amazement, then tightened with anger. Her nostrils flared indignantly. She opened her mouth to speak, only to close it with an almost audible snap as the man from the doorway stepped in front of her and flashed his credentials.

"Miss Maeve Nolan?" He didn't wait for an acknowledgment; just flipped the small leather case shut and replaced it in the pocket of his trench coat and nodded toward the Saracen.

"Get in. You're under arrest by the authority established through the investiture of the Special Powers Act."

"Well," she said softly. "It did not take you bastards long, now, did it?" Her face hardened. "Under what charge? That much, you *spalpeen*, must be told despite the Special Powers. What charge?"

"Suspicion of terrorism," he said curtly. "And that, *madame*, is all you have to be told. Take her," he said to the others who had, by this time, encircled us. He nodded at me. "Him, too."

"Need any help, Billy?" one said to the fellow behind me.

"No," he said. He cuffed me alongside the head with the hand bearing the pistol. My head rang. " 'E's a good lad. You won't be causin' me any problems, will you, mate?" He cuffed me across the head again and, although I knew the time-worked cliché well, the words spilled from my lips without thinking.

"The hell I won't," I said hotly. "I'm an American citizen employed by the *Times*, and when I get done with you, you rednecked peckerwood, you'll be willing to kiss my ass in Trafalgar Square at high noon by way of apology."

"Ooo. 'E's a right proper one, ain't he, Billy? Give us a crack at 'im?"

"Right. 'Ere yuh go. Catch." With a sudden thrust of his arm, he spun me toward his friend. I staggered, windmilling my arms to keep my balance. I never saw the fist that buried itself in my stomach. I fell to my knees, my chin rasping against concrete as I retched coffee and rolls into the gutter.

"You fucking animals," Maeve hissed. A hand cracked against a cheek. Someone yelled, " 'Old the vixen," then gagged and moaned, "Bloody bitch!" I was roughly dragged erect.

"Right," my tormentor said, his cockney properly subdued. "Now, we'll 'ave no more of that or we'll 'aul you away in pieces. Makes no difference to us which way." He shoved me toward the Saracen. Hands grabbed me and unceremoniously tossed me into the interior. I fell hard against the rough metal-troughed floor. Moments later, the air rushed from my lungs as Maeve landed on top of me. O'Bannion, hands shackled behind him, was hauled in, struggling weakly against his captors. The door clanged shut and the Saracen heeled hard to its left as it spun 180 degrees and accelerated away.

"Are you all right?" Maeve's voice whispered anxiously in my ear.

"Yes," I gasped as she rolled off me. "And you?"

"Oh, yes," she said, then added uncertainly, "For now. I can't say for later."

The words didn't register. I forced myself to sit up and face her. Even in the dim light of the Saracen's hold I could see a deep bruise forming on her left cheekbone. Her lower lip had been split and was puffed to twice its size.

"Good God," I muttered. Immediately a slap behind my ear drove me back onto the floorboard.

"Shut yer foackin' mouth!" a harsh voice demanded.

"Dirty bastards!" O'Bannion said thickly. A meaty thud followed his words. I tried to rise up, but a boot roughly jammed my head hard against the floorboard and held me there as we drove the rest of the way in forced silence to the RUC interrogation center at Castlereagh.

FOUR

The door to my cell burst open with an eardrum-shattering *clang!* A sudden agonizing light poured into the previous pitch-blackness, stabbing a white-hot flame into my dark-accustomed eyes. I gritted my teeth against the sudden agony and clapped the palms of my hands hard over my eyes.

"On your feet," an impersonal voice ordered. Obediently, I stood, bare toes recoiling from cold, stone floor, genitals shrinking from sudden awareness of nakedness in front of a clad stranger. I peeped through my fingers at the doorway and saw a shaven-headed jailer, uniform crisply starched in creases, a three-foot ash billy clasped in his hands. The turquoise tile of the hallway gleamed surgically behind him. I inhaled deeply, smelling the clean Lysol of the outside in contrast to the unwashed, dry-dung-covered walls of my cell. The clean smell made me gag, and the knowledge that cleanliness had produced this reaction in me triggered a guilt complex that made me feel ashamed.

"Outside," the voice ordered, and I stumbled out the door and leaned against the wall as the jailer slammed my door to and locked it. What for? my mind asked. There is nothing there but dung-encrusted walls, an out-of-order toilet, and a tin can filled with brackish water. The jailer's billy prodded me in the ribs.

"Down there. The cellar. You know the way," he said, his voice as empty as a politician's promise.

I did, though how many times over how many days I had visited it, each time as naked as a church bell, I had no idea. I walked slowly, stiffly, down the corridor to the barred hall door and waited at the line painted across the floor four feet from the door. The cell door slammed behind me. The jailer moved down the corridor, the taps on his shoes echoing and suggesting that he was clothed and, therefore, a person while my nakedness reduced me to primitive man. He moved past me to silently open the door. He motioned me through. He did not say anything; he didn't have to. The sense of vulnerability in one's nakedness makes him willing to meekly follow all directions.

I stepped through the door, stopped at the next line, and waited as he locked the door behind me. He moved in front and looked dispassionately at me. "Okay," he said, and I obediently walked to the iron steps that led down two flights. A steel door opened onto concrete steps emptying out into the cellar and a series of bare wooden doors, behind which were large rooms fitted, I had been told, with various items that were designed to help or improve one's memory and willingness to talk with certain Special Air Service (SAS) representatives. I had been in only one room, and that held nothing more frightening than a table and chair with a second chair, bare iron, bolted to the floor in the center of the room. I wondered if this time I was going to see one of the other rooms. My fears were laid to rest, however, when my guide indicated the same room.

"Go in," he said mechanically. "They're expecting you."

I opened the door and stepped in. A man I had never seen was seated behind the table. My clothes were neatly folded on the table to his left. A folder lay open on the table in front of him. We were alone in the room.

"Mr. Edwards," he said. His words were clipped in the manner of a Sandhurst graduate. "I am Captain Wilson." His uniform was immaculate with knife-edge creases, his dark hair cropped close to his head.

"I wish," I said, pausing to painfully swallow past a dryness in the back of my throat, "to call the American consul." It was the preamble to all my answers made in this room. He eyed me speculatively for a moment, then indicated my clothes.

"That will not be necessary," he said. "You are free to go."

"Yes?" For a moment, the words didn't register. Then a

sudden surge of relief made me weak, and I held the back of the fixed chair until the feeling passed.

"Yes. Well. There is one small prerequisite, you might say." One eye stared hypnotically into mine, cold, black, that of a viper; the other was covered with a film.

"Uh-huh," I said. "And what, pray tell, would that be?"

"Your signature on this document testifying that you were allowed in Castlereagh for purposes of background study and that you will not allow to be printed any story without first sending it through the proper office for security clearance."

"And if I do not," I said, "I suppose I do not leave here?"

He regarded me for a second as he would something foul on his shoe, then faintly smiled. "I presume you do want your passport back, Mr. Edwards. And I do not believe a man such as yourself would find great comfort in one of our security camps."

"You realize that you are violating international law," I said quietly.

"Here, Mr. Edwards, I am the law. And, although I know it sounds terribly melodramatic, I have a long arm in case you harbor a plan to willingly commit perjury by signing this document, then writing an exposé later when you feel yourself to be safely out of Ireland. Do not plan to be deceitful, Mr. Edwards. Simply sign the paper. Forget what you have seen here at Castlereagh. Wipe it out of your mind." His voice was calm and dispassionate.

"What about Maeve Nolan?" I asked.

"Who?"

"The woman who was arrested with me. Will she also be freed?"

"I do not recognize the name," he said in a neutral tone.

"What about Richard O'Bannion?" I asked.

"I do not recognize the name," he repeated in the same voice.

"Now, just a minute," I said hotly, throwing caution to the winds. "Demanding silence for security reasons is one thing, but to blatantly deny the existence of someone like a despotic Big Brother fresh from an Orwellian nightmare—"

"That," he said icily, "will be enough, Mr. Edwards. Do

you wish to sign or not?" I drew a deep shuddering breath, then reached for the paper and pulled it to me.

"Tell me, is your name really Wilson?" I asked. He smiled faintly and held out a pen. I signed. I had no choice. Not if I did not want to disappear as Maeve Nolan and Richard O'Bannion apparently had. I had little doubt that Captain Wilson meant what he said. I did not doubt his autocratic power or his ruthlessness. Perhaps it was the primitive brutality behind the porcelain smoothness of Wilson's face: nearly an exact replica of Dali's portrait of Judas Iscariot, eyes close-set beneath wide forehead knobby at the temples, nose sharp, nostrils pinched, mouth a knife slash beneath hollowed cheeks, the right one bearing a long scar running down his face from a dead eye covered with a film to disappear beneath the collar of his tunic; the type of face one would never lift a glass to, for that would be tantamount to saluting death. It really didn't matter what caused the feeling; I had to get out of Castlereagh because I would find no help in there and pointless sacrifice serves no purpose. Movement was essential, and in a narrow six-by-ten cell, movement is at a premium. Remember, I kept telling myself as I dressed, the most important aspect to any revolution is staying alive. Martyrs are only today's news quickly forgotten on the morrow. Yet even as I tried to convince myself with this logic, I still could not help feeling like a traitor as I was led through the maze of corridors to the front gate, each step taking me farther and farther away from Maeve, intensifying my sense of her isolation.

Outside it was raining; not one of those gentle, soft rains spoken of in the tourist folders but a hard, lashing, lusty rain that pelted the skin and scourged it clean. The gate slammed shut behind me. I lifted my face to the heavens, opening my mouth to taste its purity. Then I pulled the collar of my coat up around my neck and turned to walk from the RUC interrogation center. I did not travel far before a black Ford Cortina pulled up beside me and the door opened.

"Get in," a cold voice ordered from the inside. I leaned down to stare into the thin face of Tomas Fallon. He made a small gesture with his hand. I looked down at the seat between us. A sawed-off shotgun stared back. "Get in," he repeated. I stepped into the car and closed the door behind me.

"Where are we going?" I asked, but received no answer as Fallon expertly piloted the car over the wet streets. I sighed and leaned back against the seat, closing my eyes. It is true, I thought, life does imitate art, even down to the clichéd melodramas produced by 1930s Hollywood directors.

I would never be able to duplicate the bewildering route Fallon took that dark night. When we pulled up behind an old Georgian tenement, I didn't even know if we were in Belfast, Antrim, or Ballymena. I do know we drove for what seemed hours. When I opened the door of the Cortina, I could smell the stench of wet garbage and cautiously followed Fallon from the car to the back door of the tenement. He knocked twice, paused, then thrice more and opened the door. A sudden blaze of light spilled out into the yard, and I realized the building had been blacked out.

"Come in, my friend," a voice quietly called as I stood foolishly blinking in the harsh light.

I stepped through the doorway and, as Fallon closed the door behind me, faced a somber Conor Larkin.

FIVE

"Conor!" I exclaimed, and involuntarily took a half-step to him. I pulled up short when he did not rise to greet me.

"Surprised?" he asked softly. "You were not expecting me?" His face was frigid, eyes like ice cubes, blue-gray and hard behind thick, wire-rimmed glasses. If he had been standing, he would have been shorter than I and thinner, what we used to call "wiry." His hands, slim and long-fingered like a pianist's, were clasped on the table in front of him. When I had last seen him surrounded by teetering piles of books in the library at Trinity College three short weeks before, he had appeared a perfect parody of Mr. Chips. That illusion was gone.

"No," I said slowly. An uneasiness spread over me. I looked around the room, noticing the others for the first time. Mac-Cauley sat behind Conor. I peered at a shadowy figure in the corner and gave a start as I recognized O'Bannion.

"Dickie!" I exclaimed. "How did you get away?" An uneasy look passed over his face, then disappeared as a stern mask settled over his features. He shrugged.

"Liam got back to the boys after he got away, so they were ready when the Prods decided to transfer me to the barracks. The boys rammed the car with a milk truck." He motioned with cupped hands. "Caught one bastard across the face with the cuffs—caved his face in—and had his pistol. The others were still dazed from the crash. After that, I just nipped out the door and away. I was lucky." He touched his lip, split and swollen twice its size, and his right eye welled nearly closed from an ugly bruise beneath it.

"Good," I said. "What do you hear about Maeve?" No one

answered. I looked at the still faces solemnly regarding me. A chill of apprehension swept through me. "What's wrong?"

"Coincidence," MacCauley answered gravely, making the word sound like a vulgarity. "That's what's wrong: coincidence. We don't believe in coincidence. Anyone who does gets dead very fast."

"Coincidence? What are you talking about?" I asked. My tongue seemed too thick for my mouth, the words stilted.

"It's like this," MacCauley said patiently as if reasoning with a child about to be punished. "You come to Belfast seemingly for a story. Being new to the area, Conor arranges for Maeve to be your guide. Eventually, you show up at Gram's where you meet us. You get your story. And names. Most importantly, names. Including some that you were told were off-the-record but could be used to verify some facts. Then suddenly you and Maeve are snatched. Both of you go into Castlereagh, but only one of you comes out and it isn't Maeve. And"—he paused, staring hard on me—"an hour after you're picked up the Prods raid The Wild Duck looking for a man called O'Rourke. Strange, don't you think, given that that information had just been told you by Dickie only minutes before your arrest? Coincidence?" He shook his head. "If I was a betting man, I wouldn't take those odds."

I stared in disbelief at him. "My God," I said softly. "You think I'm a spy?"

"Actually," he said, " 'tis the doubt we're giving you to disprove that out of respect for Conor and Dickie here, who feel this just may be coincidence after all." He grimaced. "I would just as soon execute you and be done with the trouble."

. "My paper—" I began desperately, then stopped as I realized the futility of trying to exploit the power of the press. There was no power here, as my death could be arranged a hundred different ways to reflect credibly upon the Provisionals.

"Your paper will be of little help to you now, I'm afraid," Dickie regretfully said. I sensed a hint of pity in his voice. His eyes refused to meet mine. A tiny muscle ticked at the corner of his jaw.

"I am afraid," Conor said quietly, "that you haven't much time."

"But how?" I asked, raking my brain for an answer, for proof. What could I tell them? What Castlereagh was like? In desperation, I began describing the humiliation, the sensory deprivation caused by black hoods tied over one's head for hours at a time, the exposure to continuous monotonous noise, being forced to stand supporting one's weight against a wall with his hands, and last, the terrible screams that kept one from sleeping whenever he tried to close his eyes.

"And Maeve?" Conor asked when I finished. "Did Maeve go through this as well?"

"I don't know," I answered dully, suddenly exhausted. "They kept us separate."

Conor nodded and after a moment spoke. "He's all in. Take him upstairs and let him sleep. Relax," he added, as I stiffened in alarm. "We believe you. No one could remember all the details who had not gone through what you did."

"I'm sorry, Con," Dickie said, running his fingers through his hair. Large bags suddenly appeared under his eyes, and he swayed drunkenly. I realized he was worn to exhaustion trying to find out what had happened to us. Gratitude licked at the edges of my weariness.

"Thank you," I said warmly, then turned toward Conor. "What about Maeve?"

"We'll see," he said gently. He motioned to Fallon. "Take him upstairs, then rejoin us."

I felt a gentle pressure on my arm and blindly followed its direction. We climbed a short staircase to a Spartan room containing an iron bedstead and bureau upon which rested an ewer and basin. I shrugged out of my coat while Fallon disappeared and immediately returned with a bottle of Jameson and a glass. I sat down on the bed to remove my shoes only to fall into a deep, dreamless sleep while listening to the whiskey gurgle into the glass.

SIX

A rough hand shook my shoulder. For a moment, I dreamt I was still in Castlereagh, then a heavy mug filled with steaming tea heady with the smoky scent of whiskey was thrust beneath my nose, and I remembered where I was.

"No, thanks," I said to Fallon, pushing the mug away. "Just tea, please."

"Drink it," he said softly, his voice carrying the musical lilt of the born tenor. "You'll be needing it. Conor wants to see you downstairs as soon as possible. Your clothes are there." He pointed to where they hung, freshly cleaned and pressed, on hangers from a door hook. My shoes, buffed and polished, rested on the floor next to the bureau, new underclothes still in their packages on top.

"Thank you," I murmured, and took the cup, sipping carefully. Almost immediately, I felt new life buzzing through my veins. "Have they made plans?"

A sudden grin flashed across his face. "Sure, and grand ones at that. I'm after thinking Finvarra will soon be welcoming a few Brits to the kingdom of the *Daoine Sidhe*. Best hurry if you don't want to be left out." He stepped lithely through the doorway, gently closing the door behind him.

I rose, placing my mug on the bureau, and thoughtfully dressed. I wondered how I could possibly be of any help. Like most mortal men, I wanted revenge against the state that had locked me away, then attempted to tie my hands to prevent my indignation from becoming a public outcry. I also had a healthy abundance of fear remembering Wilson's warning, but I remembered Jefferson's maxim that fear was no justification for nonaction. There are times when a reporter's noninvolvement is worse than creating news.

The faces in the room at the foot of the stairs still had hard lines etched into them. But the hardness was reserved for the job ahead. They greeted me casually. Conor even had a smile for me that, coupled with the deep pouches beneath his eyes, made him resemble a Sassanid satrap I had seen in a painting by a nameless Titian imitator titled "Administrating Justice." Appropriate, I thought, given the temper of the meeting.

"Feeling better?" Conor solicitously asked, although the question was more rhetoric than concern. I nodded. "Good. Now, then, let me explain what it is of you we want." He leaned forward over a map spread wide on the table in front of him, tracing a route on the map with an elegant forefinger.

"Soon, the RUC will move Maeve from Castlereagh south on M1 to the Women's Detention Center near Lisburn. We intend to intercept them here," his finger stabbed down, "at Dunmurry: far enough from Belfast that the guards will relax some, not near enough to Lisburn for help to be immediately available. Just before the cars arrive, we'll cover the road with 'knickknacks.' " He held up a small ball with four prongs an inch long forming a pyramid emerging from it. "Handy little things. The partisans used them in the war." He turned back to the map. "Immediately after the cars hit the knickknacks, we'll close in on all sides and release Maeve." He paused and looked expectantly at me. A vague uneasiness settled over me. I glanced at MacCauley and O'Bannion first, saving Fallon for last. The first two appeared worried and grim, Fallon just calm and assured. Suddenly, I realized Conor had just told me the entire plan. In that instant, I knew what I had to do. It wasn't noble or for any romantic idealism of D'Artagnan, it was for self-preservation. I directed my attention back to Conor.

"I see," I said slowly. "And just what am I supposed to do?"

He threw a quick look of triumph at MacCauley, who shrugged and shook his head. O'Bannion grinned and nodded. "Good lad," he said. "I knew you wouldn't let us down." Fallon had a faint grin on his face, and I knew that he was fully aware of the real reason behind my "enlistment."

"Simply this," Conor said, drawing my attention back to the map. "As soon as we free Maeve, you will leave with her for Clifden here," pointing with a finger, "on the coast near Mannin Bay in Connemara. She'll travel with you as your secretary-guide, appointed by the *Bord Fáilte*, the tourist board, to help you with a series of articles you are planning for your newspaper. We have papers certifying this, plus new identity cards for Maeve. She'll travel as Mairead Maguiness. The first name is close enough to her own to allow for mistakes if you forget and call her by her own. Now, this is very important: You *must* travel this route we've laid out for you. We have arranged for checkpoints along the way to help you if you get into trouble. If you miss *one*, an alarm will be raised. The SAS and RUC will think the Wild Geese will be flocking south after the raid, as indeed we shall, but you will be going west to Clifden. To find the cottage, go to The Hour-Glass, it's a pub, and ask for Michael John. Tell him *'pogue ma hone'* and he'll take you to the cottage. Have you got that?" He leaned forward, his hands splayed flat over the map.

"The Hour-Glass. Michael John. *Pogue ma hone.* Right. Do I get the map?" He nodded. "Then I can see no problem."

"Good," Conor said. He grinned. "We'll go south until everything has cooled down. In a week or two, I'll join you at Clifden." His face became serious. "You must get her away. Maeve's sympathies are well-known. Understand?" I nodded. "Good." He clapped me on the shoulder.

"Just one thing more, lad," O'Bannion said, a slow smile breaking across his face. "After you tell Michael John *pogue ma hone*, be sure to duck."

I looked at the others, grins splitting their faces from ear to ear. "Why?" I suspiciously asked.

"Because," he said slowly, relishing the moment and memory, "it means 'kiss my arse.' "

"Oh, God," I said. They laughed at my chagrin, and O'Bannion slapped my shoulder with delight in the Irishman's love of gallows humor: the need to find laughter in the blackest situation. But I realized that, too, was natural; this generation had known no other situation since birth and had carved the ability to laugh from the dark mine of despair fate had thrust them into. It was a role impossible for any other to play: the stage Irishman for whom the entire world feels pathos.

SEVEN

We had all memorized Conor's plans and were impatient to put them into operation. But the RUC and SAS did not cooperate and we waited, maintaining contact with the Provos inside Castlereagh while our tempers drew taut like nautical ropes in a high storm. At last, twelve days after my release from Castlereagh, the RUC and SAS decided to move Maeve from Castlereagh to the Women's Detention Center. I had just returned from filing a volatile interview with Ian Paisley, who spoke at length—sometimes for fifteen minutes or more—in answer to each question I posed him, causing me to also write a column I subtitled "Portrait of an Egomaniac" in which I likened him to Machiavelli's Prince. The piece was one step shy of libel, but I knew Paisley wouldn't sue, for most of the interview was repetitious oratory. Like most eager politicians, Paisley fell a rung or two below competency. He had made a career for himself by alternating descriptive adjectives on shopworn topics. He was completely unable to see into the future or comprehend present problems and societal fluctuations. Tunnel-visioned, but wily, he carefully manipulated the fears of others to satisfy his own bigotry. Still, he was copy for people more willing to believe empty flamboyance than competent ability.

I knew something had happened the moment I stepped over the threshold of the "safe" house in the Short Strand district of Belfast. A certain intensity, almost electric, crackled in the air. Reckless smiles stretched tight lips on MacCauley, Fallon, O'Bannion, and Conor. Their eyes danced with an eagerness normally seen on soldiers readying for leave.

"What is it? What's wrong?" I asked, alarm making my voice perceptibly climb.

"Good news," Conor said, glancing up from a final wiping of a Sterling submachine gun already glowing in readiness. "O'Rourke called. They're moving Maeve this afternoon at three."

My heart lurched from a sudden surge of adrenaline. I leaned against the wall of the room to let a wave of dizziness pass, fervently hoping my own insisting bladder would not independently empty itself. Conor grinned bleakly and pulled his revolver from its shoulder holster.

I watched the others: Fallon checking a sawed-off automatic shotgun, O'Bannion oiling a Thompson submachine gun, while MacCauley loaded an Ingram submachine pistol. All had .45 caliber semiautomatic pistols in shoulder holsters except Conor, who carried an old .38 caliber, long-barreled revolver, the blue of its barrel worn to metal shiny from long use. He caught my glance and smiled softly, a touch of bitter resignation in his eyes.

"An old friend," he said, hefting it familiarly. "Or perhaps beguiler. I thought I was done with all this." He swept the room with sad eyes. He suddenly looked old and benevolent, sad and wise, a tired soldier being pressed back into service for one last battle because there was no one else who could do the job.

"Why do you do it?" I asked curiously. He looked faintly surprised.

"For Maeve."

"I meant before," I amended.

"It was something to do."

"Not for love of country?" I asked, surprised. "Not to unite the six counties?"

"I'm not Balzac," he said, giving me a crooked grin. "But love, well, that is a different story. Perhaps I'll tell it to you one dark and stormy night in front of a fire with a bottle of *uisce beatha* on the table between us." He laughed and stood, sliding the pistol in his belt at the small of his back. He rammed a clip home in the Sterling and laid it on the table in front of him. He lifted his jacket from the back of the chair on which he'd been sitting.

"You're an incurable romantic," I said.

He laughed, shrugged into his jacket, and said, "Romantic, perhaps. Incurable, most certainly. It is the adventure calling, the wailing cry of the wild geese. Or," he added, "maybe it's just insanity. You knew, did you not, that the Irish are men that God made mad?" He smiled mockingly at me. "But what about you? What are you doing throwing in your lot with four mad Irishmen, for, as everyone knows, sanity visits the Irish only on those months during the second cycle of the moon."

"I want to write the truth," I said.

"That," Conor said, settling his coat over his shoulders, "is nigh impossible, my friend. Truth is a will-o'-the-wisp, a faerie, a changeling, different to each man."

"No," I said stubbornly, shaking my head, "truth is truth. Like man, it can be dressed in many clothes, but also like all men, it is the same when naked."

He looked at me in surprise. "A philosophic newsman. I never thought I'd see the day."

"But will he carry a gun," MacCauley said, impatiently interrupting. "And if so, what would be suitin' you?" He belligerently thrust his chin forward. Light reflected from his high, white forehead.

"No guns," I said, placing my hands in my pockets and hastily backing away. "Sorry. I'll drive, I'll run with you. But no guns."

"Ahh," MacCauley said, disgustedly turning away. "Little good. Little good."

"It is for people who do not carry guns that we do," Conor murmured. "Or have you forgotten why we are fighting?"

"I have not, Conor Larkin," MacCauley said, turning to face him. "But it's also because of people like him that we must do this, I'm thinking."

"You never had a thought in your life. You're a soldier, nothing more. Don't be giving yourself airs, Seamus Mac-Cauley," Conor said dangerously. His brogue deepened. His eyes turned flat and cold. My flesh pebbled in the room's sudden chill.

MacCauley's face flushed dark red, and his hand tightened on the grip of the Ingram. "Another time, in another place, you'll answer for those words, Conor Larkin."

"Perhaps," Conor said. A reckless grin flashed over his lips. "And then again, maybe it'll be tonight that I hear the drums of Brian Boru." O'Bannion gave a short bark of laughter at Conor's irreverent indifference to what waited ahead for them. Even Fallon gave a tiny, cold smile, and MacCauley was forced into humor in spite of his anger.

"Ah, Conor," he said, shaking his head. "How do we ever get along without you?"

"Sure, and if it's not the same thing I've been thinking," Conor drawled, deliberately lengthening his vowels in near perfect imitation of an uneducated bog Irishman. We all laughed at his mimicry. Tension fled from the room. Once again we were united in a universal brotherhood of chivalry, off to do battle with the dragons lurking beneath the flag of St. George. It was melodramatic as all hell; the type that would be booed off the stage anywhere, or if written, cast aside in disgust by an editor. Yet, at the same time it was wonderful.

The four drove in twin black Fords ahead of me. I followed well behind in a red Austin Mini. We made our way from the Short Strand district down Divis Street and Falls Road, covertly watched by Catholic eyes as we cut through their districts on our way to M1. As we drove past Balkan Street at the corner of Grosvenor Road, I caught a glimpse of a group of leather-jacketed youths watching the two black Fords cross in front of me. One glanced to his left, saw the red Mini, and raised a surreptitious thumb in good luck. I waved back and followed the Fords through the intersection, concentrating on maintaining the distance between the Mini and the Fords.

As we left Belfast and neared the turnoff to Dunmurry, the weather changed from overcast to drizzle. I could feel the surface of the highway change beneath the wheels of the Mini, causing them to slightly plane. I eased up on the accelerator and followed the Fords onto the turnoff and to a small lane cutting through high bushes. We pulled behind the bushes and stopped. I left the Mini beneath the low-hanging branches of a pin oak and crossed over thick, long grass to the second Ford with Conor and O'Bannion. I opened the door and climbed into the rear, closing it behind me.

"Foul day," I said. O'Bannion shook his head.

"No, a good day," he contradicted. "It will make the Prods drive slower than usual and make them easier to stop with less chance of harm to Maeve." He glanced into the rearview mirror, noticed my skepticism, and laughed. "The cars will go into a skid easier on a wet road," he explained. "While they're slidin', they're not shootin'. That will give us more time to neutralize them before they can do anything."

"What are you going to do with those following them?" I asked. O'Bannion shrugged and shook his head.

"They will have seen us," he said. "If we leave them alive, they'll raise the hue and cry faster than otherwise."

"Otherwise?" The word felt hollow and stupid in my mouth, for I knew the answer even as I voiced the question. O'Bannion and Conor left me to the horror of my own discovery.

We sat in silence and growing darkness for about an hour before Fallon left the other Ford and loped through the rain to us. Conor opened his window a crack. "They're coming," Fallon said. "*Three* cars," he emphasized. "One lagging a bit behind." A wintry smile frosted his lips. Conor swore.

"*Three* cars?" I parroted. "I thought . . ."

"So did we," Conor spat. "But we can deal with the change." He faced Fallon. "Swing wide in front of the lead car and force it to brake," he said, speaking tersely. "But don't stop. When you pass the second car, have MacCauley get the front tires with the shotgun. Block the road behind the second car and send MacCauley down to the bend with the knick-knacks. Dickie, you'll have to get those in the front car immediately with the Thompson. Don't miss or we're dead. I'll ram the second car. Fallon, you take out the guards with the shotgun. Be careful!" Fallon nodded and ran back to the other Ford. "Two minutes, then we go."

Conor turned in the seat to me, his face drawn and white, eyes flat pools with tiny fires hungrily licking in their depths. "Best get back to the Mini, now," he said, adding not unkindly as I stepped from the door, "Remember, Con, we're in a war."

He closed the door firmly behind me. I hurried to the Mini and settled myself behind the wheel, making sure the passenger door was unlocked. I fervently prayed that I would not miss my timing and tried not to think about what was about to happen on the highway. Then the Ford's taillights blinked, and it was gone, wheels tossing huge gouts of mud as the car spun out of the lane back toward M1. I began counting, heard a frantic blaring of horn, a grinding crash, then the familiar sharp staccato of guns rapidly emptying their clips punctuated by the deep booming of Fallon's shotgun, a brief silence, then the shriek of tires skidding and a second staccato followed by a crash. I counted five more seconds, then drove as fast as I could down the lane and back to the highway.

Three cars identical with the Fords I had followed were in the ditch at the far side of M1. A body hung limply from the broken window of one. Broken glass sparkled like a carpet of crystal around it. Fallon methodically walked around each car, giving each body an insurance blast from his shotgun. Conor impatiently stood in the middle of the road, his arm supporting a weak figure. My heart lurched, and I turned the steering wheel hard to the right to present him with the passenger door. He angrily jerked the door open and with surprising gentleness eased Maeve onto the seat beside me.

"Is she—" I began, but he savagely interrupted me.

"She's not hurt," he panted, his eyes blazing with anger. I flinched from their intensity. "At least, not from this. But . . ." He shook his head. "Oh, the bastards! The bastards!" He drew a deep ragged breath to steady himself. "Remember to follow the route. Now go! Go!"

He slammed the door. I needed no second urging to get away from that bloodbath. I gunned the engine and popped the clutch, corrected for the sudden skid, and rapidly worked my way through the gears as I headed west. Only after I had passed Lisburn and was through Lurgan did I glance at Maeve. I almost swerved off the road in shock.

She stared woodenly ahead, hands loosely clasped in her lap. Her hair hung in oily strands down pasty cheeks. A thin filament of saliva dripped from slightly parted lips. Her skin seemed sclerodermatous from what I could see beneath the man's trench coat with which she'd been covered in a flitting gesture toward propriety.

I turned my attention back to the road in front of me. I felt the sudden, savage delight of judge, jury, and executioner. When law becomes corrupt, men are forced to reinvent justice.

EIGHT

I drove the rest of the way to the border, anxiously watching my rearview mirror for signs of chase. I crossed the border at Belcoo in County Fermanagh, the waters of Upper Lough Macnean flipping whitecaps in farewell on my right. I was surprised at not being stopped by a security check but reasoned that the lateness of the hour and the ninety-plus miles distance back accounted for our easy arrival in County Cavan in the Republic.

I breathed a little easier and tried to talk to Maeve, but she continued to stare blankly through the windshield. I gave up and concentrated on driving the remaining distance to Sligo on the coast where we traded the Mini for a van, our contact glancing only once at Maeve before turning away to spare her embarrassment, muscles bunching along his jawline, a string of obscenities softly falling from his lips.

I made good time and slowed after passing through Leenane, found a lane leading off to the right, and took it, trusting to blind luck that I had made a wise choice. It was too early yet for the pub to be open, and I didn't want to park in front of the pub for every curious passerby to inspect us.

I pulled up on top of a small hill and turned the van around to face the way we had come. I turned the engine off and leaned back in the seat to silence broken only by the dim sound of the sea behind us. I impatiently waited for the time when I could drive into Clifden and meet Michael John at The Hour-Glass. I turned to Maeve and placed my hand on her shoulder, gently shaking it. "Maeve," I said. "Maeve?" She blinked once, twice, then turned to face away from me, a lone tear trickling through the grime of her cheek.

"No more," she whispered, cowering away from me against the door. "Please. No more."

"Shh," I said soothingly around a lump in my throat. "It's all right now. You're safe. You're safe. We need to clean you up a bit before we go into the town, that's all. Here. See?" I produced my handkerchief, moistened an end of it, and slowly, carefully, began to wipe her face. Her eyes fearfully watched me, the sclera startlingly clear around the emerald. I did the best I could and tried to put some order to her hair with my pocket comb, but the result was little better than before. At least, she looked as if she had been up all night rather than like a slattern. I hoped Michael John knew a doctor who could keep his mouth shut.

I drove back down the lane and turned right to skirt Benna Beola, The Twelve Pins. Two hours later, I came to Clifden, a sleepy-looking village, two church spires standing tall on small hills above the town, stone walls dividing lots, and trees hiding residences in the north. A sparkling white road ran through the town, spilling out into a large commons before continuing south where it split into a Y at a large, Celtic cross. It was a beautiful little town as I remembered later, but my immediate concern was not aesthetical, but medical, and I filed the memory away for later as I drove down into town to find The Hour-Glass.

The pub stood on the northwest corner of the commons. A weathered sign painted in peeling green and cream in the shape of an hourglass hung from rusty chains over the entrance. I parked in front, cautioned Maeve not to speak to anyone, and went up the two steps of the pub and pushed open the door. A heavy, stale odor of malt greeted me. I found myself in a long, narrow room, a peat fire burning at one end. Several heavy, dark wooden tables and chairs were scattered in the center of the room, a bench along the wall. The dark mahogany bar was well-worn, the surface cracked and stained in places. Behind the bar, shelves held an assortment of bottles, most of them dusty, testament to the tastes of the locals. A heavily built bald man with a flaming red walrus mustache stood behind the bar, leaning against the beer pumps while he talked to a brawny young man in twills and checkered shirt, the sleeves vainly rolled up to reveal bulging biceps. I glanced around; the room was nearly empty, but it was early yet. A man sat in a corner reading *The Irish Independent*, a half-full glass of stout on the table in front of him. Two others hunched over pints at one of the center tables. All turned to look at me as I walked in, closing the door behind me.

I crossed to the bartender and said, "I'm looking for Michael John." The bartender's eyes automatically shifted to the man in the corner, then snapped back to meet my own.

"And what will you be wantin' with him?" he growled, his eyes wary with that suspiciousness reserved for strangers.

"Never mind," I said, and crossed to the man in the corner. "Michael John?" He was tall and solid with broad shoulders and the ruddy cheeks of a drinker. His hands, square and blunt, showed scars across the backs of the knuckles, testifying to his willingness to accommodate people.

"Perhaps," he said, his voice cocky with self-assuredness. "It depends on what yer lookin' for."

I took a deep breath and said, *"Pogue ma hone."*

He blinked and stared disbelievingly at me. Behind me, someone drew a quick breath and whispered "sweet Jaysus." Slowly, he neatly folded the paper and placed it beside his glass.

"Yank," a voice called from behind me. I looked over my shoulder. The youth grinned at me. "You just committed suicide. 'Tis not holy ground we'll be buryin' you in."

"Ground's ground," I said, turning away from him as the smile slipped from his face.

"What was that?" Michael John quietly asked, squinting at me. His hands pressed hard against the table.

"Pogue ma hone," I said.

"Mister, either yer crazy and know what yer saying, or someone's playing a terrible joke on you."

"I know what it means," I said. He flushed and started to rise. I quickly leaned over the table to add in a voice only he could hear, "Richard O'Bannion told me."

He froze and slid back into his chair. He lifted the glass and drained it in one gulp. "St. Brigid and St. Colombine preserve you," he said. An explosion of pent-up air burst in amazement behind me. "There was supposed to be two of you. That's what threw me," he said softly.

[65]

"There is," I said, equally quiet. "In the van. We need a doctor. One who can keep quiet."

"Jaysus," he muttered, scrubbing huge hands over his face. "Bullets?"

I shook my head. "The RUC and SAS got a bit carried away, I'm afraid. Can you help?"

"I can," he said. He rose, tucking his paper into a side pocket of his tweed coat. He pulled a scully cap from the other pocket and clapped it on his head. I followed him toward the door.

"Getting old, Michael John," the young man said as we passed. "Old and toothless, when you back down from an old foaker like this." He jerked his thumb at me. Michael John stopped and faced him.

"We don't have the time for this," I said hastily. A half-smile crazily spread across his face.

"This won't take long," he said lazily. "Old, is it? Tooth-less?" He grinned to show white teeth. I didn't like the smile and took a step backward and to my left well behind him. The young man looked a little concerned about the attention he was suddenly getting from Michael John but, with the foolish-ness of youth, refused to recant.

"You are," he defiantly said.

"Ah. Well. It comes soon enough, lad, along with wisdom, which you surely do not have." With that, he looped a right hand into the young man's mouth, splitting lips and smashing teeth in a bloody splatter. His left hand caught the young man by the collar to keep him from falling while the right dropped down to seize his belt. With a grunt, he lifted him high in the air, tossing him into the corner formed by the wall and bar. The young man lay quietly in a crumpled heap.

"Well," Michael John said, dusting his hands together. "D'yuh see what I was sayin'? Now, let's be going. You take care of him, now, Rúairí," he said to the bartender. "An' you'll not be chargin' him for sleepin' over, you hear?"

The bartender gave us a gap-toothed smile, nodded, and began filling a pitcher of water as we left.

"How is my good friend Richard O'Bannion?" he asked,

then stopped his lively banter as he saw Maeve. "St. Brendan help us all. What have they done to you, girl?"

"Look," I said. "Conor said you have a safe house for us. I think we'd best get her there before people become too suspicious."

"Yes. Yes. Yer right, of course . . . er . . ." He looked questioningly at me.

"Con Edwards," I said, and shook his hand.

"Follow me," he said crisply. "I'm parked just around the corner." I slipped behind the van's wheel as he hurried around the corner. I followed his lorry south out of town then west along a narrow lane toward Mannin Bay.

The cottage was three miles from town; not far enough to be distant, but far enough to discourage the curious. The cottage sat on the edge of a windblown cliff not far from a dark cleft that dropped away to the sea. The gray cliffs were jagged and fearsome as if sliced by a savage knife. Below, the sea crashed wildly over elephantine rocks, trying by force to conquer the land. Far out away from land, the sea appeared a luxurious purple touched here and there by a golden glow. Little vegetation grew near and around the cottage save for sparse gorse and a reedy weed that by a miracle found a foothold in the rocks and a small saxifrage thing blue in color.

The cottage itself was whitewashed, stone-walled, and slate-roofed—unusual for this part of Connemara, for thatch was much cheaper if less durable—with a stone-flagged floor and low ceiling supported by black oak beams. There was one central room with a stone fireplace so large that an inglenook with a bench had been built on either side. A rustic table and four chairs plus two easy chairs and a heavy sideboard and counter completed the furnishings, except for a calor gas stove recently added to save cooking in the fireplace. To the left as one entered was a short corridor leading to a pair of small bedrooms in the back, a small bathroom with a cold-water shower stall separating them. I gently led Maeve into the largest of the bedrooms while Michael John hurried for a doctor he knew in Ballyconneely.

I pulled a chair into Maeve's bedroom and waited with her

as she lay unmoving on the bed, staring at the ceiling. I wanted to talk to her, ached to talk to her, but could think of nothing to say. I had not known her that long. I felt a helplessness, a quiet desperation, for I knew, and felt cheap and mercenary for knowing, that without her I had no story, and she was not there.

NINE

A week after our arrival at Clifden, word came for Michael John
to meet Conor at the pub in town. A few hours after he left, I
came out of the small cottage to discover Maeve standing at
the cliff's edge staring seaward. The cliff fell away to a shallow
shale beach tucked under an overhang and reached by a narrow,
twisting trail beginning behind the cottage and looping back
and forth across the face of the cliff. She wore a white sweater
in fisherman's weave and white canvas trousers, both old and
soft from many washings. Her hair blew in soft waves around
her neck from the offshore breeze. I cautiously moved toward
her, fearful that I might startle her. The doctor had examined
her and quietly explained that it would take some time for the
shock to wear off to the point where she would be able to
function.

"It could, of course, occur any time as well," he added, his
voice deep in an Aran Island dialect. "Right now, she is blank-
ing out everything that happened to her as well as the present
for fear of what could happen. It'll just take time."

"What did happen?" Michael John asked. The doctor shook
his head.

"All, I cannot tell you," he said. "Burn scars, a cigar, I'd
say, from the size of them. Bruises from beatings. And . . ." He
hesitated, lips compressing into a thin line. "She's been raped
and sodomized. Repeatedly."

"Jaysus," Michael John breathed, his face going white.
"This will set himself off for sure."

"Aye." The doctor nodded. He crossed the room to the window and gloomily stared out at the sun beginning to sink into the ocean. "Twice in a man's lifetime is too much for any man, let alone a man like Conor Larkin."

"Twice?" I asked, puzzled. "This has happened before?"

"Oh, not to her, but to his sister, aye," the doctor sighed. He stepped to the table and removed a cup of tea prepared by Michael John when the doctor and his wife were busily taking care of Maeve. The doctor's wife was still with her. "That is what drove Conor Larkin from Trinity the first time in the fifties. 'Twas a terrible revenge he took; one that lasted 'most twenty years. A lot of people died."

"And his sister?" I asked.

"She wasn't as strong as that one," he said, raising the mug in unconscious toast to the hallway. "They didn't believe her when she told them she didn't know anything about the IRA. She just happened to be in the wrong place at the wrong time and got caught up in a RUC sweep. She hanged herself in her cell one night after interrogation. She was sixteen."

"And now Maeve," I murmured.

"Yes," he said, finishing his tea and placing the empty mug back on the table. "And now Maeve. I'm after thinking that there'll be a widow's run on black crepe long before this is over now."

I reached her side and gently spoke her name. "Maeve?" She didn't answer but continued to stare out to sea. It was a foul day, but a curragh defiantly moved against a quartering sea, lurching between the troughs, then shuddering as waves broke over the bow. The wind felt almost cold on my face, and, although we were too high up for the spray to reach us from where the waves crashed over the rocks, I could still taste salt on my lips. Overhead, lonely curlews flew forward and backward, chased by sea gulls when they flew too close to nests in the cliff rocks, dipping occasionally to the shale beach, their cries filled with haunting despair.

"Maeve," I said again and waited. Slowly she turned her head and stared at me. Something stirred and flickered—memory?—in the emerald deepness of her eyes but was quickly masked.

"They won't make it," she said softly.

"Who won't, Maeve?" I said, pressing the point and trying to keep my voice normal.

"The sea," she said. She looked back at the curragh, and I knew then what she meant. Even as we watched, the prow of the curragh rose high in the air and slammed into the next trough, disappearing as the wave washed over it. Miraculously, all stayed with the curragh though it was filled with water. The pilot turned the prow, cunningly timing his motions so as not to present the curragh broadside to the waves, while the others furiously bailed.

"Why do they do it?" I said, meaning the question to be rhetorical.

Maeve shrugged. "If they do not fish, they do not eat. Tonight, there may well be empty bellies."

She fell silent as the curragh rounded the head to the north and disappeared.

"Would you like to go see if they made it, Maeve?" I asked.

"No," she answered. "They made it. Have you not heard of the fishermen of Connemara? They are the souls in Purgatory that come back to habitations and familiar spots to relive their transgressions until at last they know the consequences of those transgressions. Then the sea will take them."

"Maeve," I said carefully. "Do you know who I am and where we are?"

Her eyes widened in surprise, tiny wrinkles of concern forming themselves between her eyebrows. "Of course. You're Con Edwards and we're in Connemara."

"And do you know how we got here?"

"Drove. How else? What's the matter?" she asked, alarm beginning to show in her voice. She turned to face me. "What are you trying to do?"

"Do you know where you were before we came here?" I asked, ignoring her question. The frown deepened between her eyes. She quickly looked away, back toward the sea.

"No," she said in a small voice. "Is it important?"

I hesitated before answering. It was absolutely vital to the story I had planned on the RUC and SAS not to mention the Ulster 'B' Specials. I was sure that she would remember if I pressed her further; the line of questions I had posed had set up the row of blocks in her mind that the answer to her question could topple. But leaving what behind? A shattered shell? Sudden shame made my cheeks burn. Why did I think I even had a chance?

"No." I tried to make my voice sound casual, offhand. "Don't worry about it. Just curious, that's all. What do you want for lunch?"

She said nothing for a long minute, then slowly turned and buried her face against my chest, arms tightly hugging me. Awkwardly, I patted her shoulder and stared out across the sea while tears came; mine, not hers, for she did not cry. She was not yet ready for tears. I wondered if she ever would be.

"Ain't this a touching scene," a voice spoke from behind us. "Now, tell the truth, Billy: ain't it a touching scene? Herself all cozy with an outsider?" I twisted around, shielding Maeve with my body, protectively holding her close. Two men dressed in working clothes faced us, lips parted in wolfish grins. One was larger than the other with a shaggy mop of black hair and clumps of scar tissue bulging over humorless black eyes. The other had sandy hair thinning back from a widow's peak, blue eyes, and a single, twisted yellow tooth hanging down in front like a fang. Both held pistols pointed at us.

"What do you want?" I asked. My legs trembled. I tightened the muscles, trying to stop them.

"Would you listen to him, Harry?" the shorter one said. "Ain't very friendly, is he?"

"That he ain't," Harry answered. "That he ain't. An' after we be comin' so far to find 'em."

"Con," Maeve whispered from beside me. "Who are these men? What do they want?" I tightened my arm around her, pressing her close to me.

"Shh, Maeve," I said, trying to keep my voice from shaking. "I'll handle this."

"Now, how do you suppose you'll be doing that?" Billy said. "Do you hear him, Harry? This foacker's going to handle us. How do you suppose he'll be doing that?" His face tightened as he turned back to face us. "The boys have sent us," he said harshly. "Turn around."

"What for?" I asked.

"Man, are you failing in the head?" Harry said. " 'Tis judgment yer facin'."

"Whose judgment?" They whirled to their right to face an unsmiling Conor Larkin and Michael John. Behind them stood the doctor and his wife. Conor's face was frozen into a cold mask, the skin pulled tightly over the skull like Death suddenly transfigured. Even without the pistol in his hand or the shotgun in Michael John's hands, I felt the fear our two would-be assassins felt.

"Whose judgment?" Conor repeated. "I'll not be asking you again."

"*Sinn Fein*," Harry muttered. Conor shook his head.

"I think not," he said softly.

"Think what you like," Billy answered sullenly. "The council passed its decision."

"When?"

"Two days ago," Harry said. Conor smiled, a tight lifting of his lips that did not touch his eyes.

"Why?"

"None of yer foakin' business! Now!" Harry shouted. He swung his pistol toward Conor. Conor's bullet struck him in the throat. I flinched as the air filled with a fine mist of blood. Michael John's shotgun boomed. Billy flew backward, his chest disappearing as the charge blew him over the edge of the cliff. I became aware of Maeve's keening through the ringing in my ears. Her nails dug sharply through my sweater into my chest.

"It's all right," I said, swallowing convulsively against the ringing. The doctor's wife hurried forward, making soothing noises. I let her take Maeve from me and they slowly moved back to the cottage. I looked at Conor and tried to smile.

"You can't believe how happy I am to see you," I said. He curtly nodded.

"I think I can," he answered. He motioned to Michael John, who laid his shotgun on the ground and effortlessly picked up Harry and threw him over the cliff's edge.

"What was this all about?" I asked. "What did they mean by 'judgment'?"

"They meant you'd been found guilty *in camera* and sentence passed," Conor replied, frowning.

"What?" I said. He nodded. "But that doesn't make any sense!"

"I know," he answered. "I know." His eyes looked off into

the distance. "Somebody has gone to a lot of trouble," he mused. "These two were sent to the far south around Bantry after they became too well known by the Prods and Brits in the North. But not everyone knew that. Word was given out that they had left the country for America. If they were caught, this would automatically have been considered an IRA operation." He frowned. "This doesn't make sense. The council has declared the Republic off-limits for operations of this sort. We need to maintain good relations with the government to ensure a haven for operators such as these two. Who would want to jeopardize that?"

"Provos?" I asked.

"No. They wouldn't have gone to so much trouble. And it wasn't the *Sinn Fein*. They want no trouble in the Republic to threaten their legitimate status." He shook his head. "None of this makes any sense. But I intend to find out. Will you be all right?" I nodded. "Good. I'll stay in touch through Michael John." He looked toward the cottage. Pain flickered across his face. "It's a terrible thing," he said softly. "A terrible thing." He turned back to me. "Michael John will post some of the boys around the cottage. You'll not be bothered again. Say goodbye to Maeve for me, will you? I think it best she not see me just now."

"I will," I answered. He nodded, gripped my hand tightly for a moment, then left. I watched him leave, then turned to look out at the sea, trying to make sense out of what had happened, but I couldn't. None of it fit into any logical pattern. At last, I gave up and turned back to the cottage, hoping Conor would be able to resolve the situation. Two weeks passed before he returned, bitter at having discovered nothing. In the meantime, though, Maeve and I tried desperately to purge the past by creating our own private world. I thought we had succeeded, but Conor's return made a lie of my reckoning. Mortals cannot walk beside gods.

Part Three

1979

ONE

Large, soft, white flakes filled the air as Maeve, Liam, and I pulled into a parking lot across the street from The Black Dog pub in Belmont and parked in the middle of three stalls. We pushed our way through the heavy snow rapidly covering the ground and entered the pub. A roaring fire at one end greeted us as we stepped over the pub's namesake stretched across the inner threshold. The low ceiling held in the heat and smell of porter and, today, the odors of nutmeg and cinnamon mixed in mulled claret and eggnogs and hot, buttered rums and beneath that the satisfying hints of pub stew and steak and kidney pie.

We ordered large whiskeys to drive off the chill and carried our drinks to a small table and chairs by the fire. I took a sip of my whiskey, sighed with contentment, and stretched my damp feet toward the fire. Maeve shook the snow from her coat and hooked it by its arms over the back of her chair toward the fire before sitting, while Liam casually tossed his on the seat of an empty settle before joining us. We drank in silence for a moment, banded together by our memories of the funeral and Conor, kindred spirits reunited by the present. The wind moaned through the eaves of the pub. At last, Liam broke the silence among us.

"To Conor," he said, lifting his glass. "May the devil pass him on as a fearful adversary." Solemnly, we raised our glasses in ritual toast and drank, letting the warm whiskey loosen the coldness upon our minds and throats.

"So," I said. "How did you get on with TRANCO, Liam? I would think a company that big would be a bit leery about hiring someone who had been with the Provos."

"Plain luck. I went to interview Joe Killian when Killian

[77]

Shipping announced its merger with TRANCO. He was quite interested in my past. His grandfather was a cautious sympathizer in the old days. You know the type: the ones who like to appear mysterious when it suits their needs."

I nodded. "The hint of danger but not the risk. But it gives one a sense of nationalism that provides invigorating conversation in the club without the smell of cordite, the sound of explosions, or getting one's hands bloodied."

"Exactly. Joe Killian grew up listening to his grandfather's stories. Seems like the old man was a pretty colorful gent. He had friends in the IRA and went to dinner parties at Classiebawn Castle with Lord Mountbatten. Seems the two of them became friends during a sailing regatta at the Isle of Wight. Strange combination, don't you think? Anyway, Joe's like his grandfather, an incurable romantic. Having a former IRA man around convinces him he's part of the Rising." He shrugged. "It's not so bad, I guess. I was the public relations officer so I wasn't just window dressing. When TRANCO and Killian Shipping merged, the entire Killian staff went along, too."

"What are you going to do now?" I asked.

"Back to Manchester, I guess," he said. "TRANCO's beginning to organize the Porcupine Banks Project, and I have to begin putting the public relations office together."

"I thought TRANCO already had a PR office," Maeve said.

Liam smiled. "It does. But this is to be a subsidiary undertaking. TRANCO's merging with Killian Shipping in a few days to gain the work ships it needs to cover Porcupine Banks."

"And you, Maeve?" I asked. "What will you do?"

"Dublin first, then London," she said. "Trinity's asked me to finish the term Conor began. After that, I'll go to London as a consultant for a proposed television special on the 'troubles,' " she explained.

"What about you?" Liam asked, sipping his drink. "What's up for you?"

I shrugged. I seemed to be the only one without firm plans. "I suppose back to London for a start. Paisley's in town making a big noise again about England's responsibilities to Northern Ireland. So far, he's being tolerated, but I don't think it'll take much before the politicians turn against him. The general feeling I'm getting is that most of the people would just like to have the situation settled. Paisley's keeping it stirred up."

"Of course he is," Liam observed. "If peace actually does come, then he goes back to being just a minister, and a poor one at that, instead of the celebrity he is now. His ego won't let that happen. Has he ever forgiven you for that article you wrote about him?"

"No," I answered. Maeve grinned, shook her head, and raised her glass in mock salute to me. "But I'm not too upset about that. I just want to be around to pick over the pieces when his tower is finally pulled down."

"Do you think that will happen soon?" Maeve asked.

"There is a possibility that it will," a rich baritone said. We looked at the speaker and recognized the older of the two men from the cemetery. He wore tweeds of a careful cut and carried a glass of whiskey in a manicured hand as if it were crystal. But it was the younger of the two I remembered. He wore a carefully pressed suit, but the cut showed that it had obviously come off the rack of Marks and Sparks. It was a far cry from the tailored uniform I remembered at Castlereagh.

"Hello, Wilson," I said with distaste. A tiny smile moved the scar on the side of his face.

"Edwards," he acknowledged.

"You two know each other?" the older man said.

"We've met," I answered. I looked at Maeve and Liam. "In the basement at Castlereagh. They're SAS."

Blood drained from Maeve's face. She stared bleakly at Wilson. Liam made an unintelligible sound in his throat.

"Ah, actually, I'm from Special Branch. Denis Naismith. We've been put in charge of . . . things."

"What happened, Wilson?" I asked. "You use a cattle prod on the wrong person?"

Wilson regarded me stonily, a faint flush appearing in his neck just above the stiffly starched collar of his shirt.

"A political move," Naismith said smoothly. "There was an unfortunate incident at Castlereagh that caused a bit of a problem. A lack of communication. Special Branch now coordinates affairs."

Liam gave a short laugh. "Bit of a problem, you say. I think it was a bit more than that. The European Court of Human

Rights found Britain guilty of inhuman conduct and treatment of prisoners. Something about sensory deprivation, wasn't it?"

"Do you mind if we sit down?" Naismith asked. Wilson pulled two chairs to the table without waiting. Naismith frowned at the deliberate rudeness.

"I don't think we really have anything to say to you," Liam said stiffly.

"Are you sure?" Wilson said softly.

"Please," Naismith said. He shook his head warningly at Wilson.

"SAS," Liam said disgustedly. He picked up his glass of whiskey, draining it. "Or Special Branch." He shook his head.

"There *is* a difference," Naismith said mildly. He signaled for a round of drinks.

"A bastard's a bastard by one name or another," Maeve said.

"Er, yes," Naismith said. A pained expression crossed his face. Wilson stared coldly at her. "I can understand a person in your position adopting that attitude."

"And what position might that be?" she asked.

"Shall we say as friends and wife of a recently deceased Irish terrorist." He brushed an imaginary speck of lint from his trouser leg. "One wanted by the authorities for the past fifteen years."

"Go away," Maeve said, leaning back in distaste. "This is a private wake. Billy-boys aren't wanted."

"You do not understand," Wilson interjected. "You really don't have much choice in the matter."

I stared at him for a moment, then turned back to Naismith. He seemed a bit embarrassed by his partner's truculence. "Is he serious?" I asked.

"Please excuse him," Naismith said apologetically. "He spent a long time in Belfast. It takes time to, er, readjust one's thinking."

"Don't apologize for me!"

"Shut up, Wilson," Naismith said tiredly. "Wait for me at the bar." Wilson started to argue, but one look from Naismith sent him climbing stiffly to his feet. He left his chair pushed away from the table. His partner reached over to pull it neatly to place.

"He lost a brother in the 'troubles,' " he said by way of apology. "I'm afraid he takes things like this a bit personal at times. Especially in, er, present company."

"Maybe he should be reassigned," I said.

"Perhaps," Naismith said. "But, in a way, he is correct, you know. We do have the right to ask you some questions."

"Is this an interrogation?" Liam asked.

"Does it have to be? What are you afraid of?"

"Nothing," Liam snapped. "Conor Larkin was a friend, a good friend, but that's about all I can tell you."

Naismith's eyes flickered to Maeve. Tight lines appeared around her lips. "Conor Larkin. Age sixty-four. Professor at Trinity College, Dublin. Wife. No family."

He sighed and raised his glass, slightly wetting his lips. At that rate, I figured it would take him about a month to finish the drink. "And, of course, you have no idea why he was alone on the docks so early in the morning and why he was buried at St. Brigid's and not taken back to Ireland, right?" Maeve did not answer. "You really disappoint me."

"Sorry," she said. "It must be an aversion to authority born from years of disillusionment."

"And, of course, his presence would have nothing to do with the Porcupine Banks Project, would it?"

I cast an involuntary look at Liam. Naismith caught my glance and smiled. "What do you think, Mr. Edwards?"

"Why should that interest you?" I countered.

"A question with a question. Now I know why you are such a good reporter, Mr. Edwards," he said. "By the end of the year, an exploration grant will be awarded by both the Republic of Ireland and Great Britain to Transcontinental Oil. TRANCO, however, wants to make sure that its investment will have some measure of security. Consequently, Her Majesty's government has been secretly negotiating between Stormont and Dail representatives for the past few months. If a truce can be achieved, Ireland's economy will receive a large and needed boost."

"And," I murmured, "Great Britain will receive the interest off TRANCO's increased dividends and levy per barrel on import-export duties."

"There is that, too," he calmly said. "The pound sterling

could use some new blood. But consider that Ireland's economic growth has fallen to less than one percent. Inflation has risen to eighteen percent, mainly through the increase in the price of imported oil that supplies seventy percent of the country's energy. The establishment of drilling platforms over Porcupine Bank would ease the heavy loan deficit the current government under the *Fine Gael* party has been forced to run up to keep the economy moving. Ireland needs that oil development."

"But what does this have to do with Conor Larkin?" I asked.

"The part of the docks where he was killed belongs to TRANCO," he said. "Naturally, given the, ah, delicacy of the situation a sudden unexplained gun battle in which a notorious IRA killer is slain makes people a bit edgy. I'm sure you can understand that."

"Gun battle?" I asked, my pulse beginning to quicken. "There was no mention of a gun battle. I was led to believe that Conor's death was more of an execution."

"It wouldn't do for the public to know too much, now, would it?" he asked. "From the splotches of blood we found in several places, I think it is safe to assume that he took a few with him. Now, will you help us?"

I glanced at the others, who sat tight-lipped, watching him. I shook my head. "I'm sorry, but we know nothing about the death of Conor Larkin."

"I am sorry, too," he said, rising from the table. "If you change your mind, leave a message for me at the home office." He paused. "Sorry if we've caused you any inconvenience."

"Are you?" Liam asked. He didn't answer but smiled, politely nodded at Maeve, and motioned to Wilson.

"What do you think?" I asked, watching the door close behind them. I shivered as a gust of wind rushed across the room from the door to fan the fire. Flames danced high in the fireplace, then settled back to lick the logs. Liam made an abrupt gesture of dismissal.

"Forget him," he said. "Those people are always heralders of doom."

"It would explain what Conor was doing in England," Maeve said thoughtfully.

"Searching for an informer?" Liam asked, his voice skeptical. "In England? Isn't that a bit odd?"

"I don't know," Maeve said. She bit her lip, thinking for a minute. "A few months ago, he told MacCauley he thought he had an informer somewhere in the ranks. That was right after the SAS caught Cavanaugh and his boys with the gelignite at the depot, remember?"

"Yes," Liam said. "And the investigation turned up nothing. Cavanaugh had been drinking in The Arms and Swan the night before and probably said something. I'd like to be thinking you're right, but it doesn't make sense. Why look for an informer, a *gombeen* man, *here*? 'Tis in Belfast you'd have better luck."

"Then what was he doing on the docks?" she demanded. "Why risk his freedom coming to England?" Liam ignored her question.

"You forget that MacCauley warned him after he kept insisting there was an informer," Liam said.

"He also threatened to kill Conor the day we freed you, Maeve, so I don't know how far you can trust MacCauley. But what was that about an informer?" I asked. The two of them looked at me in surprise.

"It's true," Liam said defensively. "Conor was told to let it drop and stop pressing on about an informer in the ranks. MacCauley didn't want anything to create ill-feeling, what with this business about Porcupine Banks coming up. But Conor kept chipping away at it until finally MacCauley closed the door on him. Told him to stay out of Belfast."

"And that's why he must have come to England," Maeve said. A strange light began to shine from her eyes. "There was no place else for him to go. You knew him, Liam. And you, Con. Once he had hold of something he wouldn't let it go." She shook her head. "Even if it meant coming here. It was the romantic in him. He *had* to do it."

"Maeve," Liam sighed.

"Please, Liam. Con," she said quietly, "for my sake. What will it take? A few minutes here and there. I'm not asking for the two of you to drop everything."

"Well," I said, looking at Liam. "I can take some time off. What do you say?" He shook his head, avoiding Maeve's eyes.

"Bad timing," he said. "We're just getting started. But I'll do what I can. I have to be in Manchester for a while. I'll see what I can find out. Mind now," he said admonishingly, holding up a warning finger, "I'm not promising anything."

Maeve clasped his arm for a moment. "Thank you, Liam," she said.

"To Conor," he said, reaching for his glass. "He's probably laughing and kicking his heels at the devil over all of this." Solemnly, we raised our glasses. I felt a strange exhilaration, a satisfaction that Conor's death had not been at the hands of a solitary assassin. He had died as he lived, a Spenserian knight to the end. But what had he been doing on TRANCO's dock in the first place?

The snow had doubled its efforts when we emerged from the pub, Liam and Maeve to return to their hotel in Manchester, and I to meet them there the next day for breakfast. When we reached the Volvo, Liam reached with his key to unlock the door, then hesitated, frowning at the ground behind the Volvo.

"What's wrong?" I asked, my teeth chattering from the cold.

"I don't know," he answered. Maeve impatiently stamped her feet.

"Hurry up, Liam! For God's sake!" she complained.

I looked at the ground at the back of the Volvo, trying to see it through his eyes. For a moment, I couldn't understand his perplexity; then I saw it. My teeth stopped chattering.

"Maybe it's nothing," I said. He glanced at me.

"You really think so?" he asked.

"What?" Maeve asked, mystified.

"No," I said.

"The snow," he answered. He pointed to the snow at the side of the Volvo, smooth and neat where it had fallen like a blanket, then to the back where it appeared ruffled and lumpy, as if someone had shaken the blanket and carelessly let it drop. "It looks as if someone had tried to cover something." He carefully brushed the snow away away from the back of the Volvo to uncover bare ground. He glanced at me, and fell to his knees. Slowly, he worked his way under the Volvo, careful not to touch any part of the car. Suddenly, his movements stopped.

"Con," he said softly. "You'd better see this. But, for God's sakes, don't touch the car!"

I hesitated, then dropped to my knees, awkwardly crawling after him. He pointed to a small gray brick attached to the gasoline tank with a single strand of friction tape. A heavy wire leading from it was tightly wrapped around the drive shaft. I knew what it was: a motion bomb. The drive shaft in turning would wind the wire around itself, pulling the bomb from the side of the tank. The fuse, undoubtedly fulminate of mercury, would detonate the bomb. Simple and highly effective. If it had not been snowing . . .

My mouth went dry; I felt alone, colder than I had ever been before. "Who?" I asked past dry lips.

"I don't know," Liam said. We looked at each other and carefully slid out together from under the Volvo.

TWO

My eyes felt gritty from lack of sleep when I joined Maeve and Liam for breakfast the next morning in the Grand Hotel dining room. As I approached their table, I could tell they had spent an equally sleepless night: Maeve's hair hung limply around her jaw like dank seaweed and Liam's five o'clock shadow had moved to at least eight-thirty. I pulled out a chair and sat. Liam poured a glass of orange juice from a pitcher near his elbow. It was cold and fresh, and I began to feel better.

"I ordered scones," he said, nudging a plate toward me. "Unless you'd rather have something else?"

"These will be fine," I said, lifting the cover. I slid two onto my plate. "What time did the police leave?" Liam made a face and poured black coffee into his cup.

"About two hours ago. I don't think they believed we were innocent about how the bomb got there."

"That one inspector—what was his name? Wentford?—didn't believe us," Maeve said. Her voice was husky from lack of sleep. "He thinks we planted it ourselves. He was more interested in the fact that we were Irish than that we were victims."

"Too many bombs have made them suspicious of all Irish," I said. "Some sort of collective responsibility, I suppose. You're Irish, therefore you must be guilty."

"Christ," Liam said irritably. "It's too early for arcane logic and poor syllogisms." He directed a casual look around at the others in the dining room, then lowered his voice. "I called himself after the police left. He's checking to see what UDA boys handy with explosives are out of Belfast."

[86]

"Did he give any ideas as to why?" I asked. Liam glanced at Maeve, then back to me.

"Not really," he said. I could sense the lie in his casualness. "Speculation only. It might be a backlash at Maeve. She is, was, Conor's wife and since Conor obviously took a couple with him—"

"The revenge angle?" I interrupted with misgiving. "I doubt that. Conor was killed. It died with him."

"I think so, too," he said dryly. "But there is more, you know. Maeve is herself. You haven't exactly been quiet about the 'troubles,' my beauty. You and that Devlin woman have kept things pretty stirred up lately. Remember Derry? Mothers and fathers who have lost sons want to believe the loss was worthwhile."

"Possible," she said. "But why now? Here?" He shrugged and leaned back in his chair. He picked up his coffee and took a sip.

"Opportunity. *Carpe diem*, and all that rot. Everyone knew you'd be here. Someone obviously followed you and planted the bomb when he could."

"Then why not at the cemetery?" I asked. He gave me a disdainful look.

"Ah, use your head, man! The Brits were all about. Remember those two yesterday in the pub?"

"Yes," I said, adding slowly as the thought manifested itself, "and we discovered the bomb *after* they left." Silence held at the table for a long moment as they played with the implication in my words. Then Maeve broke the silence.

"I'm not saying you're right, and I'm not saying you're wrong," she said. "But I'm thinking that it's the latter. The Brits are smarter than that. They wouldn't want to create a martyr on their home soil. Much better to have it done back in Belfast where it could be explained away a dozen different ways. Besides, the Brits are really only a part of this out of a sense of obligation."

Liam frowned at her words. I could tell he wanted to believe that the British were responsible, but Maeve's words had a ring of truth to them. It was highly unlikely that the British had placed the bomb. But that also suggested something even more frightening.

"What if," I asked slowly, "somebody *wanted* to create a martyr? Especially if someone had been making herself a bit of a nuisance?"

Maeve's eyes widened. Liam indignantly shook his head.

"You forget," he said. "MacCauley was just as surprised about the bomb as we were."

"Would you expect him to admit otherwise?" I asked. "Those whom the gods wish to destroy they first put at ease."

"Christ," he sighed. "We're right back where we started. Who do we believe?"

"Not quite," I said. "At least now we know who to avoid."

"Yes," Maeve bitterly enjoined. "Practically everybody."

We visited a while longer, making plans. Liam had to stay in Manchester but promised to continue contact with Mac-Cauley and to put out feelers of his own among contacts he had on the docks. Maeve and I would continue together to London where I had arranged for Ed Logan, a friend from Vietnam days now with Reuters, to cover for me while I took a week or two vacation, and Maeve finished some groundwork with the BBC proposed special.

We left the dining room together. Liam had volunteered to give the two of us a lift to the railroad station, from where we would take the next train to Euston Station. When we emerged from the hotel, heavy gray clouds hung over the city, threatening to blanket it with another snowfall. I automatically turned to a black Volvo parked to my right, but Liam placed a hand upon my arm to stop me. A man brushed by us and hurried to the Volvo, keys impatiently jingling from his hand.

"I changed cars," he said, indicating a red Morris parked by the curb. "I felt a different car might be safer. A bit paranoid, I suppose."

"Makes sense to me," I said. I heard the slam of a car door followed by a blinding flash of light and an ear-ringing blast. A shock wave threw us back. I gasped as the hotel door edge bruised my ribs. My head struck the wall, and the street swam in and out of focus for a minute. Shards of glass and metal rained down around us; the Volvo's hood hurtled past. Then my sight cleared. I looked at the remains of the Volvo: a leg lay in the street; the rest of the body, torn and twisted, sprawled half in and half out of the car. I swallowed to relieve the ringing in my ears. The stench of cordite drifted to us.

"Good God," I said. Maeve gripped my arm, hard.

"Con," she said. Her voice sounded strangled.

"Somebody is very determined," Liam said grimly. "Perhaps it would be a good idea to disappear for a while."

"So it would appear," I answered. I looked back at the debris in the street, anger slowly replacing the earlier fear.

THREE

The crossing from the Isle of Man to Dublin was one of the worst in recent memory, according to the captain of the Douglas Line. I had wanted to take the ferry from Holyhead in Wales to Dublin, but Maeve firmly vetoed that as being too obvious for anyone who wished to enter Ireland quietly. The British employed watchers who reported directly to the RUC and Paisley's boys. The best way, she argued, was a circuitous route on the Douglas Line from Fleetwood to the Isle of Man (crossing time: three hours) and from the Isle of Man to Dublin (crossing time: four and one-half hours). I argued for an airplane (crossing time: one hour), then the ship from Holyhead (crossing time: three and one-half hours) but was sneeringly dismissed as an amateur in the great game of international intrigue. I guess only professionals spend six and a half hours more than is necessary traveling from Britain to Ireland. But I gave in to her.

Three weeks had passed since Maeve and I had left Manchester to wrap up our business in London, she to finalize an agreement as a consultant on the proposed television special on the "troubles," and I to arrange for Logan to cover for me while I took a couple of weeks vacation. Things had not been as simple as I had thought, for I had to cover the summit talks between Roy Mason, newly appointed secretary of state for Northern Ireland, and Ian Paisley following the awarding of the exploration grant to TRANCO.

Halfway to Dublin, the Irish Sea roared up to greet us. Huge waves crashed over the bow of the ferry in frothing welcome as an unseasonal storm suddenly crashed down from the North, laying waste to the weatherman's "cheery and bright" outlook. By the time we finally docked, Maeve would have been eating humble pie if she could have kept it down and was vowing that the sea had seen the last of her if she had to spend the rest of her life captive on the Emerald Isle. But, to give the witch her due, we disembarked at a dock empty save for one bored customs officer who made a cursory check of all baggage by casting one eye upon it to see if it was light enough to be hand-carried before waggling a thumb of dismissal toward the empty gates.

The gloomy, damp Dublin weather greeted us as we stepped out of the customs shed and caressed us with wet arms as we made our way to Grafton Street, where Maeve had arranged for us to stay with friends. I thought we were carrying subterfuge too far but held quiet and allowed Maeve to "smuggle" us into the inner-city life. We passed many pubs emitting strong stout smells and tearooms advertising a variety of teas with scones and cream and homemade jams. My mouth watered in anticipation of what awaited us, for we had not eaten since leaving Castletown.

We followed Grafton Street up to St. Stephen's Green and took a quick jaunt down what seemed a cobblestoned alley but was in reality one of those small streets dead-ending into an inn built across the street to stop its advance two hundred years ago. The Hound and Bird smelled of horse piss at least a hundred years old and was run by two of Maeve's friends who appeared to be siblings but were, instead, lovers with a penchant for unisex clothes. Dear, dirty Dublin. The whole affair reminded me of a scene from *The Informer*. Any minute I expected to be accosted by Victor McLaglen demanding I stand him a pint. It was a case of students determinedly living the role of revolutionaries complete with cold tea and hard biscuits accompanied by a slab of stale cheddar. I rebelled.

"This," I said to Maeve after we were alone in a garret room, "is carrying things too far."

"We must be careful," she said soothingly. She sat on the bed and sank two feet to the tune of protesting springs.

"We're not even in Northern Ireland, for Christ sakes," I complained. "If we were, then maybe I could understand a part of this. But we're not. The *Garda Síochána* isn't looking for us, the SAS is not looking for us, the RUC isn't looking for us, and I don't have, to the best of my recollection, any creditors in Ireland. Now, I don't mind sharing a cold, bare room with a beautiful woman, but I absolutely, positively, draw the line at this"—I waved a disgruntled hand over the tray that had been brought to our room—"*sorry* excuse for a meal."

She looked around the room, at the tray, then stared thoughtfully at me. Her lips parted in a slow grin. "Yes, perhaps it *is* a bit much. We Irish tend to be a bit overdramatic sometimes. Now, what would you be wanting?"

I felt my mouth salivate as I fantasized a gastronomical adventure. "I want," I said softly, reverently, "medium-rare roast beef and Yorkshire pudding, with a bottle of Beaujolais hand-warmed to match the roast beef. For dessert, I want Pavlova with kiwi fruit or whatever fruit is in season followed by a glass of brandy in front of a fire."

"Very well," she said. "I suppose allowances for the proto-revolutionary are in order. Would the grill at the Gresham be satisfactory?"

"Quite," I said, mocking her accent. "And I'll even pick up the tab."

"You'd better," she said, shrugging back into her coat. "I don't fancy washing dishes."

Half an hour later, I was contentedly sipping a Blarney Stone cocktail, waiting for the first of our order. I looked around the room with its dark wood paneling polished to a glow and smugly said, "Now, you have to admit this is much better than what we left."

"Yes," she acknowledged. "But is it as safe?"

I leaned toward her. "It's probably safer because anyone who might be searching for us will think to look in the usual places, like that dump we just left. Besides, we haven't done anything. I tried to tell you that back in London. Who the hell cares if we come to Ireland anyway? Everything is so far in the past that we're just tourists now. Or lovers," I wistfully added.

She laughed, glancing over my shoulder, then the laughter caught in her throat, and twin frown lines appeared between her eyes. I twisted in my seat to see what had suddenly caused her concern and found Liam Drumm weaving his way around the other diners toward our table.

"Maeve! Con! How good to see you!" he said upon his approach. "Imagine meeting you here. This is totally unexpected!" I stood to receive him, and he grabbed my hand, enthusiastically pumping it. I forced a smile.

"What are you doing here? How did you find us?" I asked him, pitching my voice low enough so that others could not hear the words but loud enough to avoid looking conspiratorial.

"Accidental, believe me," he said, beaming for the sake of any watchers while pitching his voice low. "I'm just here for a brief meeting with the Dail, then it's back to Manchester. I thought I'd better say hello in case someone saw us and wondered why we ignored each other. What the devil are you doing here? I thought you'd still be in London." I caught a heavy scent of porter on his breath.

"We finished early," Maeve said. "And if anyone followed you from Manchester, they've now found us." She gave me a disgusted look. "Your stomach may have blown our cover."

"Our 'cover,' if that is what that circuitous route we took here was supposed to supply, was probably blown long before Liam said hello. If people wanted to find us, they most certainly would have covered that cloak and dagger route." Liam looked half-worried as he tried to follow our argument.

"Excuse me," he said apologetically. "Is something the matter?"

"No problems," Maeve said disgustedly. "At least, I hope not. Are you going to be here long?"

A look of relief crossed his face. "Not long," he said loudly, his accent deepening, thickening to a stage Irishman's as he tried to convince anyone watching that our meeting was indeed accidental. "A night and day only. Then it's back to Manchester, and sad I'll be to leave the green of Ireland for the satanic mills of that gray English town. But, my beauty, the worst will be the taking of my leave from you."

He seemed to have the need to hold the center of attention, of the action: his fingers moved in mystic maunderings, his feet dancing a sycophantic suite in sambic measure as he cariocaed around the table to the side of her chair. He reached for her hand and kissed it with a stage flourish. Maeve gracefully pulled her hand free, archly eyeing him from a distance, slipping into the role he had elected her to play.

[93]

"Perhaps," she said, her voice slipping into an accent to match his. "But, sure, and you've been playing with the Fenians and dealing in money tainted with their blood."

"And sure it's not that I've been doing," he protested, casting nervous glances around to see if we'd been overheard. He lowererd his voice. "And, Maeve, my beauty, ye'd be doin' me a favor if ye'd be forgettin' the name of those rabble-rousers and others of their ilk. 'Tis dangerous talk."

Maeve gave him a beautiful smile, then innocently asked, "Why, Liam! Sure, you, being a newsman sworn to the truth, would not fear those you've sworn to expose: the traitors, the terrorists, the *gombeen* men. You won't be suggesting now, would you, that complicity might be existing? 'Tis positive I am that it's not fear you'd be confessing, for that to the newsman would be castration. So it's only a spot of fun you're having with us." She finished, a touch of acid in the last of her words.

Drumm flushed at the stage parody and sheepishly smiled. "Sorry. Guess I became a little . . ."

"Dramatic?" Maeve suggested, eyebrows raising. "Do not be blaming Willie Yeats now for your shortcomings, Liam Drumm. Nor your heritage. The truth be known, 'tis an onager you've become along with your riches. Do you fancy yourself another Croesus?"

" 'Tis another Croesus I wish I'd become," he said ruefully. "These togs cost a pretty shilling or two."

"Will you join us?" I asked hastily, indicating an empty chair at our table. He regretfully shook his head and dropped the stage-Irish brogue.

"Sorry. But I'm meeting some people about this TRANCO thing. Business, you know." He winked. "It is true, don't you think? Clothes do make the man." He turned slowly to let us admire the cut of his suit. Tiny lights flashed from the inlaid *R* on his moccasins.

"In some cases," Maeve said. "At least you look the part. But can you play it?" He beamed and again grabbed her hand, wetly kissing it.

"And what Irishman couldn't, given the chance? Take care, my beauty." His voice dropped. "And I'm sorry if I've complicated your situation, but it *was* an accident. Please believe that." He straightened, touched the knot of his tie, nodded at me, and left our table. I watched him walk the tables, treating their occupants as old friends on his way to the stag bar off the dining room.

"Well," I said, turning back to Maeve. "Hale friends heartily met and all that."

"Yes," she said, absently toying with the silver by her plate. A frown settled over her face as her eyes turned inward, racing along a hidden path of memory. Her mouth drew down into a hard, thin line.

"Maeve? What is it?" I asked, gently touching her hand lying on the table between us. "Maeve?" I gripped her hand harder and was rewarded by a tiny flutter of her eyelids and a sudden surge of warmth through her cheeks.

"Con?" she asked, puzzlement showing in her eyes. "What's wrong?"

"You tell me," I said, holding tightly to her hand. Her fingers automatically moved against my palm. She shakily laughed and withdrew her hand to reach for her wineglass.

"Sorry," she said, then paused to take a deep gulp of wine. "For some reason, Castlereagh suddenly seemed very close." I felt cold.

"What do you mean?" I asked.

"I don't know," she said. Color began to return to her face. "Just that for a moment, I could hear it and smell it again. Isn't that strange?" She tried to laugh again, but the sound was harsh and brittle.

"Not really," I said, refilling her glass. "I know of several cases when former soldiers suffered agonizing flashbacks. Psychiatrists call it 'posttraumatic stress syndrome.' It's very evident in those who have suffered severe trauma."

"Has it ever happened to you?"

"I have occasional dreams," I admitted. "But that's all."

"I envy you," she said. "To have such peace of mind must be gratifying. Conor never had that." Back to Conor again. I was beginning to see a pattern developing within her: a retreat into her marriage during troubling memories.

"I have many dreams," I said. "The result of many years."

"You can't be that old," she said.

"It's not the years," I said. "It's the mileage."

She laughed. "If that were true, why then I would be an old hag."

"That is an impossibility," I said gallantly.

She inclined her head. "Why thank you, kind sir." We both began to helplessly giggle, caught in the absurdity of the moment. It was a welcome change, but I recognized a trace of a dark secret beneath her laughter and wondered if the fear and hate she experienced at Castlereagh had been responsible for her strange, almost endogamous, marriage with Conor. Suddenly I had a brief insight into Conor: he had had an elemental desire for immortality that he pursued under the guise of nobility, like Spenser's knight knocking too boldly on the iron door.

But what did that leave for Maeve? I tried to keep the atmosphere light and happy through dinner against the threat of black recall.

"Well, kind sir," she said, pulling her coat collar tight around her neck as we emerged from the Gresham into an evening of mist, "you have been wined and dined, and now it's off to bed." I grimaced as I thought of The Hound and the Bird and the room waiting for us.

"Must we?" I wistfully added. "There's the Sherbourne and at least a dozen others not far from here." She shook her head and firmly hooked her arm through mine.

"Now. You promised."

"I know," I sighed. "I know. But I can always hope you change your mind." She laughed, throwing her head back, exposing the strong lines of her throat.

"Not a chance. Come on. Time's a-wasting, and we have a long day tomorrow." Resolutely, I turned my steps toward the inn. By the time we reached the front door, I had reluctantly changed my mind. My feet were wet, my coat soaked, and the temperature had fallen a good five degrees.

"At last," I murmured to Maeve. I reached for the door-knob, then froze as I noticed the door ajar. A familiar tingle settled sickeningly into my stomach.

"What's wrong?" Maeve asked. I shook my head, backing away from the door.

"I don't know," I said. "Something. Maybe nothing." I

pointed at the door. She frowned, biting her lip. "Maybe someone just left the door open by accident."

"And maybe not," she said. "Come with me." We squeezed between the inn and its neighbor, carefully feeling our way through the blackness to the rear of the inn. My feet slipped on the wet cobblestones. I tried to breathe through my mouth as the stench of rotting garbage floated up from the stones. My stomach rolled, threatening to purge itself. "Here we are," she said, pausing before a door. She gently lifted the latch. We squeezed through the narrow doorway and found ourselves in the inn storeroom. Bottles shone dimly in the pale light. The room was musty with an acrid smell to it.

We groped across the room and opened the opposite door a crack and peeped through. The interior looked empty. Together, we cautiously stepped into the room. Her friends were behind the counter, roped and gagged, staring sightlessly at us. Maeve turned away. I forced myself to take a closer look: each had been shot through the knees, then through the back of the head with a small-caliber pistol. Surprisingly, there wasn't much blood. I heard the stairs creak behind me. My heart lurched in my chest. But it was only Maeve climbing to the rooms above us. I followed. Only two other rooms had been rented besides ours. Their inhabitants had been executed in a like manner: bound, gagged, bullets in the knees and the backs of heads.

"Jesus," I breathed.

"Yes," Maeve bitterly said. "They were thorough."

"I'll call the *Garda*," I said. I made a move to the door.

"No," she said. "Not yet. We have to be gone before they arrive."

"What?" I asked stupidly. She impatiently shook her head.

"Who knows who'll arrive first? We have to be careful. Someone's after us. Otherwise, these people wouldn't have been killed. They were looking for us. Come on." We hurried to our rooms and gathered our bags, carefully wiping our fingerprints from whatever surfaces we might have touched.

"Who do you think did this?" I asked. "Provos?"

"Who else?" she bitterly rejoined. "Come on!"

We hurried downstairs toward the door when suddenly a

memory flashed through my mind. I grabbed Maeve's arm and dragged her back away from the door.

"What's the matter?" she asked, her voice rising in alarm.

"The door," I said. "Why was it left ajar?"

"Maybe they left in a hurry?" she said dubiously.

"I doubt it," I said. "Leave a door open for any passerby to see?"

"This is an inn," she said, continuing to play the devil's advocate.

"Uh-huh," I said. I carefully stepped to the door and studied it. I almost missed the thin wire running from the door through an eyelet on the jamb to a hand grenade taped to a two-gallon pickle jar filled with liquid detergent and gasoline. "Here," I said, pointing out my discovery. "Instant napalm. This old building would have burned fast with us in it. We'd better call the *Garda*."

"From the box on the corner," she said, adding to my raised eyebrow. "The telephone could have been fixed, too."

We slipped out the back door, retracing our steps through the narrow passageway to the telephone booth. I impatiently waited while Maeve made the call to the *Garda*, feeling the eyes of shadows on the back of my neck. At last, she was through. We hurried through the mist to the Shelbourne, a hundred years away from The Hound and the Bird.

"We shouldn't have gone out," Maeve bitterly said as we hurried through the streets. "If we had stayed there—"

"—we'd have died the same way," I snapped. But I felt the guilt for the death of her friends heavy upon my shoulders, accepting her pain, her anger, her frustration directed at me for stubbornly insisting that we go out for dinner. I had caused their deaths—of that, I was positive. But I did not understand how—or why.

FOUR

I groaned and tried to ease my legs in the cramped front seat of the Ford Cortina as Maeve recklessly drove along the narrow back roads paralleling N6 toward Galway. Maeve's plan was to take the coastal road around Connemara to County Sligo like a pair of tourists, with a stopoff in Clifden to visit with Michael John.

A search of Conor's papers had revealed nothing regarding the Porcupine Banks Project, leaving us with little choice but to seek answers elsewhere. The only "elsewhere" either of us could think of was Mullaghmore, the port designated in the exploration grant given to TRANCO.

I gritted my teeth as the Cortina dropped deep into a dip in the road, then rose and violently swung left between two stone walls. If we met another car, the result would be murderous. "Wouldn't we be better off on N6? It is a primary road."

"And easier to follow us," she said impatiently. "Although we may go a bit out of our way, it'll be a safer route."

"How?" I closed my eyes as we swung dangerously close to a wall.

"We have friends this way," she explained. "Have you forgotten Michael John?"

"No," I said meaningfully. "I haven't forgotten anything about Clifden."

"Some things," she said softly, "would be better forgotten."

I twisted in my seat to look fully upon her. "Maeve," I said carefully, "why are you doing this?"

"I told you."

"Conor's dead, Maeve. Why are you doing this?"

She sighed, threw a quick look at me, then said, "If you are looking for a deep psychological reason, you won't find it. I've already been through that."

"Now it's all patriotism? The search for an informer, a *gombeen* man? You expect me to believe that?"

"You don't have to be here," she flared. "I'm sure I can find someone else to help me."

"Like Michael John? Liam Drumm?"

"Yes," she said, her voice rising defiantly. "He's more than capable."

"Oh, forget it," I said crossly. I turned back to watch the countryside speeding past. The gorse, shaggy on top, was bright green dappled in pink. On the high hills in the distance, I could see sheep grazing. I wasn't mad at her—it was more frustration than anything. The argument, I knew, was an attempt to avoid the inevitable question and answer that had been dangerously close to being voiced. Sooner or later, we would have to face it, but this was not the time. As afraid as she was of the question, I was equally afraid of the answer.

We didn't stop in Galway, the City of Tribes, but continued on west, following the twisting, scenic route along the north shore of Galway Bay toward Clifden. I was mesmerized once again by the *côte sauvage* coast, a craggy landmass stubbornly resisting the Atlantic pounding. From time to time, we ran past clusters of lined cottages with thatched roofs and nets drying on broken spar racks, picturesque and poor, but showing a proud, quiet spirit.

Maeve cleared her throat and in a neutral voice said, "I still do not see any connection between Conor's death and TRANCO."

"Neither do I," I answered, glad for a chance to break the strained silence between us. "But Conor was killed on TRAN-CO's docks. Maybe the informer worked for them."

She shook her head. "I don't think so."

"Still, we need a starting point. I'm afraid TRANCO's all we have. Besides," I added, "why else would Special Branch be so interested in questioning us after Conor's funeral? Where did Conor get his information about an informer?"

"From Liam. Apparently the night after I was freed, Liam was tipping a few pints with a Brit sergeant in a pub, and the sergeant let it slip that the RUC was upset because they didn't know about the attempt to free me in time. They got the call too late to stop the boys. As it was, they just missed intercepting you that day."

"Lucky," I murmured and stared out the window.

"Is something the matter?" Maeve asked.

'Should there be?" I countered.

"Now, stop that," she said, grinning, a soft admonishment in her words. " 'Tis something you're thinking about. What?"

"Well," I said, "for a bog-trotting Irishman 'tis sure a fine set of feathers our Liam's been sportin' lately. A regular trimmer, that one." Laughter exploded from her in a series of high giggles that forced her to ease up on the accelerator lest we graze a wall on one side or the other.

Finally, she daubed at her eyes with the back of a wrist. "I really do not think you have to worry about Liam Drumm. We practically grew up together."

"Yes, I know," I said, remembering the story about the banns. "But people change."

"Not that much," she said. "Anyway, if he was the informer there are others more important than myself he would be concerning himself with. Why would he risk telling Conor about the Brit sergeant?"

"I don't know," I said. "You're right. Christ. Liam. I'm just looking for a starting place. Something. Anything. Do you have any ideas?"

She shook her head. "No. And I doubt if TRANCO's the answer. Maybe Michael John can put us onto something."

"Maybe," I grunted doubtfully and again turned my attention to the scenery as she concentrated on coaxing another few miles per hour from what seemed to me an already overtaxed engine. The feeling of helplessness was beginning to make me moody, but I could not find any parallels, any leads. Our only hope was to snag something. So far, logic was useless. I winced as the Cortina bounced through a deep hole. If, I privately amended, we survive this trip.

FIVE

Clifden hadn't changed—the stone walls, the large commons, the quiet streets—and Michael John a solid fixture in the corner of The Hour-Glass, reading *The Irish Independent*, a pint on the table before him. The young man who had been at the counter the last time I came to the pub was missing, but I thought I recognized one of the patrons, a ferret-faced man nursing a pint of Guinness. I crossed to Michael John.

"Some things," I said dryly, "never change." He raised his head, a brief look of annoyance flickering before recognition.

"And, in truth, why should they?" he asked, eyes twinkling merrily from rubicund face finely reticulated. "Aren't we all just figments of our own imagination?"

"Or others'," I said, holding out my hand. He grasped it firmly. "How have you been, Michael John?"

"As well as can be expected," he said. "It's been a long time. Have a drink."

"Maeve's waiting," I said by way of refusal. "Outside. In the car."

Caution touched his eyes. He picked up his glass and drained it. "Herself, is it? Ah. A sad life she's led." He shook his head and stood, carefully pulling his scully cap down over one eye. "But, then, he brought it upon himself, I suppose. More's the pity." He moved toward the door. I fell in beside him.

"What do you mean?" I asked. He looked blankly at me. "About bringing it on himself?"

"Shh. 'Tis no place to be talkin' treason," he said warningly. His eyes flitted around the room. He stepped closer and confidently leaned toward my ear. I smelled the sweetness of the porter on his breath. "You've been gone so long you cannot have known. 'Tis a thing kept from her as well."

I grabbed the lapels of his coat. "Conor Larkin? Traitor? What madness is this?"

"Easy, now," he said admonishingly. He plucked my fingers from his coat. " 'Tis the truth. Seamus MacCauley himself charged Conor when he kept insisting there was an informer in the ranks. And what else could MacCauley have done, the Brotherhood existing solely on trust and all?"

"MacCauley? I would have thought he would have been most interested in seeing if Conor was right," I said.

"Conor's accusation came at a bad time," Michael John said soberly. "There was a chance we could all get together— the Fenians, the Provos, the Republicans—but Conor's accusation toward the Provos made the others uneasy. MacCauley had little choice, man! United, the war would have lasted no longer than a couple of months!"

I shook my head and stepped away. "Truth is the first victim of war and its expounders the second."

"Ah, now, don't be a-taking it that way," he said, following me to the door. "I'd sell the soul of me own granmuther if it would mean a united Ireland." The man at the bar raised his head at this to stare at us. I lowered my voice.

"And put a bounty on the heads of men like Conor Larkin? Some prices are too dear. What good is a country without honor?" I threw open the door and stepped outside. I drew deep breaths to clear my head. "So, who had the contract?"

He looked curiously at me. "On Conor Larkin? Are you daft, man? He was still Conor Larkin."

"You mean . . ." I paused to stare at him. He nodded.

"Yes. That's what I've been telling you. 'Twas only if he went north did he have anything to worry about. Or," he emphasized, pitching his voice lower as we neared the Cortina where Maeve patiently waited, "if he ever involved himself in Provo business again."

"And the Manchester docks?" I hurriedly asked. "That was Provo business?"

He stopped and stared at me, lips curling into a mocking grin. "And from which port do you think most of our arms come? But they didn't kill him, Con. They didn't kill him. Maeve!" Beaming a welcome, he walked rapidly toward her, powerful arms spread for a hug. I turned to close the door. The man with the ferret face had gone back to his pint.

I shook my head in despair. The story seemed directionless, a piece of flotsam aimlessly drifting on the whims of tide and current.

"Con!"

I shook myself from my thoughts and obediently hurried forward at Maeve's beckoning.

The twilight was a long gloaming as we neared the cottage on the cliffs outside Clifden. Maeve and Michael John kept up an excited chatter, playing the what-has-happened game good friends always play after a separation of any length longer than a month. A flock of corncakes, black and raucous, sprang into the air as we turned off Highway N59 onto the dusty road leading to the house on the cliff. Ahead of us, a sliver of blue showed above the line of the cliff and the house. An ache struck my chest as memories tried to crowd into my mind, but I forced them away by concentrating on the dialogue between Maeve and Michael John.

"It hasn't changed much now," Michael John said, keeping an anxious eye on Maeve.

"Oh, a bit," she said softly. "All things change. For good or ill." She slipped out of the Cortina and slowly walked toward the house.

"Er . . . yes . . . now . . . uh," Michael John stuttered as he untangled himself to follow her. He threw a desperate look in my direction and scurried after her. I sighed and stepped out of the car, stretching cramped legs. I was tired and hungry. I didn't know how Michael John was going to explain what he knew about Conor's death to Maeve, but explain he would have to, for she had a right to the truth and would, I knew, accept nothing else. After the explanation, we would have to worry about how Maeve handled being here, not before. She could either withdraw from the world as she did when I first brought her here or become a *Leanan-Sidhe*, the bloodsucking vampire of Irish legend, muse of poets, vengeful spirit. I feared the latter more than the former. Nightmares feed upon themselves to replenish their purpose.

"Is she all right now, do you think?" Michael John anxiously asked, returning for the fourth time within the past five minutes to watch Maeve out on the cliff's edge. She had waited until halfway through the evening meal before asking the question Michael John had dreaded. At first, he'd stammered and lied, then suddenly blurted out the story he'd told me in The Hour-Glass. She sat quietly until he finished, then rose and went outside.

"Yes," I said. "For now. Want some more tea?" I held the pot over his mug. He shuddered and hurriedly covered it with his hand.

"Tea? You'll have me running to the jakes with tea. Give me something with more body. There's a bottle in the cupboard." He sighed with frustration and scrubbed his hands across his face. "Ah. The poor thing." I fetched the bottle and set it at his elbow. I sat across the table from him, refilled my mug, and contemplated the plate of crumbly orange Irish cheddar and processed Galtee cheese remaining from our Spartan dinner.

"What happens now?" he asked, expertly removing the cork from the whiskey bottle with a wide thumb. He poured a generous measure into his cup and thirstily drank.

"I don't know," I said. "I suppose up to Sligo."

"What do you hope to be finding there?" He poured another dram into his mug, caught my eye, and said defensively, "There's no satisfying the devil once he's in your throat. A powerful thirst." I shrugged and looked out along the cliff. "Well?"

"Nothing," I said. "Not anymore, anyway. But I had hopes when we started this."

"Of her?" he asked quietly. I turned in surprise toward him. "It's no secret, you know. Not when one sees how you look at her."

"Is it that obvious?" I reached for the bottle and laced my tea.

"To everyone but her, I'm thinking," he said. "But, then, Conor Larkin is too close to mind and all men pale before the memory of that one. Until now, maybe," he added. "God and St. Brigid help me!" He grabbed his mug and brought it to his lips.

"She really wasn't in love with him, you know."

"How's that?" he asked suspiciously. He placed the mug back on the table. "She married him, man! Of course she loved him!"

I shook my head. "She needed him. And, I think, after a fashion, he needed her, too. But need is not love, and they were not in love."

"Then what was it?"

"I think a sense of belonging," I said slowly. "All that they once were had been taken from them—Conor, his sense of justice, his truth, his honor by the people who negotiated the early treaties and the Provos; Maeve, her self-esteem and pride by the animals at Castlereagh. It was completely natural for them to come together as they did."

"Like two lost sheep in a fold?" Maeve asked from behind me. Michael John cleared his throat and reached for the bottle. His hand halted at Maeve's cutting remark. "Is it a wake you're thinking of having, Michael John? If it is, and it's Conor you're thinking of, you're a month too late."

"Now, Maeve," he lamely said, "that's no way to be talking. Me and Conor were friends."

"I know," she said, her voice perceptibly softer, "but don't be dirtying his memory for the sole purpose of drinking." Chastened, he looked away, his face burning bright red. She crossed from behind me and patted his shoulder. "I'm sorry, Michael John. But please stop treating me as glass. I won't shatter if you tell me the truth. You," she said, turning to face me, "are quite the psychologist, Con. But in one aspect you're wrong."

"Perhaps. It doesn't really matter, does it?" I asked. "You've already made up your mind, haven't you?"

A faint smile played around her lips. "Yes," she said. "I have."

I nodded. "Somehow, I was afraid of that. Is it for Conor or yourself?"

"Does it really matter?"

"No," I said heavily. "I guess it doesn't. Either way, you'll do it." I reached for the bottle; Maeve reached for a cup. I poured. Michael John sighed contentedly.

"Sure, I know what you two are about," he said. "But, if you're going to be opening the bottle again, I think I'll be joining you. For myself, Maeve, for myself," he hastily added.

Maeve grinned and nodded. I topped off his cup. Michael John sighed. "You've a fine, steady hand," he said to me. We took a silent drink together. The wind moaned outside. A stone clinked against the wall, breaking the moment of reverie. "Now. What are you two about?"

"Sligo first, then on to Belfast if we turn up nothing there," I said. He stared at us for a moment, then shook his head.

"Mary, Mother of God," he groaned. "Can't you see the wrong of it? There's too many of them for you to find the one you want. Too many who would as soon kill you as take the trouble to deal with you. None of the bailiffs will be helping you, and none but the Holy Father'd be taking notice of the likes of you."

"Maybe," I said, noting the Connaught thickening of his words from the whiskey. "But we intend to try anyway."

"Why not stay here?" he pleaded. "Can't you sit in by the hearth with the light lit and herself in the room beyond? There's many a quare fellow getting his death in Sligo and Enniskillen. No need to be adding more to them."

"Michael John," Maeve said gently. "Have you something else to tell us?"

He sadly shook his head. "The only friends you'll be finding up north will be the bloody Brits, and then only if you're willing to be sheared like Wicklow sheep. Or the holy brotherhoods."

"Tell us what you know," Maeve said sharply.

"They're a heartless crew, Maeve," he said after a moment's hesitation. "They wouldn't give a *thraneen* to save you if they wanted. A last warning on the head of him who utters Conor Larkin's name."

"Last warning?" I asked.

"Kneecapping," Maeve said impatiently. "Someone puts a bullet through each kneecap, and it's off to the Royal Victoria for an artificial fitting. It's a fright surely, Michael John, but aren't you a louty schemer to go on a-keening like a mourner at a wake? It's a poor thing for a man such as yourself to be doing to a poor widow. A spavined tinker's mule has more honesty in his backside than you have in your black heart."

"Faith," he said, " 'tis a sharp tongue you have, Maeve Larkin. So you want my drift, do you? There are other things I could be telling you. Won't you be having them?"

"I'll be having what you know about Conor Larkin, Michael John, or it's your name I'll be giving to a poet!"

"By the murdering saints and the mother of blessed Saint Brigid! Maeve, none will help you! The rising tide has washed all traces of Conor's memory from man. The word was passed by MacCauley himself, who at this moment is keeping the gobshite Prods from changing Sligo into another Belfast."

"What's this?" I broke in. "MacCauley? In Sligo?"

"And where else would he be what with TRANCO hiring? Do you think we'd be letting the sons of a scabby tinker wench have a free hand with the hiring and firing in the Republic as well as the counties? He'll be giving bad cess to them who try to ram their brogans down our gullets. O'Bannion, too. And Fallon." He rapidly crossed himself. "And may God grant His indulgence to those who cross that one. You see now, Maeve darling, why you can't go?"

"Where in Sligo?"

"Maeve, it's an appointment with death you'll be keeping if you go to Sligo now. And for what? Conor'll be after knowing nothing about it and caring less."

"Honor, Michael John," she said quietly. "Conor's honor."

A stone again clinked against the cottage wall as he opened his mouth to answer her. I held up my hand in warning and motioned at the window. Maeve frowned. His eyes narrowed and he nodded, silently rising.

"Honor, Maeve," I said conversationally as Michael John soundlessly glided to the door, "has caused the needless deaths of too many people. Will it make Conor's grave any the warmer?" Michael John lifted the latch and slipped out into the night. "Will it change others' opinions of him? To the rest of the world, he is still a legend that will live on long after we are gone." A large thump by the wall beside the window accented my words. Moments later, the door burst open, and the ferret-faced man from the pub stumbled into the room propelled by an angry Michael John.

"Would you be lookin' at what I found lurking about outside?" he said angrily. "Careful!" The man whirled, a flick-knife appearing in his hand. Michael John caught his wrist with one hand, twisted his arm straight, and struck his elbow hard with the flat of his hand. The elbow popped. The man screamed and dropped the knife. He grabbed his elbow and sagged, gray-faced, against the wall of the cottage. Michael John clucked his tongue. "Foolish man."

"How long do you think he was there?" Maeve asked. I shook my head.

"I heard something about an hour ago, but thought it was the wind," I answered.

"So. It's safe to assume he heard everything." I nodded. She turned back to him. "Who sent you here?"

"Me arm," he moaned. Michael John made a threatening move. He flinched away, sliding down the wall to cower in the corner. "For the luv-o-God! I don't know! 'Twas a telephone call along the network. You know how it works!"

"Who called you?" Michael John asked. "It's no Clifden man you are. That, I know."

"Dublin," he said sullenly, wincing. "I got the call in Dublin."

"I thought I recognized you," I said. "You picked us up at the Gresham, didn't you?" He hesitated, then nodded. "Then you're the one who tried to kill us at the inn." His eyes widened, and he violently shook his head.

"Before God, no!" he said. "That was none of my doing! Nor of the lads, I'm telling you!" He looked imploringly at Michael John. "Faith, you know the policy in the south! Any who'd do that digs his own grave!" Michael John caught my eye and nodded.

"There's truth to those words," he said grudgingly. "By now, we'd know if the council had directed that operation. But," he added threateningly, turning back to the man, "that doesn't mean it wasn't your dirty hand stirring the mess."

"Sweet Jaysus," he breathed. "I didn't even know anything about the two of yous until I got the call. I went straight to the Gresham and stayed with you ever since."

"I believe him," I reluctantly said. "Don't ask me why. How did you get here ahead of us?"

"I heard you talkin' about comin' here," he said sullenly. "When you turned off south to come the back road, I came up N6." I turned to look meaningfully at Meave. She ignored me.

"What were your instructions?" she asked. He shook his head and made a sudden leap for the door. Michael John threw out his arm like a bar, catching him in the throat. The Provo's legs kicked up in front of him, and he crashed to the floor, cracking the back of his head against the corner of the table on his way down. Michael John hastily bent and pressed two fingers against his throat, feeling for the pulse. He thoughtfully pursed his lips and peeled back the man's eyelids, checking the pupils. He shook his head and rose.

"Sorry, Maeve. He'll be out for some time. Maybe morning."

"That's all right," she said. "Couldn't be helped."

"What do you want me to do with him? Over the cliff?"

"No!" I said loudly. They looked at me curiously. "Good God! That would make us no better than he is."

"We aren't," Michael John said softly. "You have to be like them, if you want to continue with this. It's safer over the cliff, Maeve."

"Maybe," she answered. "But we'll be long gone before he wakes up. Then what can he tell them? That he failed? You know what that'll mean. No, he'll lie and say he lost us after having a motor breakdown. Take him south and leave him at Carna. There's no telephones there," she said. "It'll take him a few days to make his way to Galway."

"It'd be easier over the cliff," Michael John argued.

"But a senseless death," she said. "No, take him to Carna."

"If you say so. And what about yourselves?"

"You know where, Michael John, and I'll be thanking you for the name now."

"Ah. Now." He rubbed his palm across his lips as if to wipe the words away before they sprang free. "You'll be going, I suppose, whether I tell you or not?" She nodded. "God help me and keep Conor's spirit from my bedside." He paused a moment to reflect and gather his thoughts. "They'll be staying at a safe house. Father Mahon will know their lay-by."

"*Cullen* Mahon?" Maeve asked. "I thought he was down at Dingle."

"North he is now," Michael John said. "Still saying the Mass after drinking till the red dawn. He's got a proper devil in his throat, does that one, but he's stayed true to Conor. 'Tis the best I can do for you, Maeve. No one'll harm you with him for fear he'll read their names in the Mass on Sunday. Except Fallon. That one has no soul, but he will listen to MacCauley. And, of course, O'Bannion. That one has never stood queue for confessional."

Maeve rose and walked around the table to him. She bent and kissed him on the cheek. "Thank you, Michael John," she said. "For Conor. Thank you."

"Enough of that, enough of that," he said gruffly. "I'm feeling I've piped the long car for you, Maeve Nolan-Larkin. And you, Con Edwards. It's certain I am that you'll be following a blind lead, for neither one of you knows enough to beware the young streelers trailing after MacCauley seeking his approval. But," he added, his voice softening, "I'll be giving you the blessings of all the saints and try and join you in a day or two. Remember, though," he cautioned, "the truth is not what it seems in the Western world. We've hidden it far too long here. You'll have to find it on your own."

His words held a terrible finality that did little to reassure me. He bent and unceremoniously draped the man over his shoulder. "I'll be going now," he said. "It's a wee way to Carna, and I want to be shot of him 'fore it's light. So, I'll be saying good-bye and God bless." Maeve rose on tiptoes and kissed his leathery cheek.

"You're a good friend, Michael John," she said. "Thank you."

"Go on with you," he gruffly answered. "You watch yourself up north. 'Tis no game they're playing. One last thing, Maeve. This wasn't the doings of MacCauley."

"How do you know?" she asked.

"The call came in Dublin," he answered. "The lads are all in Sligo now. No, Maeve, darlin'," he added, shaking his head. " 'Tis someone else responsible for this business. MacCauley has authority only in the North. But you know that." He nodded and left, closing the door behind him. It seemed terribly abrupt and final. I looked at Maeve. She smiled and reached out to squeeze my hand.

"Thank you, too," she said.

"For what?" I said. I held her eyes for a moment. "Maeve . . ." I stopped as she made a tiny movement with her hand.

"I know," she said. "I know. And so does Conor."

I felt his ghost move between us again and bit my tongue against the thoughts I wanted to voice. They would have been useless words anyway, for she already knew them. Too many memories remained in the cottage for them to be spoken now.

Together, we sat at the rough-hewn kitchen table through the night, watching large bugs click against the lantern, murmuring slight remembrances of Conor Larkin, and reliving memories of what had been against the uncertain and uneasy future.

SIX

Tension seemed to build within the car as we drove into Sligo. The trip up from Clifden had been fairly quiet, the raw beauty of Connaught sliding unnoticed past the car windows as we silently contemplated what waited for us. Even the stately and serene abbey on sylvan Kylemore Lake could not induce us to make more than a passing commentary.

Sligo appeared asleep as we pulled into the city in midafternoon. It seemed different this visit: the buildings weathered, facades cracked as was the tarmacadam in places on the streets. Signs hanging from creaking chains showed fading letters advertising products no longer for sale. Windows in a few places had been boarded over. The few people in the streets wore serviceable clothing, unfashionable among their peers in "dear, dirty Dublin."

The fishing boats were still out after salmon when we slipped past the harbor and the flour and sawmills still open along the Garavogue River. It was evident that Sligo had been waiting for an economic surge since the Irish had been sent to Connaught by the mercenaries of William of Orange.

We found the Roman Catholic cathedral near the college, both built in the Norman style—huge, gray granite blocks forming crenellated walls and towers fairly covered in ivy.

Inside the dimly lit sanctuary, the well-varnished pews softly glowed from the burnish of many hands. The air seemed heavily laden with incense and sins. I thought I heard the clacking of ancient rosary beads, but it was only imagination. A few elderly people patiently waited in line a discreet distance from a confessional box. A faint chant touched my ears from the central altar, a priest busily at work cleaning the vessels:

Ut queant laxis Reasonare fibris.
Mira gestorum Famuli tuorum,
Solve polluti Labii reatum,
Sanete Joannes.

I nudged Maeve and nodded toward the priest. "You don't suppose he could be the one?"

She shrugged her shoulders. "I'm thinking there's only the two. One in the confessional and himself." She walked determinedly down the aisle, deliberately not genuflecting. I followed behind. She paused in front of the communion railing. "Is it Father Cullen Mahon I'm addressing?" she bluntly asked.

He paused and looked up, gray eyes warily flashing, eyebrows knotted in perplexity at the lack of servility in her voice. Irish priests are used to the deference shown to them by the populace, most notably the women.

"Perhaps," he said softly, his eyes sweeping the cathedral behind us. "And if it is Father Mahon I am, what would you be wanting with him? If it's confession, Father O'Donnell is available now."

" 'Tis not the confessional I'm after, with its stains of lies and false hopes," Maeve answered tartly. His eyes narrowed at her sacrilege. " 'Tis himself we want."

"For what purpose?" His words held an undercurrent of anger.

"Before God and all?" Maeve asked, raising her eyebrows at the foolishness of the question. She looked pointedly at the line of confessors by the side of the church. "But then what else should I expect from a Sunday Fenian?"

He started, darting a quick, anxious look at the confessional. "God's grace, woman! Has the devil got you by the tongue? Who are you?"

"Maeve Larkin," she said. "And this is—"

"Con Edwards," he said, lips thinning as if he'd bitten into a lemon. "Word has been passed. Come with me."

We followed him through the vestry to a small, cluttered office. He swept a pile of books off a couple of chairs and motioned us to them. He slid behind his desk and opened a drawer, producing a bottle of Black Bush.

"Would you be taking a jar?" he asked solicitously. We nodded. He reached back into the drawer and removed three squat glasses. He poured liberal dollops into each and passed them around before leaning back in his chair with a sigh, the nearly filled squat glass firmly clutched in right hand. "Now," he said, tasting the whiskey, "what is all this nonsense you're on and about, Mrs. Larkin—or is it Nolan once more? And what do you mean running in here and casting aspersions without so much as a by-your-leave or a showing of proper respect for the Lord? 'Tis a careful line you're treading, Maeve Nolan, with these sacrilegious panderings."

Maeve gave me a thin smile, then directed her attention back to the good father. "Then if you'll be pardoning my saying so, Father, I'll be getting on with telling you—if you'll shut your gob for a minute." The priest flushed, the knuckles of his hand holding the glass suddenly white. Maeve ignored his anger and smoothly continued. "It's information I'm after, as you're well aware. Where do we find Seamus MacCauley and Richard O'Bannion? And don't be telling me the tale while you're about it."

He took a healthy jolt from his glass and shook his head. "And what makes you think I'd know the whereabouts of the likes of them?"

"First, you're a priest—even if you are a rogue priest—and the boys have a need for such as you now and again. Secondly, there's nowhere else to go in Sligo to be safe."

He scratched the back of his head and tugged at his forelock. "Well, for Seamus, perhaps, there's need of a priest, but it's a dark day since Dickie O'Bannion set foot in the church door. But, aye, I know their whereabouts. Little good it'll do you, Maeve Nolan, wife of Conor Larkin, for you've no right to be asking and the door being closed to you."

"And why is the door closed to me?" she asked, her voice suddenly soft.

He shifted his weight in the chair and looked uncomfortable before her scrutiny. "Now, you know full well why Seamus had to close the door to you, what with Conor going on so and you followin' in his steps. 'Tis true. 'Tis true," he said, holding up a hand against her objections. "At first, the possibility that he might be right was considered, but nothing was found. And how could there be? He had no names, no witnesses, only a few happenstances that could be but more than likely were not. And where was Seamus to go with the likes of that? 'Twas sedition Conor Larkin was preaching, and at an ill time. Progress was being made in negotiations. Talk of an informer was harmful to our stand. What else could the man do?"

"And so we ruin a man's reputation for the sake of a few words that had the ring of truth to them? A man whose entire life was given to uniting Ireland?"

"Where was the truth?" he demanded.

"In the man himself," Maeve answered. "In Conor Larkin. Now in his memory."

Father Mahon stared unblinking at her for a long moment, then wearily shook his head, raised his glass, and drained the contents. "All right. I'll take you to them. It's another jar we'll be needing before we face them and that devil's breath, Tomas Fallon. We'll take a touch with us as well, for we've a ways to travel, and I can feel the change of the sea a-coming."

Mullaghmore lies only about thirty short miles north of Sligo on a small point of land jutting into Donegal Bay. Close to five hours, though, passed before we reached it after leaving the church. Father Mahon insisted we follow a route that explored the back country of his parish and the neighboring ones of Rosses Point, Raghly, and Grange. My eyes felt gritty, and my mouth had a foul taste from frequent nips at Mahon's flask. A small ache had settled behind my right eye by the time we pulled into a farmyard just on the outskirts of Mullaghmore. The false light of early dawn showed grayly in the east. All was quiet, although a thin plume of smoke rose from the chimney and held low against the heavy dampness. The black windows of the farmhouse malevolently watched as we stiffly climbed from the Cortina. I turned to look over the farmyard, pretending a casualness I did not feel.

The farm had not been properly managed for a long time. The outbuildings badly needed paint. A broken pitchfork with rusty tines lay against the barn wall along with pieces of broken machinery. The yard itself was bare, rock-hard from well-packed earth. Some stones had fallen from the wall and lay where they had fallen, now covered with lichens. The gate swung drunkenly on one hinge, the slats splintered. Father Mahon caught my eye and shook his head.

"Ah, now, Dan's a fine man, I'll have you know. 'Tis through no fault of his that the ground goes a-wanting for hands to work it. His son cools his heels in The Maze and his daughter has taken up with a British captain in Ballyclare," he said, his voice tightening with anger at the last. "He has only a wastrel of a man who thinks himself a prophet and healer and his wife, Dan's niece—a poor, misguided creature without a mind of her own—to care for him." He lifted his flask, took a short drink, then spat upon the ground. "To think a good Christian lass would fall for the platitudes and posturing and preaching of that profane whited sepulcher! 'Tis enough to curdle good whiskey in an honest man's throat."

The door behind us opened. We turned as one to face Tomas Fallon leaning against the doorframe, eyes casually studying us from a face as white as a priest's Easter alb. He wore a black leather jacket over a black turtleneck sweater, black leather pants, and black ankle boots. An UZI carelessly dangled from thin fingers.

"What do you want, priest?" he asked, his voice soft yet carrying the distance to us.

"Himself," Mahon said, muttering under his breath, "and may the saints keep us safe."

"You were told not to bring them, priest," he said, his eyes flicking back and forth between Maeve and myself. It was a simple statement, yet the threat was there with his presence. A sudden chill brushed across me.

"I'll answer to himself," Mahon said. "Not to you. Be good enough to announce us, if you will."

A smile suddenly flashed and disappeared across his face. "Before his morning coffee? Aren't you the brave one?" He pushed away from the door frame. "But you'll be coming in anyway while we wait. It won't do to have you standing about in the yard like a band of gypsies."

"Band of gypsies?" Mahon's indignation could be heard in

his voice. "You'll be showing some respect, Tomas Fallon, or I'll be reading your name in the Mass!"

The flash appeared again, and I realized it was as close as Fallon ever came to smiling. "Suit yourself. 'Tis only your own breath you'll be wasting, priest. And that you know."

"Yes, but I still have hope," Mahon said resignedly and led the way inside the house. We passed through a short hallway and emerged into a large kitchen, once-white walls now showing a tinge of gray. A large table buttressed by twelve chairs stood opposite a huge cast-iron stove next to a large fireplace with a baker's oven built into the side. At the far end, a towering escritoire with shelves and nooks crammed to overflowing with paper stood next to a large sideboard laden with plates and vessels. A door left ajar at the corner showed the pantry. A woman paused from rolling out dough to consider us as we came through the door. She wore a carefully ironed red-and-white checkered dress covered by a long white apron. Her honey blond hair was tightly pulled back from a round and pleasant face. Laugh lines appeared at the corners of her lips, but her blue eyes carried a certain vacuity that bothered me.

"Yes, Mr. Fallon, and is it guests we'll be having for breakfast?" she asked.

"Yes, Sarah, it is," Fallon said softly. " 'Tis coffee, though, I think they'll be wanting now. They've come a long ways."

"Ah! Be seating yourselves, sirs, and I'll be bringing you a cup. Perhaps the missus would be wanting to freshen up a spot?" This last to Maeve, who nodded.

"Yes, I would, Sarah, if it's not a bother," she said tiredly. Dark smudges appeared beneath her eyes, and one curl had broken free and lay dankly across one cheek.

"Tch. Bother me not!" Sarah said, and taking Maeve's elbow, firmly led her down the hallway.

"Make yourselves comfortable," Fallon said, waving the UZI at the table. "I'll tell Seamus you've arrived." He moved lithely down the hall and disappeared.

Mahon sighed and crossed to the stove, pausing to hook two thick mugs by their handles. He filled each from the coffeepot and carried them to the table. "Might as well seat yourself. No telling how long we'll have to wait. 'Tis the game, you know. They'll be hoping we'll get nervous and uneasy at being made to wait." He sipped at his coffee, frowned, and pulled out his flask. He dribbled a little whiskey into his cup, tasted, and nodded with satisfaction. I refused his offer of the flask.

"It would appear," I said, "that we might have something to worry about."

He frowned. "Maybe. But I'll be damned if I'll give them the satisfaction of the knowing of it."

A step sounded in the hall, and an old man appeared in the doorway. He paused upon seeing us, then shuffled to the stove to pour himself a cup of coffee.

"A sad affair," Father Mahon said softly, nodding in the direction of the old man. "He was once one of our best brigade leaders." He shook his head with regret and raised his cup of coffee. "Now his mind is mostly gone."

"What happened?" I asked.

"He killed too many Prods and Brits and had too many of his own killed," he answered. He looked pointedly at the door as Fallon stepped into the kitchen. "For those like Dan here, the killing was only a means to the end. For others, it has become a way of life as necessary as the odd pint in the pub after a long day's work."

The old man shuffled to the table, pulled out a chair, and sat. He blew on his coffee and noisily slurped at it, fixing us with rheumy eyes.

"Will you be knowing my oldest son, Billy?" the old man asked me in a reedy voice. "Second Brigade, he is, with Perry."

"Dead he is these past eleven years. As is Perry," Father Mahon breathed quietly from behind his cup.

"No, I don't," I said. I glanced at my cup while I raised it. Looking into the eyes of the past is like looking into the eyes of the dead.

"More's the pity," he said. "A fine lad, my boy Billy. He'll do well by Perry, and sure if Perry won't return the favor. Father Mahon, will you be remembering my Martha in the Mass tonight? 'Tis five years since she left us."

"More like twenty-five," Mahon muttered, then said loudly, "Of course I will, Dan-boy. And Billy, too, if you want."

The old man stared in disgust at him. "Sure, and have you lost what little sense you were born with, Father Mahon? What would be the need of that with Billy alive and a-kicking up his heels with the Sligo *colleens*?" A string of saliva ran unheeded from his mouth to the table in front of him. "Don't be putting the curse upon him now just because you've buried one of us. 'Tis a long time before you'll be saying a rosary at the wake of any more."

"Right you are, Dan-boy," Father Mahon said easily. "Sure, and if my mind isn't still upon the Widow O'Donnell. And her having such a hard time of it now with the men all gone."

"Ach," the old man said, slapping his hand hard on the table. "So it's silent the tongue-waggers have been with you, is it? And herself just getting a ticket and passage money from her youngest in Boston across the waters the week before last. 'Tis there she'll be moving and soon. Frank's his name."

"Sedition, Uncle Dan?" a voice asked, a hint of mockery underlying the words. "From such as you, the darling of *Sinn Fein*?"

I didn't care for him before I lifted my head to see who had entered the kitchen. A short, round man with a chubby face and pig's eyes behind wire-rimmed glasses rocked back and forth on his heels at the head of the table. He wore the Sacred Heart lapel badge of the Pioneer Total Abstinence Association below the collar of his workshirt, which he obviously wore for its intrinsic purpose only: the shirt was too clean to ever have known a day of farm duty. I glanced at his hands: soft and pudgy, the nails clean and pink, the hands of an altar boy. The nephew, I thought. Sarah fluttered like an aged butterfly behind him back to her bread dough. The old man bowed his head until his nose almost touched the coffee cup in front of him. "Me nephew, Seamus Halloran," he muttered, giving a slight nod in the direction of Sarah. "Hers," he needlessly added.

"I apologize for my uncle, gentlemen," he said, suavely molding his words. "I am afraid reality has bypassed him." His lip curled slightly, and he raised a knuckle to brush across the smudge of a mustache on his upper lip. It was not, I thought, much of a mustache.

"We are well aware of what each is at this table," Father Mahon calmly said, and deliberately turned back to the old man. "And would you be having a touch of poteen about with which to take off the chill, Dan-boy."

The old man raised his head, his rheumy eyes suddenly crafty. He darted a glance at his nephew, then conspiratorially leaned over the table. "If you'll be following me out to the shebeen, Father, we'll be seeing what's laying about. But be careful of him." He nodded at the nephew. "He's a Pioneer, one of the worst of those drum-thumping pietists. Come along, and we'll drink to stave off the total madness from what the bloody bastards have imposed upon us."

"Or," the nephew snapped, eyes sparking with righteous fire, "bring it on again. Mark my words, Uncle Dan, and you, Black Priest, those who drink seek the spirit of the devil, forsaking the spirit of our Lord and Saviour Jesus Christ. 'Tis as sure as I am standing here before you that you damn your souls, blaspheme the work of our Lord and Creator, by placing the cup that contains the devil's spit between your lips. Drink puts liquid fire in man's blood and keeps him senseless under the heels of his enemy. And the Church, Black Priest, that Holy Catholic Church with its acceptance of drink, has had much to do with the plight of the Irishman, for it has always reaped its fields with British scythes!" he finished, panting. I glanced at Sarah standing beside her table, gazing with rapturous eyes upon her husband. Father Mahon ignored him and left with the old man by way of the back door. He turned, looking in triumph at Maeve and me alone at the table.

"You see," he said, again molding his words.

"You mix your metaphors," Maeve calmly said. He stared at her in disbelief. A quiet chuckle came from the hall entrance.

"Always had a sharp tongue, didn't you, Maeve darling?" Seamus MacCauley said, stepping into the room. Richard O'Bannion followed, detouring to the stove to collect two cups of coffee, bringing them to the table. He grinned and toasted me with his coffee.

"A long ways from Marta's house," he said. "How have the lads been treating you?"

"Fair," I said easily. "But you'd know that, wouldn't you?"

"Contrary to popular belief," O'Bannion said, "we don't know everything. But some things we do know, and," he added meaningfully, "some things we don't want others to know. Maeve, how have you been since Conor's death? A long time for my asking and for that I apologize, but the time for pleasantries and paying attention to the proprieties has passed for those of us in Ulster."

"Fine, thank you, Dickie. It's good to hear that. For a while, I thought you had forgotten Conor." O'Bannion turned a shade red at her mild admonition. She looked at MacCauley. "Seamus. It's a pleasure to see you."

"Is it, Maeve?" MacCauley asked. He straddled a chair.

"Good morning," the nephew began, then fell silent as MacCauley negligently waved his hand in dismissal. "Leave us for a while, there's a good boy. Tomas?"

The nephew flushed and tried to draw himself up into a stern and forbidding figure. But a quick look into MacCauley's eyes was enough to send him from the table.

"Come," Sarah said, opening the oven door and drawing forth covered platters, piling them on a large tray. "I'll be setting a place for your breakfast on the good table."

"I'm not hungry," he snapped, and marched from the room, head held valiantly high. Sarah scurried after him, heavy tray clutched high in white-knuckled hands, face set in anxious long-suffering.

"Bastard," Maeve muttered, eyes following the small parade from the kitchen.

"Undoubtedly," MacCauley agreed distastefully. He turned to fix us with cold eyes. "Well?"

"The question," Maeve said quietly, "should be mine. Why did you declare Conor persona non grata?"

"Expediency's sake," MacCauley said, his words clipped, precise. "His accusations were a threat to the organization. You were told this." Maeve's eyes narrowed at the blunt warning in his last words.

"Don't threaten me, Seamus MacCauley," she said.

"Or what? Conor Larkin is dead, Maeve. You have nothing to bargain with."

"She has me," I said, trying to keep my voice casual. MacCauley's eyes swept over me, reflecting puzzlement for a moment, then cleared as the implication of my words registered.

"The press?" A thin smile flickered across his lips. "We've dealt with crusaders before."

"There's crusaders and then there's crusaders," I said. "It all depends upon how big a crusader a person is."

"And you think yourself big?"

"No. But my paper is."

I was running a bluff; my sudden disappearance or death would be good for maybe one front-page story followed by maybe a week of follow-ups as the story marched page by page through the various editions, leapfrogging over the comics and sports and society news until, at last, it fell against the classifieds before being buried in the morgue along with thousands of other clippings of dead news. I was gambling that Mac-Cauley would remember that the majority of Provisional IRA financing came from America.

"I don't believe you," he said after a long moment. "But I do admire your courage. And, perhaps, we owe you a favor. The articles you wrote after your release from Castlereagh greatly helped us." He pursed his lips, considering Maeve and me for another long moment. Then he nodded. "Very well. This time and this time *only*. Understand?"

I nodded. Maeve hesitated, then slowly agreed.

"Ask your questions," he said, settling back against his chair. O'Bannion gave him a surprised look and opened his mouth to speak, then changed his mind and followed Mac-Cauley's lead. He twitched his eyebrows at me and shrugged.

"What did Conor know? Did he give any names?" Maeve asked.

"None," MacCauley said. "He saw us twice. The first time he explained why he thought it was an informer that put you away." He shrugged. "It made sense—then. Why else should you be detained? To be forced to reveal where we were hiding? The Brits knew the minute you were picked up we would be moved to another safe house. No, there had to be another reason."

"What? I couldn't tell them anything even if I wanted," she said.

"True," MacCauley said. "We think that was a gamble. But they had to know who, and that could have only come from an informer. Later, it seemed just a coincidence. You were a known critic; you were known to be familiar with certain members of the IRA; you were easy to find *and* very visible to the public. Your arrest made sense on that score. But Conor didn't think so. He was adamant about there having been an informer. Reluctantly, and against my better judgment, I let him continue although our investigation had uncovered nothing. At the time, I could see no harm in it, and if he wanted to pass his time in that matter, let him. What I didn't know was just how far Conor was going to go with his search. Later, when he saw us the second time, he thought he had uncovered another conspiracy. Well, Maeve darling, enough is enough. I tried to reason with him, but he would hear nothing of it. Finally, I had little choice. I had to close the door."

"What was the second conspiracy?"

"Something to do with sabotaging the Porcupine Banks Project," MacCauley said. "When I tried to question him, he refused to say anything more about it. Just that someone was trying to destroy it."

"But why?" I interrupted. "Did he tell you that? It doesn't make sense. The Porcupine Banks Project could be the economic transfusion Ireland needs to allow her to escape the bonds of England. Everyone—Catholic and Protestant alike—would support that. It would finally mean total freedom. For once, there would be a united Ireland and . . ." I became aware of everyone staring at me. I flushed and tried to sink into my chair, lamely finishing, "uh, well."

"Yes," MacCauley said, graciousness masked by officiousness. "We are fully aware of your meaning. That precisely was *my* argument. But he was insistent. You know how stubborn he could be, Maeve." She nodded. "Finally, I had little choice but to declare him bane." The archaic term reminded me about the simplicity of the man—a simplicity that made it easier for him to be ruthless.

"I see," Maeve said. She sat quietly for a moment, her eyes turned inward, examining the information from various angles. Finally she spoke. "I am most sorry, Seamus MacCauley, but I can't let it drop. Conor knew what he was doing even if his actions were a bit strange at the last."

" 'Tis your death warrant you'll be signing, you know

[124]

that?" O'Bannion said. His eyes had a strange fire lurking in their depths.

"And mine?" I said challengingly. "Is it to be my death warrant as well?"

He shrugged. " 'Tis a shame. We had a time together. But some things are larger than feelings. We'll dig the grave a bit deeper. A few shovelfuls of dirt; that's all it will matter. But"— he looked fondly at me—"I will be missing you, and that I want you to know." He turned to MacCauley. "Should I be giving the contract to Fallon or will you be putting it out to the others?"

"Now, just a damn minute!" I said hotly. "Your word is not divine. What harm are we going to do? You already have the project."

"That's true," Maeve said. Her eyes shined with new intensity. "The hiring has already begun. It will make no difference if we see what we can find."

"Don't listen to them," O'Bannion argued. "As sure as I am sitting here there will be no good coming from their poking and prying. We've come a long way, and the end is now in sight. You cannot take a chance. Too much of the lads' blood has been spilt to get this far. I say put a stop to it now."

"No," MacCauley said thoughtfully. "They're right. The contracts are out. It won't hurt any but themselves to be looking around for what doesn't exist. Where do you think about starting?" O'Bannion shrugged and swung away in resignation, picking up his coffee cup and heading for the stove to replenish it.

"I think with TRANCO's officers," Maeve said. "Conor was killed on TRANCO's docks in Manchester. That seems a good place to begin."

"Yes," MacCauley said, eyes narrowing slightly. "But take care not to be making any waves. A *quiet* inquiry, if you please." Maeve nodded her agreement. "Very well, then. You'll be keeping me posted. And, if not me, him." He nodded at O'Bannion. "Now, mind you," he said closely, eyes shifting pointedly from Maeve to me, "there will be no upsetting the good people of TRANCO. Even," he said, his eyes settling warningly on me, "for the sake of a story."

I flushed and started to reply, but the back door flew open.

Father Mahon and the old man entered, their eyes bright sparkles, their faces ruddy, "The Rising of the Moon" falling from their lips.

They paused in the doorway, blinking owlishly at the gathering by the table.

"God bless all here," Father Mahon piously intoned, then pitched forward onto his face. The old man sadly looked down at the priest and shook his head.

"By Jaysus," he sighed. "What is there left to this world when a man's own priest can't withstand the drawing of a cork?"

SEVEN

The drive back to Sligo was uneventful save for one brief stop
for Father Mahon, who hastily disappeared behind a low stone
wall while muttering imprecations against "the divil's dew"
that kept threatening to "spew forth" from his stomach. He
emerged long minutes later, white and shaking. When we left
him at the rectory, he paused only long enough to sketch a
hasty blessing upon us before rushing inside.

We found TRANCO's offices in a converted warehouse on
Canal Street. So rapid had been TRANCO's move that the
front of the building still appeared to be little else than a
warehouse. The boards were split and cracked in places around
the windows. Mortar crumbled from between old bricks so
weathered they more closely resembled moldy straw than
Georgian red. The sole newness could be seen only in the new
sign nailed above the door and the fresh lettering on the
windows. Inside, the smell of fresh paint and newly laid carpet
barely disguised the mustiness of age. The walls cast a soft
glow from rich panels, yet the overhead lights still shone with
brutal brightness.

A cheerful, middle-aged woman greeted us after we pushed
through the outer door and crossed the waiting room to her
desk. I was impressed already by TRANCO; no vacuous, feath-
erbrained, young woman with blond, metallic hair and alpine
peaks for breasts here. Miss Digby radiated confidence and
competence.

"May I help you?" she briskly asked, her voice carrying
the polished accent of a BBC commentator. Her brown eyes
flicked once over each of us as if taking a picture and filing it

away for future reference. I had the strange feeling that every-thing about us was already on the data card in her mind. I summoned up my best smile.

"I hope so," I said. "My name is Con Edwards. I'm looking for information on TRANCO for an article I'm doing for the *Times*." I deliberately avoided introducing Maeve, hoping that Miss Digby would categorize her as my secretary.

"What type of information?" she asked.

"The Porcupine Banks Project," I said. Tiny frown lines of irritation appeared between her eyes.

"I presumed as much," she said. "Otherwise, you would have contacted our home offices in Manchester. Could you be more precise?"

"Would you happen to have anything on the officers-in-residence on the project? And a copy of the grant and initial seabed exploration soundings that I might see? Has TRANCO compiled an economic feasibility study yet and a policy pro-cedure handbook governing employee relations? Those would be of immense help."

She slowly blinked, thoughtfully considering me for a long moment before speaking. "Precisely what type of article is it you are planning, Mr. Edwards?"

"A series," I said easily. "My office sent me here to cover the initial stages, but since TRANCO so recently received the exploratory grant from Eire and Great Britain, there is a lack of depth of background material. Other than the initial releases I received at the announcement, I have very little I can use. I thought that by now TRANCO may have put together a press packet."

The frown lines deepened as she considered my request. "I'm afraid not much is back from the printer, but what we have is certainly available to you. If you'll give me a moment, I'll get the public relations officer for you." I nodded, and she rose, pausing for a moment to be sure her desk drawer was secure, glanced disparagingly at Maeve, then disappeared through a walnut-paneled door behind her desk.

"Very efficient," I murmured to Maeve. She nodded and suddenly grinned wryly.

"And I'll be thanking you for letting her think me your poppet."

"All famous journalists have poppets," I said loftily. "It's part of our image. What do you think?" She glanced around the hastily furnished office.

"It seems sterile," she said.

"Sterile?" The word confused me. "Rich" I would understand, for it took money and lots of it to make the sudden transformation that had taken place in the warehouse. I would even accept "opulent," "mellow," maybe even a stretch at "fertile," but "sterile"?

"It seems contrived," she said. "Here, in Sligo, it is only a little better than Belfast. The walls of most places are plaster and the floors scarred wood. This is a place for tourists, not reality. If you pull the paneling from the wall, you'll find the reality: stark brick, probably crumbling from age, but an honest ambience. This is all a facade: sterile."

I thought about telling her she was reading too much Jung into a simple remodeling job but refrained. If she wanted to see Evil in a few sheets of paneling and a few yards of carpet, there was nothing I could say to change her mind. Instead, I changed the topic.

"I wonder what this place was used for before TRANCO moved in," I said, pretending to consider the cavernous ceiling above the walls.

"Probably a storage place for flour or cured salmon," she said testily. "Maybe lumber. Who knows?"

"Sorry," I said. "Just making conversation."

She touched her hand to her forehead and gave me a rueful smile. "No, I'm sorry for coming off at you that way and you having put up with so much."

"Forget it," I said. "Besides, there's a story in all this someplace."

"A story. Yes, a story," she said, her face growing thoughtful. "It begins to make one wonder, doesn't it?"

"What?"

She started to answer, but the door opening behind the receptionist's desk interrupted her. We turned as one to greet her and the public relations officer. My stomach involuntarily lurched as Liam Drumm stepped through the doorway.

He smiled broadly at us. "Surprised? I almost told you back in Dublin that we were moving the office to here but thought that would be tactless." He managed to convey a modest look despite being obviously rather pleased with himself. I realized I was staring and forced myself to stretch forth my hand.

"Congratulations," I said. I nudged Maeve, standing open-mouthed near me. She blinked and forced her lips into a smile.

"Yes. Of course. It's about time that something good should be happening to you, Liam Drumm." Her words were warm, and he basked in our well-wishes.

"Thank you, Maeve," he said. "I am so happy to be hearing that from your lips." His eyes brightened and he snapped his fingers as a thought occurred to him. "Would the two of you be taking supper with me one of these early nights?"

"Perhaps," she said, then gently added to bring the topic of our visit back around, "Maybe when this business about Conor is laid to rest."

"Good," he said. "That's good. It will be like old times again." Maeve gave him a tiny, noncommittal smile, but one that allowed hope to be read. He briskly rubbed his hands together. "Right. Now, what can I do for you?" He shifted his eyes at Miss Digby and frowned warningly. I caught his drift and continued my role of journalist in search of materials for an article. He listened, nodding thoughtfully until I had finished, then smiled.

"Of course," he said, "I hope you realize that I cannot do much for you at the moment. We are just beginning to develop these offices. The project is so new," he continued apologetically, "that not all the needed material is back from the printer yet. Sure, and aren't we still in the process of hiring staff and personnel? But," he added, frowning slightly, "I can give you a few copies of second carbons in manuscript if that will help. I am sorry, but that's the best I can do. At least you'll be able to have a bit of information on the project directors. That should be of some help, I would think."

His voice sounded odd, and then I realized he was making a concerted effort to erase the brogue from his speech in favor of the polished tones of a BBC commentator.

"Thank you," I said. "We'll take whatever we can get."

He smiled and turned to the receptionist. "Would you make a copy of the directors' biographies we sent to the printer,

Miss Digby? Thank you." He beamed benignly at us. "It will only take a minute. Now, is there anything else I can do for you?"

"No, I don't believe so," I said. "Given the situation, this is more than one could hope for."

The door closed behind the secretary and he dropped the act. "So. Have you had any luck?"

I shook my head and briefly outlined what had happened to us since we had left him at the Gresham. His eyebrows rose when I related the events at The Hound and Bird.

"Drop it," he said flatly after I had finished. He looked sternly at Maeve. "It isn't worth getting killed over, Maeve. Go back to London and finish the special, then retire to Trinity and take Conor's position. That's enough to honor his memory."

She smiled and shook her head. "It's a bit late for that now, Liam."

"Not if you drop this quixotic search of yours," he said stubbornly. "The boys would be willing to listen to reason. You've earned that yourself, Maeve."

The door opened and Miss Digby reentered the room. Liam switched smoothly into his public relations patter.

"You know, this is a great economic boon to Ireland. Even if the project eventually proves untenable, the amount of money budgeted for expenditures is a definite transfusion into Ireland's economy. Of course, I don't need to tell you what it will mean if the feasibility study proves positive, now, do I? Sure, and won't it be bringing peace to the troubles?"

"Are you anticipating any trouble from environmentalists?" I asked. He frowned slightly.

"Of which environmentalists are you speaking?"

I shrugged. "None that I know of. But projects such as this normally bring them out. You know: Save the Whales. Save Our Seals. Greenpeace. The Sierra people. The environmentalists will be sure to find some reason to keep you from stirring up the ocean bed, displacing protozoan life, whatever. Have you made any plans contingent upon that happening?"

He shook his head. "No," he slowly said. "At least, nothing that has been made known to me. I'll have to check with Mr. Macreedy."

"Who?"

"William Alan Macreedy," he said. "He's the geologist. I suppose it wouldn't hurt to have something prepared ahead as a precaution."

"Might be a good idea," I said, filing away Macreedy's name. "Radicals are so damn unpredictable. Just when everything's running along smoothly, suddenly they're there, throwing the organization into total chaos. But," I laughed, "what am I doing telling an Irishman about radicals? Coals to Newcastle."

He laughed along with me. Miss Digby took the moment to hand him a slim envelope with three pages tucked under the flap. He glanced at them, nodded his thanks, slid them into the envelope, and handed them to me.

"There," he said. "Sorry that it isn't more, but we should have the brochure back from the printer within the week. Will you be staying in Sligo that long? Shall I have one sent around to your rooms?"

"I don't think that will be necessary," I said. "We'll be in and out quite a bit before then. You should be able to catch us."

"Out at Rosses Point. The Ballineor House," Maeve said. His eyebrows rose as he glanced from Maeve to me.

"Rosses Point? A bit out of the way, isn't it?" he asked. "I should think you'd be staying at Sligo Park."

"A bit more private at the Ballineor," she said. He shrugged.

"There's that, of course," he said. "Although I cannot imagine Sligo Park throwing bids open to peepholes in the walls. Well, I'll be sending the material around to you as soon as it comes in if I'm not after seeing you before." We murmured our good-byes and left, shaking hands like old friends between whom bad words had never passed.

"Now, what—" I began as soon as the door closed behind us, then stopped as Maeve motioned me to be silent. I watched curiously. She seemed to count slowly to herself before turning the doorknob and reentering the warehouse. Drumm gave us a surprised look and pulled the telephone from his ear, hugging it to his chest.

"Sorry," Maeve said. "But I forgot to ask: where is the dockage for TRANCO?"

"Out at Mullaghmore," he answered. "They're redredging the harbor for deepwater berthing. Sligo is too shallow and would be too expensive."

"Oh. Well. Thanks again." She waved her fingers at him and pulled the door firmly behind her.

"What was that all about?" I asked. She shook her head and hurried down the street with long strides, her tweed skirt tightening across the fronts of her thighs. I fell in beside her, my calves already beginning to burn from the unaccustomed haste.

"I was wondering how long it would take him to telephone MacCauley and O'Bannion, the little toad," she said.

"How do you know that's who he was talking to?" I asked.

"I don't," she admitted, suddenly looking foolish. "Aren't I the paranoid one? But at least we have a bit more information: we know where they're doing their hiring."

"And," I reminded her, "where we're going to stay. Why Rosses Point?"

"I don't know," she said. "For some reason, I simply did not want to stay in Sligo. Sorry. We *can* stay at Sligo Park if you like?"

"Rosses Point is fine," I said, opening the car door for her. "Maybe it was a pre-Neanderthal vestige, a form of ESP. Rosses Point is somewhere between Sligo and Mullaghmore, isn't it? More ideally located than Sligo Park?"

She laughed and affectionately squeezed my hand. "You're too good for me, Con. If I'm not careful, you'll be wanting to make an honest woman of me."

"Would you like that?"

The words seemed to hang in the air in front of us for a long moment. Then she gave a shaky laugh and said, "Sure, now, and you'll be having me believing it."

"Why not?" I said. "You know—"

I never finished the words. A Rover careened around the corner and headed toward us. At the last moment, I grabbed Maeve and pushed her down behind the car. I fell on top of her as an Ingram angrily chattered, slugs slamming into the body of the Cortina. Then, it was gone.

My stomach felt like a tight ball. I concentrated hard on keeping my bladder from voiding itself and soiling both of us. Dimly I heard someone shouting and slowly became aware of someone shaking me hard by the shoulders.

"Con! Con!"

The words seemed to come through an intensity of darkness, a familiar voice that I had heard in dreams. The problem, a small voice said, is your eyes are shut. I opened them and stared down into the frantic face of Maeve.

"Con!" she said urgently, giving my shoulders another shake. "Are you all right?"

"You know," I shakily said, dropping my head to muffle my voice against her hair, "this is highly erotic."

"*Goddamn* you, Con," she said, and kissed me hard on the lips.

EIGHT

The Ballineor House was warm and intimate, our rooms a study of genteel shabbiness: the veneer of the furniture showed wear, the bed linen had been repeatedly washed until the threads would not hold a crease. Yet our rooms were clean and neat, and the staff ebullient, friendly, and anxious to cater to our whims and tastes.

Our tastes were simple: a hot bath, a bottle of Black Bush, and cotton swabs and iodine for the scrapes and scratches we had suffered after our untimely contact with the pavement. We took turns with the bath and Black Bush and turns with the cotton swabs and iodine that led to much flinching and whimpering and a sudden wildness, resulting in an overpowering release of inhibitions accompanying the sexual celebration that one is still alive.

I awoke stiff and sore to find Maeve still wrapped around me, her head tucked into the hollow of my shoulder. A pain behind my right eye and the thick taste of turned cheese in my mouth reminded me of the Black Bush, which, in turn, reminded me of the night and pleasant memories that the reality in my arms assured me hadn't been a dream.

Maeve moaned, stirred delightfully, and slowly awoke. She smiled softly and nuzzled me beneath my chin, recoiling slightly from the early-morning bristle of my beard.

"Good morning," I said, kissing the tip of her nose. "Hungry?"

"Famished," she said, and yawned. She snuggled deeper into the blankets. "What's the day like?" I glanced toward the window, noting the streaks of rain across the panes.

"Raining," I said. "Should we stay here?"

"Sure, and what will they be thinking about us downstairs and me without your name? Close your eyes."

"They'll think nothing," I said, automatically following her bidding. "And why should they? We took separate rooms."

"Of which one has not been used, as they well know by now," she said. The bed shifted as she slid out. I opened my eyes to Aphrodite in pink and alabaster: high, saucy breasts, gently swelling hips, hair so red to appear burnished bronze.

"A gentleman would turn his head the better to allow a lady some decency," she said, pulling the coverlet from the bed and wrapping herself in it.

"A madman might," I said. "But a gentleman would remember everything and would want to see the loveliness he'd explored the night before by the light of the new day."

"Indeed! Aren't we the bold one?" she said, the color rapidly rising in her cheeks. "Have you forgotten what happened yesterday?"

"Not one thing," I said. "The *Garda* almost arrested us for lewd public behavior."

"Con!"

"Sorry. No, I haven't. Any ideas?"

"I'm afraid MacCauley may have been having second thoughts," she said, picking up her clothes and sliding into the bathroom. She left the door slightly ajar.

"Why?" I said, raising my voice. I rose and slid into my pants. "That doesn't make any sense."

"It does if you look at it from his viewpoint," she said. "Why not put us at ease if it's our deaths he's planning? The quarry at peace with the world is the quarry easiest snared."

"What makes you think it's MacCauley?"

"Who else?" she said impatiently. "The priest? Not hardly, I'm thinking. Too many traces of past IRA operations. The Rover and machine gun have been long favorites. Too much of watching your American gangster flicks, now, wouldn't you be saying? We'll have to be sure of our movements from now on, Con Edwards, or Conor will be greeting us on the other side." The sound of the shower brought our conversation to a momentary end. I used the time to look over the material Liam had given us.

TRANCO apparently was a very conservative and cautious company. Very little of TRANCO's own money had apparently been earmarked for the Porcupine Banks exploration. Instead, a subsidiary company had been established with sixty percent of its funds coming from public solicitation, thirty percent from Great Britain and the Republic of Ireland with each contributing fifteen percent, five percent from various oil cartels in the United States and Canada, three percent from a Brazilian banking concern, and the last two percent from TRANCO itself. Yet the officers of the subsidiary company were, for the most part, British. The Bank of England was represented by James Pillars, the York man who had negotiated financing for part of the North Sea exploration and initial drilling; Macreedy, the Scottish geologist from the University of Edinburgh who had correctly interpreted sonar soundings indicating a large formation of dolomites during an exploratory voyage aboard the *Wild Goose* three years before; Harold Rowse, an independent financier from London who had a genius for bringing diverse groups together in agreement on international investments; Christopher Railey, the head of TRANCO's shipping line; Peter Keyes, representing the United States and Canada, the sole member of the board not English; and Lord Louis Mountbatten, the consultant and liaison to the British and Irish governments. An appropriate choice, Lord Mountbatten, I thought, much admired by the British and Irish alike, since he maintained a holiday home in Mullaghmore and docked his boat *Shadow V* in the harbor.

According to the report, it had been Mountbatten who had suggested Mullaghmore as the place for TRANCO's docks, as Donegal and Sligo harbors were ill-suited for dredging. Constant silting by tidal waters would have made the cost of dredging for a deepwater anchorage prohibitive. Mullaghmore, a tiny district of 629 hardy souls located between Grange and Castlegal on a south point of Donegal Bay, the northernmost point of County Sligo, was exposed to a "washing action" of the tides that would prevent silting once the dredging was completed and leave the harbor open for heavy tankers. It was also, I thought, the closest possible point to the six counties. Fermanagh ran almost to Mullaghmore's doorstep, thus making employment possible for men from either the Republic or

Northern Ireland. A politician's move, brilliant with diplomacy. Conor Larkin could not have faulted that. A deepwater port in Donegal Bay would cut oil transport costs from the oil terminal on Whiddy Island in Bantry Bay in the south and, through the jobs created with the oil terminal, provide an economic boom to the impoverished west. Even if the Porcupine Banks Project fell through, the oil terminal would continue to operate.

I set the rough copy aside and sat brooding on one of the room's two chairs. I could see why MacCauley and O'Bannion needed to be here, given the proximity of Fermanagh and the probable Anglican Church–dominated project. Even though Mullaghmore was in the Catholic-dominated Republic, the area had, I was sure, a large share of Protestants who would, with the self-assured arrogance born of three hundred–plus years of tribal unity formed by their control of the region, be pushing for the cream of available positions over the Catholics.

I needed, I decided as the sound of the shower ceased, to see the bills of lading for the day that Conor Larkin was killed on TRANCO's docks. But how was I going to get the records?

Maeve came out of the bathroom, frowning and gnawing at her lower lip. I felt a surge of wistful nostalgia. "I think we should be going to Father Mahon," she said thoughtfully. "At least, for the moment. Have you had time to look at the material Liam gave us?"

"Yes," I said, rising and stretching. "There's nothing there that I can see. Maybe we'll find something later, but right now I'm afraid it's a dead end. I would like to look back through the shipping records, the bills of lading, for the week Conor was killed."

She frowned. "That'll mean a trip to Manchester, will it not?"

I shook my head. "No, I don't think so. The connection must be here, or Conor wouldn't have been involved. Conor's whole life was Irish. There had to be a reason for him to go to Manchester, to TRANCO, but it had to originate here since this is TRANCO's only link to Ireland. Trouble is, I'm not sure how to get to the records. Liam might be able to help, but I don't want to compromise him. *And*," I added, "there is the question of his association with MacCauley."

She thoughtfully gnawed her lip as she toyed with her hair in front of the mirror. "I think," she said slowly, "that Father Mahon will be able to help us."

"A priest?" She laughed at my incredulity.

"Actually, it was some of his acquaintances I've been thinking about," she said, a twinkle in her eye. "But I have my doubts whether the good father will be willing to lend us a hand in cracking a crib. Not for fear of *meum* or *tuum*, mind you, but simply because we are beyond the pale with Mac-Cauley."

"Speaking of the devil," I said, "shouldn't we be keeping him informed? Just in case," I hastened to add as fire began to spark from her eyes, "that he had nothing to do with the Rover and machine gun? He did, I remind you, warn us to keep in touch."

The fire died to smoldering embers as she thought over my comments. "Very well," she grudgingly said. "We can ring him up from the lobby as we check out. We did not," she said emphatically, "agree to keep him informed as to where we are—oh, hell!" The imprecation startled me.

"What? What?"

"I forgot about Liam. He'll tell MacCauley for sure. St. Brigid take my running mouth!" she said bitterly. "How long will it take you to dress?"

"Twenty minutes," I said, turning for the bathroom.

"Make it ten," she said. "I'll pack."

Rain steadily obscured the road as we made our way back from Rosses Point to Sligo. At first, I feared we were being followed as a black sedan pulled away from the curb and fell in behind us. A series of twisting curves, however, left it far behind, and when I glanced into the rearview mirror as we entered the outskirts of Sligo, it was gone. You're getting too paranoid to think straight, I told myself. Best get your mind on the business at hand. Nevertheless, I circled the cathedral twice before parking, carefully watching the mirror to see if any cars were following us.

When we entered the sanctuary, Father Mahon was in his robes of office intoning the placid, quotidian ritual, *"Introibo ad altare Dei; Hoc est enim Corpus meum . . ."* in a tumid voice with a faint tussive raspness before a cathedral empty save for a few elderly still attending the morning masses of their grandfathers and their grandfathers before them. Maeve automatically puddled her fingers in a basin of holy water, crossing herself and genuflecting before sliding into a pew. She caught my eye and smiled ruefully and shrugged, nodding at the people around us. I understood. It was best not to draw attention to oneself. I shook the rain off and dropped in beside her. An elderly penitent frowned at my casualness, then slid forward onto the knee rails to dutifully voice the *Confiteor*. I ignored him as I caught sight of a familiar figure watching me with a bemused expression from a seat behind a pillar.

"Excuse me," I whispered to Maeve.

"Where are you going?"

"Nowhere," I whispered. "Just to visit with an old friend. Over there, behind the pillar." I rose and walked as quietly as I could across the aisle and behind the last section of pews.

"Pax vobiscum," I whispered, sliding in beside Denis Naismith.

"Funny," he whispered back. "Somehow, I didn't think you were a believer." He smiled slightly to show that he was not to be taken seriously.

"A bit formal for my tastes," I said.

The grin spread wider, becoming one of enjoyment rather than politeness. "Heresy in the cathedral? Spiritual suicide, my friend."

"Is it not?" I replied, gesturing at those in attendance. *"Ecce signum.* But I'm afraid more than our souls are in danger."

The smile slipped fast from his face. "Too true," he said. "I believe you have made some individuals very unhappy."

"I see. You've been following us. Maeve will be destroyed when I tell her. Everyone seems to be able to follow us. But, of course, you would have no idea as to whom, would you?" My sarcasm was not lost on him. He shook his head.

"Unfortunately, no," he said. "The man we had following you took the opportunity to nip out for a cup of tea when you went into the TRANCO offices."

"A cup . . . of tea?" I asked, incredulous.

"I gather," he said dryly, "that it had been a rather long day, and it was the first opportunity for, ah, nourishment."

"Wilson?" I asked. He hesitated, then nodded.

"C'est plus qu'une faute, c'est un crime."

"Now, just a minute," he said, his words tainted with a touch of irritation. "That's a bit harsh, don't you think?"

"So is death," I said mildly.

"Please remember that you *are* doing this by choice," he said stiffly. "You must be willing to take the risks."

"As must you," I said softly. I leaned conspiratorially toward him. "Tell me, what do you think would happen to you here if I happened to mention aloud that you are from Special Branch?"

"Good God, man!" He darted quick nervous looks around to be certain we had not been overheard. "Don't even joke about that!"

"What are you doing here, anyway?" I asked. "Aren't you a bit out of your territory?" He hesitated, and for a moment I didn't think he was going to answer. Then he sighed and pulled his ear in frustration.

"Guns," he said simply. I stared at him. He smiled ruefully. "Yes, that's what I said: guns. They have to come into Ireland some way. You don't simply drop a seed into the ground and grow an assault rifle, you know."

"Guns go into Northern Ireland," I said. "Not the Republic."

"True," he said. "But we have most of the approaches from the sea closed."

"I see," I answered. "What about Conor Larkin? Have you found anything for me?"

"Yes, we found the body of one that Conor Larkin apparently killed before they got to him. An American by the name of Joe Kelly."

"An American? Are you sure?" I sat back, puzzled, against the pew. Naismith grinned.

"Oh, yes," he said with satisfaction. "A member, we think, of NORAID—the Irish Northern Aid Committee—but we can't be sure. We do know that he entered England on the Hovercraft from Calais to Dover after checking through customs as a merchant seaman at Marseilles. We were a bit late in picking him up, as he was using the pseudonym Nigel Newton. The only reason we caught it at all was the unusual choice of an alias: the computer kicked it out. A check with Interpol showed that he had been involved in that Angola mess before dropping out of sight. We think he was at the camps in Libya for a while. You know what that means, I presume?"

I did. Several camps had been established as training centers for future terrorists in Libya's desert. Here, the debutantes of terrorism assembled for their finishing schools. Afterward, some joined revolutions as mercenaries, some simply roamed the world, inventing causes as they went.

"But why would the Provos bring in people like that? Their organization has shown itself amply capable of handling its own problems in the past."

"Yes," he said. "That is rather the general consensus. We believe the dead man was there to guard an arms shipment. We have suspected NORAID has been smuggling arms to the Provos since its founding in the United States by Michael Flannery in 1970. But most of this is only speculation, you know. Flannery is a wise old devil. Has been ever since the 1920 troubles. We have a two-inch-thick file on him. Usually, we can anticipate a shipment whenever Martin Galvin makes a crossing. On the day Larkin was killed, Galvin took the shuttle to the Isle of Man."

"But," I said, "why would Conor try to stop an arms shipment? He, of all people, would be more likely to bring it in. Of course," I added reflectively, "he was not enamored of the Provos. I suppose it is possible."

"But not probable," Naismith said. "A bit of Socratic irony, wouldn't you say? A rebel objecting to rebel dealings? No matter. That is another puzzle."

"Do you have anything else?" I asked.

"Nothing of any relevance." I detected a slight trace of dejection in his voice. "This problem is occupying too much of my time as it is. I would have laid it to rest long ago if it were not for Joe Kelly. The fact that *he* was involved makes me play what-if games."

"Such as?"

"Conspiracy," he said. "There have been a few assassinations this year that do not make sense: Sir Richard Sykes, the

British ambassador to The Hague, and Airey Neave, the Conservative Northern Ireland spokesman in the House of Commons, both in March. They could be coincidental, but I wonder."

"What makes you think conspiracy?" I asked. "Is there a common denominator?"

"No," he said regretfully. "Both were peace advocates, but so are many others. Their deaths, however, were not claimed by the Provos."

"Understandably so," I said. "Admitting to their deaths would cost the Provos the valuable backing it receives from America as long as its targets are of military value."

"Precisely," he said. A tight grin flashed. "That is the what-if. Do you have any idea what would happen if either the Provos or the Ulster Defense people were blamed for their deaths? All talks would break down, and we would be right back to the position we held almost ten years ago."

"What do you plan on doing now?"

"That depends entirely upon you," he said.

"Me?"

"Yes. As I said, I've spent more time on this than I should have, given the information available. I cannot justify a greater expenditure of time, money, or resources. My superiors, although not ecstatic about a shoot-out on Manchester's docks, are, nevertheless, not too upset about the possibility of an internal war between Irish republican factions as, on the surface, this shows all indications of being. That is why I decided to contact you and give you all I have."

"Because you feel this to be something more than a rivalry."

"Precisely."

"Where can I find this Martin Galvin?" I asked. "That looks like the only starting place."

"We don't know," he said. "He has apparently dropped out of sight. But I would encourage the NORAID connection. Besides, that's all we've got."

"Not quite," I said. "I was thinking of checking the bills of lading for TRANCO from Manchester to Ireland."

"Good idea, but don't bother," he said. "We already have.

Other than drilling equipment, we found nothing. And every container is accounted for in TRANCO's warehouses."

"Nuts," I said. He grinned.

"Like I said, NORAID's all you've got."

"And what will you be doing?"

"Oh, something will turn up to occupy my time. It always does," he said vaguely.

"Go to your homes," Father Mahon said from the front of the altar. "The mass is ended."

"I'll be in touch," Naismith murmured, sliding from the pew. He dropped a card on my lap. "My private number. Just in case you need it."

He paused to genuflect, then hurried from the cathedral, taking care to leave with a small group of elderly people. Ever the cautious man, I thought. I rose and moved slowly to the side altar of St. Brendan, where Maeve impatiently waited with Father Mahon. I shivered against the feeling of dread that suddenly fell upon me.

NINE

The gunmetal gray sea angrily crashed against the sandy shore like a rumbling, angry beast. The tiny cottage, standing well back from the shore, was well-thatched, its whitewashed walls gleaming wetly from the fine mist in the gray gloaming, shutters and lintels a shimmering emerald green. A cheerful peat fire leaped and flickered in the fireplace to the left of the door as we entered. The main room held a rustic table and chairs well polished from use and a large escritoire with many nooks and crannies. The table was laid with fresh bread and cheese along with a pitcher of dark beer and a bottle of poteen, and glasses and plates for two. I presumed Father Mahon was not staying, despite his fondness for poteen. The single bedroom had just enough room for a small double bed and huge wardrobe capable of providing service for two people. The cottage smelled of fresh polish and peat with an underlying fresh scent of lye.

"Well?" Father Mahon asked, after we made a quick tour of the cottage. "Will this do?"

"Yes," Maeve said, casting an involuntary look down the short hall to the bedroom and blushing. "Although the accommodations are a bit . . . sparse."

"It seems very neat and comfortable," I said. "Where are the tenants?"

"A retired couple taking a short vacation down to Dingle and Inch," he said. "But they take great pride in their home. It's only a wee cottage but looks like all Irish cottages should and seldom do. 'Tis no hardship upon them," he added, anticipating my next question. "They have a daughter in Dingle most gracious with her hospitality." Tiny muscles bunched at the corners of his jaw. His eyes were flat and hard.

"Something else, Father?" I asked. I was fairly certain I knew what was bothering him. I was right.

"Why not give it up and go back to Dublin?" he blurted. "Sure, 'tis a fine and noble thing that you tried to do, but now it's guns they are using and the type of guns that do not care who they hurt. You were lucky this time that no one else was around when the attempt was made upon you. But what if there had been children playing in the street?"

"Then the attempt would not have been made, Father Mahon," Maeve said. "You know the rules the same as all." He shook his head in dogged determination.

"Ah, no, Maeve," he said. " 'Twas none of the lads' doing, that one. Wasn't himself assuring me of that just this morning when I held him to account for the shooting in my parish?"

"Then who?" I asked. He looked at me as if surprised I was still there.

"Contract men brought in from the outside," he said. "But we don't know who or why." I laughed. He frowned.

"A bit like bringing whiskey to Ireland, wouldn't you say?"

"There are renegades in all societies," he said a bit stiffly. "The Irish are no different."

"And liars," I said. "You've got more than your share of them in Ireland as well."

"What do you expect?" he said sharply. "We learn our lessons well and quickly. Except here we call it 'survival.' "

"Sorry, Father," I said sarcastically. "But I'm sure you'll understand if I take a different view. You weren't the one being shot at. That tends to belie trust. I have a little difficulty seeing gunmen as saints." A sudden thought occurred to me. "You didn't happen to make mention of this"—I waved my hand around the cottage—"to MacCauley and his associates, did you?"

"No," he said, anger beginning to show in his eyes. He belligerently raised his voice. "And I resent your asking."

"Be quiet, both of you," Maeve said. "Neither of you are children." We fell silent, glaring at each other. She sighed. "Ah, me. If you must continue to bait each other, have the decency to wait until we're through with this thing."

[146]

"Sorry," I said. "I'm afraid I was looking for an argument."

"And me as well," he said, reluctantly unbending. "No, I didn't tell anyone. You're safe here. For a while," he amended. "But this is a nice, quiet little area without much comings and goings. Someone will take note of you before long, and then it will be news for all. If you follow my meaning?"

"How long do we have?" Maeve thoughtfully asked. "A week? Ten days?"

"A week at the outside. And then the news will be all over Mullaghmore. Maybe sooner if it's there you intend to ask your questions. But," he added, rising to leave, "if you won't listen to good advice and return to Dublin, then it's a fine, snug hole you've got for a while. I'll be going now. I must be returning to the rectory to ready myself for vespers. It's good luck I'll wish you, and prayers I'll say on your behalf."

"*Slán leat,*" Maeve said. "*Go raibh maith agat.*"

"*Slán agat,*" he said roughly. He clapped his hat on his head and left. Moments later, we heard the rattle of his old Morris as he overrevved the engine and the grinding of the gears as he drove away.

We stood awkwardly in the main room, avoiding each other's eyes. Maeve took an iron poker from a stand at the side of the hearth and rustled the embers of the fire. Sparks flew upward, bouncing from the bricks of the firebox to disappear up the chimney. I pulled the cork on the bottle of poteen and cautiously sniffed the neck. My nose burned.

"Would you care for a drink, Maeve?"

She gave me a quick smile and turned her attention back to the fire. "A *manglam* is it you're offering? It would be nice, if it's here we are intending to stay for the remainder of the day, and it still having long legs to it as yet." Her brogue was thick, rich from her nervousness, evident from the quick glance she again made down the short hall to the bedroom. I sighed and recorked the bottle.

"Maybe you're right," I said lightly. "Perhaps it's best not to waste any more time, given what Father Mahon said. How far is Mullaghmore?"

"Not far, I'm thinking," she said. "Just a fair stretch of the legs."

"You mean *walk?*" I asked. "Why, it's raining outside! Storming!"

She laughed and rose from the fireplace, nervousness gone in the face of my dismay. " 'Tis only a fine, soft afternoon," she said teasingly. "Besides, if we do not use the Cortina, then it'll be harder to keep track of us and place us. Being on foot also gives us more options. We can even cross the fields and pastures."

"And play leapfrog among the hummocks on the moor," I darkly muttered. "Did you ever think that we might take a chill and be in the hospital with pneumonia?"

"Not with the medicine we have here," she said, lifting the bottle of poteen. "No microbe could live in that."

"Very well," I said, resigned to my fate. "Where to first?"

She looked at her watch. "The pub," she said decidedly. "The fishermen will be in by the time we get to Mullaghmore. If the catch was good, they'll be eager to talk."

"And if the catch was bad?" I asked, playing the devil's advocate. She grinned, her nose wrinkling with the sudden lifting of her spirits.

"They'll still be eager to talk. Such is an Irishman surrounded by his friends in a pub." She opened the door and, placing the flat of her hand in the middle of my back, propelled me out into the downpour that was a "soft afternoon."

TEN

The Gallows Tree was an old pub with long leaded panes on either side of the jamb and in the door itself. Above the door, the glass of the small transom was painted with a garland of shamrocks in the shape of a hangman's noose. I had to admire the symbolism.

I pushed open the door and entered behind Maeve. The rich smell of porter made my nose twitch. A long bar ran down the wall on my right, the curved molding well polished from thousands of cloth-covered elbow caresses. Small tables buttressed by deep-backed chairs filled the area in front of us while high settles provided privacy for those wishing it. Around the wall hung many yellowed pictures of horses, hurlers, Gaelic football team photos, near record catches, and a few leather-coated, grim-faced men seemingly out of time. Conversation momentarily halted as heads swiveled to assess us. Maeve moved toward a small unoccupied table near the far corner. I crossed to the bar for two pints of stout. Eyes followed me to the table before heads turned back to conversations.

"Now what?" I asked. I took a sip of the stout and licked the brown foam from my lips. Maeve smiled and raised her glass.

"Just wait," she said. "It won't be long." She drank long and deeply, lowering the level in her glass by half. She placed the glass back on the table and leaned back in her chair. She slowly ran her tongue over her lips and sighed deeply. The level of conversation rose sharply at the bar, followed by a bark of laughter. A tall, young man, broad-shouldered in an Aran Island sweater of fisherman's weave, broke from the bar and confidently moved toward our table, pint glass clutched in one beefy hand. Long blond hair curled along the nape of his neck. He stopped in front of Maeve.

"Yes?" I asked, craning my head to look up at him. He ignored me.

"Sure," he said slowly, his eyes insolent upon her. "Sure it is I am that we haven't met before and lucky it is that now we have." He gave her a crooked smile and tried to look at her from lowered brows like Cary Grant but only succeeded in making his jowls fleshily bunch along his jawline. I winced and picked up my glass. He caught my reaction and slowly turned toward me, shifting to Marlon Brando. "You have a problem?"

"No, no," I managed, desperately trying to keep from laughing. "I just didn't expect to meet Humphrey Bogart." He frowned, unsure if he had been insulted. He opened his mouth to speak only to shut it as someone spoke from the shadow of one of the settles.

"Best if you leave them alone, Mickey," a voice softly called. "Go back to your mates, now. There's a good lad."

His eyes darted toward the voice, a red flush rising in his face. "And who," he said thickly, "would be the one with the wit of the wee people?" A quiet chuckle followed his words. A leather-clad figure moved into the light. I sighed, and nodded at him.

"Fallon," I said. "Didn't expect to see you here." Another figure emerged from the settle behind him. Seamus Halloran. "Or you," I added. The Sacred Heart in his lapel looked decidedly out of place. He gave me a sour smile.

Fallon ignored us and stared at the one standing by our table. "Ah, Mickey," he said. "You haven't been gallivanting over the moors looking for the wee ones! Not a fine figure of a man such as yourself? No? Then why would it be that you are confusing me with them?"

Mickey's face turned pasty white. He looked down at the pint in his hand. "I didn't mean nothing, Fallon. Sure, and I was just having a bit of fun."

"I know that," Fallon said calmly. "And that's why you're still standing on healthy pins. Now, be a good lad and take yourself back to your mates."

Mickey nodded, relief washing across his face. He hurriedly shuffled away from our table. Fallon turned to us with a lazy smile. "He's a good boy," he said softly. "But he's got a devil in his throat that causes him a bit of trouble from time to time. Bit off your track, aren't you, Maeve?"

"No thanks to you, Fallon," Maeve said a bit angrily. "We could have handled him."

"I'm sure you could," Fallon smoothly answered. "The question is, could he have handled you? Remember what MacCauley said about causing any trouble around here?"

"And," she said, "what is it that has caused himself to go back on his word? You missed, Tomas Fallon. Are you getting too old to be doing the job?"

Fallon stared silently at her for a long moment, then softly said, "What sedition are you spreading now, Maeve?"

"I'm no fool, Fallon," she said scathingly. "When someone shoots at me, I figure he's trying to kill me. If he misses, I figure he's a bad shot."

"When?" Fallon said. His face settled into frozen features.

"Yesterday," I put in. "As we were leaving the TRANCO offices in Sligo. A Rover and a machine gun. It was close. Too close."

He shook his head. " 'Twas not my doing," he said. "And you have the word of Seamus MacCauley."

"But," Maeve said, frustration settling in twin lines between her eyebrows, "who else could it have been?" Fallon shook his head and lifted his pint.

"I'll find out," he said. He gestured at the bar. "Meanwhile, would you be having another pint?"

"Fallon," Maeve sighed, shaking her head at his offer. She remained silent for a moment, then raised her head and spoke. "What the hell are you doing here? And with that?" She lifted her chin to indicate Seamus Halloran standing in the shadows by the settles. Fallon shrugged.

"That," Halloran said acidly, "is precisely what I would like to know. This, this barbarian. . . ."

"Careful," Fallon murmured, eyes narrowing slightly.

". . . *insisted* I accompany him to this den of iniquity." He sniffed and dabbed his nose with his handkerchief. "You can imagine the humiliation."

"Ah, shut your gob," Fallon said darkly. "Afore I shut it for you."

"Yes, I can see where you would imagine that," I said, glancing at his lapel pin.

"And what was I to do with him after himself gave me instructions to keep him out of the way." I understood he meant MacCauley. "If it's a sorry mess, it's yourself you have to thank. I had little else to do with you," Fallon said. He looked at Maeve significantly. "Making a right mess of it all, he was. Poking his nose in where it wasn't wanted."

"And what would that be?" Maeve asked.

"I had as much right—" Halloran indignantly began, then snapped his jaw shut as Fallon looked at him.

"You had no right to be questioning the negotiations," Fallon said.

"Negotiations?" I asked.

"Down at the docks," Fallon said, impatient with my ignorance. "They've been sorting out the hiring for the whole day now."

"And two Protestants from Derry they took after the last O'Donevan, and him being as good a man upon his knees as any other," Halloran said. "And all because Paisley began to preach about the type of jobs going to the Republic. Now, if it was me—"

"Which it wasn't," Fallon said rudely. "Damn me if all your nattering doesn't bring out the thirst in a man! It doesn't matter as long as both sides agree. MacCauley and Paisley being agreed and His Lordship, too . . ."

"Lordship? Who?" I asked.

"Mountbatten, of course," he said. "Do you not read the papers or listen to the radio, man?"

"And wasn't he the cool one, though, a-sittin' there passing judgment on the choices we gave 'im for his work!" Halloran snapped.

"He could have brought in TRANCO and Killian's men to work the ships, the rigs," I murmured.

A fierce light began to burn from deep within Halloran's eyes. His nostrils pinched. "No, and doesn't he know that if he should do such a thing, not a stone of his fine home at Classiebawn Castle would be left standing?" He spat upon the floor and wiped the back of his hand across his lips. "Sure, and he knows that. He's no fool. He knows whose hand controls the unions."

"I told you once to be quiet," Fallon warned. "I'll not be telling you twice."

" 'Tis a fine day when good Irish lads are forced to queue like common gypsies to get work from an English landlord. I'm quiet, I'm quiet," he said hastily, backing into the settles as Fallon made a threatening gesture.

"And how is the selection going?" Maeve asked.

"As good as can be expected," Fallon said, casting a dark look upon Halloran. "Of course, he's hiring the navvy boys and the common tote-and-fetchits and 'tis the ones with the families that are going first as is right. But the little man has a point: the overseers and strawmen are mostly English. 'Cept, a' course, for those with salt in their beards: the shipwrights and lumpers and the fishermen who've trolled the bank."

"And the riggers?" I asked. He shook his head.

"All from the North Sea fields. Good business, that, though, for what Irishman still in the Republic has worked the sea rigs? None, that's for certain, unless there's an odd two from Bantry Bay."

"But it is work," Maeve said emphatically. "Work where there's been none before."

"There's that," Fallon conceded. "And the fact that it is work is keeping the order. Still, there's been talk."

"What kind of talk?" Maeve asked. He shrugged and pulled at his ear as if embarrassed to have mentioned it at all.

"There's always a few, Maeve," he said. "Always a few who are never satisfied unless the whole cow, milk and all, is in their barns. But," he said quickly, "nothing will be coming of it. Of that, I am certain. Himself will be seeing to that. If the peace is to be broken, it'll be at the hands of Black Ian and his UDA boys. Still," he added with a grin, "I haven't given up hope." Maeve laughed.

"By Jaysus, Tomas," she said, chuckling. "One would think you to be a wild goose come home."

"Faith," he said, a tiny smile playing about his lips. "And what else is there for a man like me?" His words were touched with a sadness filled with truth for the hate that had created him out of necessity. For a moment, I thought I caught a flicker of vulnerability, of pain, in his eyes, but the moment passed. Yet it was enough to suggest the vulnerable man behind the hate.

"There'll always be work for you, Tomas Fallon," Maeve said soberly. Fallon flashed a keen glance at her.

"And there I hope you're wrong, Maeve," he said seriously. "Sure, I'd like to kill a few more Prods, but we've had enough early wakes and enough tears. It's time for those like me to find another cause elsewhere. I hear Africa is nice."

Someone in the corner began playing softly and slowly on a concertina: a mournful tune that brought all conversation to a respectful halt. It's an unusual Irishman who can ignore a sad song in a snug pub. A high, clear tenor began to sing:

> No more—no more in Castletown
> Will I sell my health by scraping
> Or at county fairs roam up and down
> And join the merrymaking
> Where mounted farmers ride in throngs
> To find and hire me over.
> At last I'm hired, my journey's done,
> The journey of the Rover.

I caught Maeve's eye and pointed at the door. She frowned, then shrugged, and nodded. We listened for a couple of verses before quietly making our way to the outside.

"Where to?" she asked as the door closed behind us. The rain had slackened, and the air smelled sour like ripe meat. I huddled deeper into my trench coat against the heavy dampness and resignedly pushed thoughts of the warm cottage and poteen jug from my mind.

"The docks," I said. "It's the first chance we've had to talk to one of the TRANCO directors. Mountbatten should be able to give us more information than Drumm."

"And if he can't?" she asked.

I shook my head, taking her firmly by the elbow and pointing us toward the docks. "I'll figure something out," I said, hoping I sounded convincing, confident. I really didn't want to tell her I had no idea at all. I knew that neither MacCauley nor O'Bannion would be willing to help us find Martin Galvin or NORAID. I wasn't sure I wanted to ask them, either. Maeve and I had almost worn out our welcome. Something like that might result in the door being slammed shut. Or a coffin lid. The thought was chilling.

ELEVEN

Fog began to roll in from the sea by the time we got to the docks. Huge, dirty gray clumps, a Victorian fog that struck the shore and spread out to creep down the streets and cover the town. A large crowd milled in the gloom outside the TRANCO offices. Some of the men adopted roles as coarse merry-andrews as we approached, making bold comments loud enough for Maeve to hear, but she ignored them and pushed her way to the front where a large man, his back to us, blocked our path.

"Excuse me," Maeve said, tapping him insistently upon the shoulder. He slowly turned, a large grin spreading over familiar features. "Michael John!" Maeve said warmly. She gave him a hug, which brought a few whistles from the crowd.

"I'm glad you're here," I said, warm relief washing over me. "You don't know how glad I am to see you."

He gave me a swift look, then frowned. "There's been trouble?"

"A bit." He looked at Maeve, who silently nodded and in a few short words tersely explained what had happened in Sligo.

"MacCauley?"

"Fallon says no," Maeve said.

"And did you expect a yes?" He shook his head. "Lass, I think it's time for you to be cutting your losses. Go back to Dublin. To London, if you can. At least till this blows over. I know, I know. There's small chance of that." He sighed. "Well, at least I can watch your back."

"Thanks, Michael John," she said. She affectionately squeezed his arm. " 'Tis an offer we'll not refuse."

"Ah, go on with you," he said and grinned. "What else would I be doing for the wife of Conor Larkin?"

"Have they closed for the night?" I asked, gesturing at the office door behind him. He shrugged.

"Well, they have and they haven't," he said. "Depends on what you want. 'Tis no more interviewing for the day, but the clerks and such are still around."

"Thanks," I said. I reached for the doorknob, then paused. "Will you wait for us?" He nodded, a grim smile playing around his lips.

"Aye. And it's a foolish man you're being if you think I won't after the last time you visited a TRANCO office."

"You're a good lad, Michael John," Maeve said. "We won't be long." She pressed forward to follow me through the door, but I blocked her way. "What's the matter?"

"Why don't I do this while you and Michael John go back to the pub. From the looks of him, he could stand a pint." She gave me a narrow look.

"And why would you be wanting to go on without me?" she demanded. "Is it noble you're getting, Con Edwards?" Her face softened as I didn't answer. She lightly touched me on the hand. "For that, I'm thanking you, but Michael John can take care of two as easily as one. Except"—she grinned, with no humor in the smile—"if it's Armalites and Ingrams they're using. There's not much he can do against the likes of that."

I gave up and opened the door, standing aside to let her enter. I looked back at Michael John. "Watch yourself," I cautioned. He grinned.

"Not to worry," he said. "You be careful in your dealings with those *gombeen* men."

I shut the door behind me. A somewhat harried clerk with tangled and twisted yellowed hair sat on a small stool behind a chest-high counter in front of us. He raised tired eyes to ours. The lines deepened at the corners of his lips. "We're closed until nine tomorrow morning," he said wearily. "You can come back then. We're not even taking applications until then."

"Is Lord Mountbatten here?" I asked. His eyebrows rose at the sound of my American accent.

"Good Lord!" he exclaimed. "First Cork, then Limerick,

now the U.S.A. I expect Calcutta to be next. There must be another depression." I laughed and passed him my credentials.

"No," I said. "Just a reporter. Would it be possible to see Lord Mountbatten, Mr. . . ."

"The name is William Baxter, sir," he said, tugging at an askew tie and glancing at my credentials. Frost seemed to settle over his features. "And, no, it would not be possible. The Queen's uncle does not give unscheduled interviews, Mr. Edwards."

"Surely something can be arranged?" I pressed, playing the reporter to the hilt. People expect rudeness and restlessness from American reporters. Ben Hecht put a stamp on that characterization with *The Front Page*. I tried to make my voice sound aggrieved. "I do have a story to file. We tried to get here sooner—Miss Nolan, my secretary, and myself—but we ran into some car trouble around Boyle that detained us. Otherwise, we would have been here earlier."

"Lord Mountbatten is not accustomed to being at the beck and call of the press," he said stiffly, making the word sound like an epithet. "If an interview is desired, arrangements must be made through the proper channels at least a week in advance."

"I just need a moment or two of his time. Perhaps in the morning?" I insisted.

He winced and massaged the space between his eyes. Tiny muscles moved at the points of his jaw. "I am afraid Lord Mountbatten has made plans for tomorrow. I presume you are aware it's a holiday. Bank Holiday Monday."

"He can't fit in five minutes?" I complained.

"No," he said shortly. "He cannot. Now if you will excuse me, the day has been very long, and I still have work to do."

"Thanks for nothing," I said, and escorted Maeve from the office. The fog had grown thicker during our visit, the chill more intense. It seemed to search us out and worm its way beneath our coats to numb our bones. Michael John materialized out of its depths to join us.

"Not—" I began, but stopped as he urgently placed a large forefinger across his lips. I raised my eyebrows in question.

"A few boy-os up to no good, I think," he said softly,

indicating generally to our right in the thick fog. "Back there. Four, I think. In the alley. A bit hard to be certain."

"Armed?" I asked. He grinned mirthlessly. I nodded, my heart sinking. "Right. A foolish question. What do we do?"

"Can you get behind them, Michael John?" Maeve asked. He shook his head.

" 'Tis a dead end they've chosen. One way in, one way out. Their backs are safe. 'Tis no amateurs we're playing with, that's for certain."

"All right," she said. A reckless smile played around her lips. Her eyes danced like starred sapphires. My stomach began to feel queasy. "Then we'll draw them out for you. Are you armed?"

"Faith," he said, a big smile stretching across his face. He raised his hands eye level. "Always."

Maeve pulled a small automatic I had never seen from her coat pocket, checked and replaced it, keeping her hand in her pocket. She tucked her left arm through mine and faced the direction Michael John had indicated.

"We'll draw them out," she softly said. "They'll follow when we pass. Be careful."

"Mind a second opinion?" I nervously asked, looking longingly in the opposite direction.

"Yes," she said. "Keep quiet." She tugged at my arm. I stumbled after her, trying to convince myself that it was the cold making my legs tremble.

We slowly moved through the fog, groping our way by feel for the edge of the road away from the buildings to force whoever waited for us from the security of the alley. I stumbled over a small pile of rubble, almost pulling Maeve down. Stones clattered over planking. I winced. My mouth tasted like copper. My imagination rapidly and wildly danced and soared.

"Damn," I complained. "I could have broken my neck."

"Watch your step," she said snappishly, jerking me erect. "Play the game," she hurriedly hissed, then raised her voice. " 'Tis not a tearoom through which you're walking. Nor," she added, "a pub for that matter. Wasn't I telling you 'twas an evening not fit for anything but a pint or two around the fire? But, no. A stroll by the docks, you had to have. Romantic, you said. Moonlight o'er the water. And how is the moon tonight?"

"Far better than sitting in a pub and listening to another Irish tenor," I said heatedly. "Poets and singers, all with the same tiresome theme: melancholy. And complaints about the Yanks. I notice, however, no reluctance in taking my money."

A quiet chuckle came from behind us. We stopped and slowly turned. Four men stood in a loose arc, their faces hidden in the darkness. One carried a piece of what appeared to be lead pipe. Another held a section of a two-by-four. The other two appeared to be empty-handed. I painfully swallowed.

"Have the good grace not to hit the man until you're married and he can hit you back," a rich baritone mockingly said.

"And who," Maeve insolently asked, "would you be who offers advice unasked for?"

"A nightmare, lass. At least, for him that's with you." They slowly began to move toward us. "And for yourself, a dream if you're willing."

"And if I'm not?"

"No matter," the voice said. "Best enjoy it—" He grunted, grabbed his back, and fell to his knees. He slowly toppled forward onto his face, the pipe falling to the ground with a clatter. A thole pin rolled to a stop by my feet. I bent to pick it up as the other three paused uncertainly. Michael John loomed behind them, a massive distorted image. He seized two by their necks, cracking their heads together like two ripe melons. They soundlessly dropped at his feet. The fourth threateningly waved the two-by-four, then gasped, his shoulder jerking spasmodically as Maeve shot from beside me. He grabbed his arm and drunkenly ran away into the fog as Michael John reached for him.

"And why," Michael John complained, "would you be wanting to do that? Just as I was about to have a bit of fun with him."

"Sorry," Maeve said. "But there's enough for the questions we'll be putting to them." She slipped the automatic into her pocket. "How are they?"

Michael John squatted and hurriedly examined them. "Ah, well," he said, sadly shaking his head. "I'm afraid these two will not be much good for you. Don't know me own strength, I don't. But the other"—he nodded toward our first assailant, who began to stir and moan—"should be willing to answer a few questions." He squatted again, seizing the man's head between two hands. He roughly shook it back and forth, forcing consciousness.

"Ah, God!" the man croaked. "For sweet Jaysus' sakes!" Feebly he pushed at Michael John's hands.

"See?" Michael John said. "Wasn't I telling you? Wasn't I, now? Sure, in an hour or two, it'll be a fine song he'll be willing to sing." He dragged the man to his feet.

"And the others?" I asked. He looked diffidently down at the unmoving bodies at his feet.

"Leave them for the gulls and corncakes," he coarsely said. "Or what the wharf rats leave for them, which might not be much given morning's such a long ways off. What do we do with this one? Best not be standing here much longer."

"Can we get him back to the cottage?" I asked Maeve. She hesitated, then nodded.

"P'raps that's best," she said. "What do you say, Michael John? Can he walk a healthy distance?"

"Ah, don't be worrying yourself about that. 'Tis only a bit of a rap that's got him addled. And," he added meaningfully, tapping the man on the chin pointedly, "if he can't, we'll be leaving him in the ditch for the *Garda*. Do you follow my meaning, my buck-o? Or is it here with your fine companions you'd prefer to stay?"

"I can walk," the other sullenly said. "Just lay off my noggin! Jaysus, but there's bees a-hummin' inside!" He gently massaged his temples with both hands.

"Ah, not to worry, not to worry," Michael John beamed, cuffing him none too gently again. "A fine stretch of the legs will clear your bell in no time. Now, let's be off. And," he said, turning to Maeve. "I'm after hoping there's a wee drop a-waiting at the end of our march?" He gave the man a negligent shove that sent him staggering down the street. He winked and moved with long, loping strides after our prisoner.

TWELVE

Although the trip earlier had taken only a couple of hours, the return trip took nearly twice that; partly because of the fog, partly because we couldn't afford the chance of being spotted and took little-used country lanes. At one point, our prisoner tried to take advantage of the darkness and escape, only to be knocked unconscious a second time by Michael John. At last, we arrived back at the cottage, our prisoner's limp form casually slung over Michael John's shoulder.

"God bless all here," Michael John automatically said, stooping to go through the doorway. He unceremoniously dumped the would-be assailant on the floor and expertly ran his hands through the unconscious man's pockets. He removed a small cosh and flick-knife. A faint sound of thunder echoed from far out at sea. He frowned and crossed to the window but could see nothing for the fog bank. " 'Tis a foul night that speaks no good for someone," he said, turning from the window. His eyes lit on the bottle of poteen left on the table. A large smile broke across his craggy features. He smacked his lips. "Ah," he said reverently, advancing upon the bottle. "And sure if St. Brigid and St. Columban and, aye, St. Brendan, too, aren't walking at my shoulder! Do my eyes deceive me or is it a drop of the dew, sweet leprechaun tears, that I'm studying?" He dropped the cosh and knife on the table.

"Would you be taking a drop, now, Michael John?" Maeve asked, grinning at his childlike pleasure.

"Don't mind if I do!" he said, scooping the bottle from the table and popping the cork in one smooth motion. He ignored the glasses and raised the bottle to his lips. His Adam's apple bobbed five times before he lowered it and took a deep breath. "A blessing against the night," he said. A long moan answered him from the floor. Reluctantly, he replaced the cork and carefully set the bottle in the middle of the table. He crossed to our captive and roughly hauled him to his feet. He pulled a chair out from the table and slammed him into it with such force that his feet bounced from the floor and his teeth came together with an audible *click!*

"Ah, no! For the love of God! Me head! Me head!" the man piteously moaned.

"What's your name?" Maeve quietly asked, moving directly in front of him, the small automatic negligently held against her thigh. He ignored her question and tried to turn to face Michael John.

" 'Tis no cunny I'll be speaking to," he began. He almost spun out of the chair as Michael John slapped him hard across both cheeks.

"P'raps not," he said. "But it's a civil tongue you'll be keeping in your head and polite words you'll be speaking. Now, answer the lady."

His eyes followed me as I crossed to the table and filled a glass half-full with poteen. I raised the glass to my lips, sipping, barely managing to keep a straight face as the raw spirits slid open-clawed down my throat. His eyes dropped to his lap.

"Kevin O'Garvey," he mumbled. His lips began to swell like bee stings. "Christ, man!"

"From where?" Maeve calmly continued, as if nothing had happened.

He hesitated, then blurted as Michael John threateningly raised his hand: "County Down!"

"Good. That's very good, Kevin O'Garvey. 'Tis a fine talk we'll be having now."

"Yer ass," he growled. The blow knocked him from his seat. He lay dazed on the floor until Michael John seized him by the collar and hauled him back into the chair.

"Now, what was I telling you about polite words?" Michael John demanded. "You're a hard learner, Kevin O'Garvey."

"Why were you waiting in that alley, Kevin O'Garvey?" Maeve asked, keeping her voice neutral, devoid of emotion. Her face could have been carved from stone, but tiny fires flickered in the depths of her eyes. I had never seen this Maeve Nolan: enigmatic, unknowable, the Deirdre of Irish legend? Perhaps. But somehow, I couldn't help but think also of the harpies of Zeus as she stood poised, leaning slightly forward, a figure of vengeance. I felt pity for Kevin O'Garvey, although I didn't want to, and, strangely, an excitement for Maeve Nolan, much, I imagined, like Jason must have felt for Medea. Mixed metaphors, perhaps, but deserving of the imagery, for she embodied the qualities of each: the legendary beauty of Deirdre, the justice of the harpies, the cruel vengeance of Medea. I wasn't sure if I wanted to see this Maeve Nolan, but I was powerless, unable to turn my head.

"We was looking . . . " he began, then hurriedly amended, "that is . . . we, me mates and me, were told to wait there for you."

"Who told you?" O'Garvey hesitated, his eyes jerking desperately between the three of us.

"There is no one to help you, Kevin O'Garvey," Maeve said. "We are a long way from Mullaghmore. No one will hear you scream except the three of us. And scream you will, Kevin O'Garvey. Scream you will, and beg us to put a bullet through your brain to end your agony. You are all alone now. Those who sent you have already forgotten about you."

His shoulders sagged as the last defiance drained from him. "Doxie Crawford. He got it from Martin O'Donnell, who got it from somebody else."

"Seamus MacCauley?" Maeve asked. Michael John gave her a swift look of concern. She ignored him. O'Garvey shook his head.

"I don't know. Perhaps. 'Twas from Belfast. The NORAID people."

"So why would NORAID want to harm us?" I said. Maeve frowned, turning back to O'Garvey.

"That, I think, is something we need to know. Mr. O'Garvey?"

Slowly his head rose, and he stared with lusterless eyes at her. "You're going to kill me, aren't you?" he said tonelessly. He looked at me, then at Michael John. His eyes were dead, his skin gray beneath black beard stubble. Twin frown lines appeared between Michael John's eyes. He placed the unfinished glass of poteen on the table and edged closer to O'Garvey.

"Now, lad," he soothingly said. "No such thing crossed our minds, did it? We may hurt you a wee bit, but kill you? Tch, tch." He shook his head. "Aren't you flattering yourself to be thinking you're worth the price of a bullet?"

"Don't matter none," O'Garvey said. He slumped in his chair, staring at the toes of his boots. "If not you, then them."

"Why would they want to kill you?" Maeve asked. He shook his head and remained silent. "Come now," she said. "Tell me. Why would NORAID want to harm us?" O'Garvey shook his head again. Maeve sighed and moved away from him.

"I can break an arm for you, Maeve," Michael John said halfheartedly. "But I'm thinking it won't do you any good."

"No," she said. "He's done. He's hearing nothing but banshees now, is that one. Sure, and there's no life in him to make him fear."

"He's Black Irish and a Donegal man, too, from the looks of him. They're a superstitious lot. Well, what should I do with him? He's not much good to anyone, much less to himself."

"Take him to Father Mahon and tell him the tale. He'll take care of him."

"That I will," he said. He paused and gently nodded at the pistol in her hand. "You know what has to be done, Maeve." She looked startled and slowly raised her hand to stare at the weapon. Woodenly, she moved in front of O'Garvey and hesitated. She looked up at Michael John.

"It has to be done, Maeve," he said softly. " 'Tis his only chance. You know that. Would you be wanting me to do it?"

"No," she said. " 'Tis a filthy thing to do to a man, but 'tis not of my choosing. Are you listening, Kevin O'Garvey? The choice was made by your ancestors and mine long before we were born. Blame them, if you must. And yourself."

She raised the automatic and swiftly shot him twice— once in each knee. He screamed, clutched his knees, screamed again, a hideous shriek exploding from primal memory. Then his eyes rolled back in his head, and he toppled unconscious from the chair to ignobly sprawl upon the floor. Michael John stood over him for a moment, the cosh swinging gently from his hand. He tossed it back onto the table and anxiously bent to check O'Garvey's pulse. He grunted in satisfaction and rose.

"And wasn't I thinking I'd cracked his skull for him," he said. He looked at Maeve. "Took it badly, he did. Never did I hear a man scream like that."

White-faced, she nodded in agreement. "Nor I. Anticipation, it was, I'm thinking. A terrible thing."

Bile rose in my throat. I lifted Michael John's half-filled glass from the table and drained it, using the bite of the poteen to purge my mouth. I gasped and clung to the table, blinking tears from my eyes, fighting the indignant roll of my stomach.

Maeve crossed to the washstand, removed a clean dish towel, and tore it lengthwise into two strips. "Bind him with this," she said, tossing one at Michael John and thrusting the second into my hands. "You can use the Cortina," she said. She abruptly turned on her heel and quickly walked from the hall to the bedroom. The door quietly closed behind her. I looked at the tattered cloth in my hands, then at Michael John.

"Times," he said, reading my thoughts. " 'Tis the times, Con, not the person. Don't be thinking too badly of her, for she'll be needing you more now than ever. And those who set this vermin on you will know 'tis no weeping Dublin lass there but a daughter of Cuchulain. Now, lend me a hand before this one bleeds to death, and I'll be taking him to Father Mahon." He bent to his task, expertly winding and knotting the scrap around the gaping hole in O'Garvey's right knee. I watched for a moment, swallowed my gorge, then bent clumsily to the task.

THIRTEEN

At first, I thought it was an echo of thunder from the heavy storm that had rolled in from the sea to lash the cottage. Then I heard it again: a low, hesitant call as if written on the wind: "Con?"

I struggled awake, confused for a moment by my surroundings. I tried to push myself erect and cracked my elbow on the stone floor of the cottage. Memory flooded back with painful force. My stomach heaved with sudden fear. A dull red glow emitted from the banked fire in the living area fireplace, making the heavy table and chairs fearful, grotesque shadows on the wall. I pulled the heavy eiderdown comforter tighter around my shoulders.

"Yes. What is it?" I said softly.

"Con? I'm sorry." A muffled sob accompanied the words.

"Maeve?" I threw the comforter off and painfully rose. My muscles protested the hours spent on the floor. "What's the matter?" I stumbled down the dark hall, my hands outstretched before me, groping between the flashes of lightning. I fumbled for the latch to the bedroom door, found it, and entered. My shin smashed against the frame of the bed, bringing an involuntary curse to my lips.

"What's wrong?" I could barely make out her dim form upon the bed.

"Everything," she said. "It's all going wrong. It wasn't supposed to be like this. I don't know what I expected, but not this."

Slowly I felt my way around the bed and gingerly sat on the edge next to her. "You've been around this all your life," I said. "What did you expect? You knew when you started this someone had to be hurt. It was almost us." She rolled over. I could feel her eyes trying to pierce the darkness.

"Yes," she said, sobs held tightly in check at the edge of her words.

"Maeve," I said, "you're no stranger to kneecapping."

"No," she bitterly said. "I'm not. But I've never done that before or been around when it was done. It would have been more merciful to have killed him."

"Probably," I said. "Especially since he's marked as an outcast from both NORAID and the IRA. He'll be shunned, and he'll live in pain, fearful that someday someone will come along to finish the job. But he'll also be a warning, and in this society that's necessary."

"What do you mean?" she asked, snuffling her words.

"Conor believed the people in Belfast have developed a siege mentality, a sort of primal throwback where violence was the accepted moral norm in society. I think he was right, but I think it goes even deeper than he suspected with all his pessimism. I believe that mentality has developed into an acceptance of blood." I settled back against the headboard, shifting my shoulders against its hardness.

"You sound like a prophet of old," she said. "No chance at redemption. I don't want to believe that. I want to believe there's hope. Is that too terribly wrong?" I shook my head, forgetting the darkness for a moment.

"No, it's not. It's like a game in which each player draws blind cards and plays them without knowing their values or possibilities. The possibility of defeat is so galling that through sheer stubbornness he attempts the game. Like all games, though, there must be a set of rules. One must follow those rules. You did." I shivered from the cold and clammy night that had crept into the warmth of the cottage.

"And what if I didn't?" she asked, her voice stronger than before. "It's a stupid and silly custom."

"You made your choice. Live with it. You'll never have the type of choice you want to make in a game like this."

"Then there never will be a united Ireland?"

I drew a deep breath and slowly let it out. "No," I said softly. "Too many years have passed with too much hatred breeding upon hatred that has become part of the new traditions. Values have changed. There is no longer any common ground upon which a temple of trust can be built."

She was silent for a moment, then halfheartedly laughed. "You're good for me, Con Edwards. And, sure, if you aren't picking up the bad habits of Irish blarney. 'Temple of trust' indeed!"

"Ah, me. Sure, and haven't I been darkly misused of late?" I tried joking, but although she laughed, it was an obedient laugh with no humor behind it. We lay awhile in the dark before she spoke again.

"Con? It's fearful cold. Would you hold me? Just for a little while against the cold?"

Silently I slid beneath the covers. She snuggled spoon-fashion into my side, her head in the hollow of my shoulder. I fell asleep smelling the heather in her hair.

FOURTEEN

Rain was pouring down when we arose in the morning, cross with each other. A dull pain settled behind my eyes as my sinuses filled from the wet and cold. I tried to call the TRANCO offices from a telephone booth in town in another attempt to find out Lord Mountbatten's plans for the day but received a busy signal. After the third attempt, I crossly hung up and slammed the booth door open. A fine mist stroked my face with clammy fingers. I climbed irritably into the car. Maeve looked at me questioningly.

"Christ," I sighed. "Now what?"

Maeve shook her head. "Maybe the docks again?"

I gestured impatiently. "That bastard Baxter? He won't give us anything." I glanced at the telephone. "I was hoping to catch a secretary or someone less pompous and officious."

"They would have told you nothing, either. You forget where you are. Protocol and tradition are rigid and inflexible."

"Not to mention security," I grumbled.

"Not to mention security," she agreed. "But there are ways around it. What have we to lose?"

"Nothing," I sighed. I motioned toward the docks.

The sun broke through the storm as we left the car at the top of the docks and strolled down to the TRANCO offices. A few bedraggled sea gulls watched with careful eyes in case we dribbled a few crumbs behind us as we passed their perches upon mooring posts. A crowd of men as bedraggled as the sea gulls milled in front of the offices.

We paused beside one of the men. He glanced at us, his look resting appreciatively on Maeve. She smiled at him.

"A fine day," she said.

"That it is," he answered.

"Have you been taken on?" she asked, nodding at the closed door. A shade had been drawn over its glass.

He shook his head. "Not yet. But I have hopes. I'm told there's a need for pipe fitters, and I have me card."

"A shame the office is closed," Maeve said. "But it being a holiday and all 'tis to be expected."

"Aye," he answered. "But I hope His Lordship might remember me face tomorrow after he passes today."

"Oh? And he'll be by here?"

He cast a quick look around. Seeing the others were beyond hearing, he conspiratorially leaned forward. "He'll be passin' on his way to his boat." He gestured down the pier.

"How are you knowing this?" Maeve asked. The man spat and wiped his lips with the back of his hand.

"Sure and isn't me sister's husband's nephew going along to work the boat while the others fish for sharks," he said importantly. Maeve threw me a quick look of triumph.

" 'Tis fine and fair. Luck to you," she said. He nodded as we casually strolled away.

"Never lose your faith in the little people," Maeve said with satisfaction. "Royalty may have its protocol, but it takes common men to run it."

"Tradition," I grunted.

"Yes. But now we know." She glanced up at the sun. "And if His Lordship is planning a day on the water, he should be showing about now." She looked over my shoulder. I turned and followed her gaze. A small group of people dressed for fishing moved down the dock toward us. Mountbatten towered over them, his silver hair carefully combed back from high forehead, tanned face bursting with life, his body hard and slender even at seventy-nine. Two casually dressed men flanked the group, doing their best to look inconspicuous.

"Now how do we get close to him?" she murmured.

"Have you forgotten I'm a crass American reporter?" I said. "I have a reputation to live up to."

I hurriedly pulled my identification from my pocket and held it high in plain sight as I approached the party.

"Lord Mountbatten!" I called. "Con Edwards from the

Times. Might I speak with you for a minute about Joe Killian? Easy now!" I said as the two plainclothesmen immediately stepped in front of Mountbatten. One looked swiftly around the pier, his gaze sharply focused on the men by TRANCO's office, his hand clutching a pistol beneath his shirt. The other stood directly in front of me, his eyes staring coldly into mine. He reached up and took my identification, wordlessly glanced at it, and handed it without looking to his partner. His partner carefully studied it, comparing the picture to me, then handed it to Lord Mountbatten.

"The *Times*?" Mountbatten frowned a bit, his speech exact, clipped, and direct. "This is highly irregular."

"I know, sir. I just need a minute or two. That's all. I understand you're a friend of Joe Killian?" I said respectfully.

He glanced at the other members of his party. "Why don't you go on ahead. I'll join you in a minute."

The others gave me a curious look, but moved away down the pier toward Mountbatten's boat. One of the plainclothesmen drifted behind in their wake; the other stayed close by my side.

"I'm afraid I don't know exactly what I can help you with. We have a man for that, I believe, who could give you much more information than I. You mentioned Joe Killian? I knew his grandfather. We were friends."

"Actually," I admitted, "it's something else I'd like to ask you if I may." His eyes widened fractionally for a moment in question, then relaxed. He nodded.

"Go ahead. But I haven't much time. I must rejoin my guests."

"It's about Conor Larkin, sir," Maeve said from behind me. I was a touch surprised at the deference in her tone, then dismissed the surprise: the man commanded it with the sheer ebullience of his nature. He waited patiently, courteously giving her his attention. I suddenly realized he had not made a connection with Conor's name.

"The man who was killed on TRANCO's docks at Manchester about six months ago?"

His face cleared. "Ah, yes. Sorry, I didn't make the connection for a moment. But I'm afraid I can't tell you anything. The whole affair was over hours before I arrived."

"*Before* you arrived?" I asked. He nodded, leaning casually against a piling, arms crossed over his chest.

"Why, yes. I was there to check the transport ships Killian Shipping was planning on transferring to TRANCO under their merger agreement. A formality, you know, what with the Environmental Protection Act and all."

"Excuse me," I said. "Isn't that rather unusual for an Admiral of the Fleet to do? I mean, wouldn't something like that normally be relegated to someone in the lower ranks?"

"Normally," he said, a smile briefly flashing. "But it was a favor to the grandson of a friend and"—he shrugged—"I like to know all I can about organizations that use my name on their letterhead."

"Then this"—I waved my hand toward the TRANCO office—"is just part of that curiosity?"

He laughed. "Well, yes, I suppose you could say that, although I think it is a bit more than curiosity in that the jobs are needed in Ireland, and the hiring in such a situation as this could lead to violence if not done in a judicious manner."

"But surely there are representatives that could handle that?"

"But not as impartially," he said, then, anticipating my next question, added, "I have a home here; it is necessary that I remain as neutral as possible."

"And are you able to with such as Ian Paisley around?" Maeve asked. His face sobered for an instant, then the serene mask was back.

"Yes," he admitted, tactfully adding, "although it is difficult at times."

"Would you consider Paisley to be a dangerous man in this situation?" I asked.

"All men," he said, "are dangerous if given a bit of authority. Some," he said, smiling faintly, "would even place me in that category. Perhaps they rightly should." He glanced at his watch. "I am sorry, but I must be going. I have kept my guests waiting long enough."

"One last question," I said. "Do you have any idea why Conor Larkin was on the TRANCO docks?"

He regretfully shook his head. "No, I don't. Although . . ." He hesitated, casting a swift look at Maeve.

"Although?" I prompted. He tugged at his earlobe for a second, then sighed.

"Special Branch believes he might have been there as part of an, er, well, an assassination plot. I'm sure there's nothing to all that," he hastened to add. "But I'm given to understand, the man was a notorious IRA leader. On that basis, I can understand such reasoning. I do not believe anyone will ever know. His purpose died with him. I am sorry," he gently added, noticing the tears suddenly gleaming in Maeve's eyes. "Please believe me when I say I believe that's all speculation."

"Thank you," Maeve said. She quickly dried her eyes. "It wasn't that. Actually, we hoped you might be able to help us."

"Ah. I see. He was family, then?" Maeve nodded. "I know what it is like to lose someone. It was a poleax blow when my wife died." He hesitated. "Well. I am sorry I can't help you further."

"Thank you for your time, sir," I said. He nodded and started to walk away. "By the way," I asked. "When you did inspect the ships did you find them satisfactory?"

He smiled apologetically. "I haven't inspected them yet. What with all the trouble and all, Special Branch requested the inspection be put off. As a matter of fact, I'm due back in Manchester next week."

"Why has it taken so long to inspect the ships since the trouble?" I asked. He shrugged.

"The ships had contracts that needed to be filled. I was trying to slip the inspection in between shipping commitments. That day was the one day in eight months when all of the ships would be in port at once. Now the contracts are all fulfilled, or will be by next week, and the ships will again be ready for inspection. It's just a formality anyway. I would like, however, to acquaint myself with that part of TRANCO's business, you understand."

I thanked him again and followed Maeve as she pushed her way through the crowd and walked down the long wharf to an isolated docking. She turned and faced the sea, letting the fresh breeze dry her eyes.

"Perhaps the good Father Mahon is right, Con," she said as I moved up to stand alongside her. I didn't answer; it was something she had to find for herself inside herself. She rubbed the sleeve of her coat across her face, blotting her eyes. "Faith," she said, trying for the stage brogue and failing. "Would you be having a look at me? 'Tis mourning the banshee's wailing, I am. And fearing the *Cailleach* for 'tis no salt I'm carrying in me pocket." She dropped the sham, choking back the sobs. "Oh, Con, he was right, he was right! Let the dead bury the dead." She turned and buried her face in my shoulder. She cried for a minute, then angrily slammed her fists against my shoulders. "Damn you! Say something!"

I held her close, once again smelling the heather in her hair. It would have been so easy to agree with her and live out my life writing the odd short story, the safe human interest article, in a small cottage tucked away in beautiful County Mayo or the Wicklow Mountains near Dublin. But I couldn't do that.

"All I've heard are 'maybes.' The decision is yours to make, not mine."

She shakily laughed and pushed away from me. She pressed the heels of her hands hard against her eyes. "Funny. For a moment there, I thought you were going to ask me to marry you."

"For a moment, I was," I said. "But the ghost of Conor Larkin would be in the marriage bed between us. Maeve!" I spoke sharply to draw her eyes to mine. "I would like nothing better than to have you for my wife. But it must be because you want me for your *husband* and not a crutch or a clone of Conor. I cannot be Conor Larkin. Nor do I want to be. I have enough trouble being Con Edwards."

She raised her hand and held it against my cheek. "Con—" she began, then jerked her hand away as an explosion sounded from the far end of the harbor.

"What . . ." I said, then flinched as the concussion struck us. Automatically, I began to run in the direction of the explosion, only to be brought up short by Maeve.

"Wait!" she yelled, grabbing my arm.

"Let go!" I said. "What are you doing?"

"Wait!" she demanded, eyes wide, lips a hard, thin line.

A second explosion ripped across the harbor, staggering us. My ears began to ring. I painfully swallowed to clear them. Maeve dropped my arm.

"Now," she said. "At times, there's a backup charge in case the first doesn't do the job."

"The IRA?" I asked.

"Who knows? Provos, maybe. It could have been Prods. Enough charges have been laid against them for a lesson to be learned. Come on!"

Together, we ran down the quay past concrete jetties and pilings. We were forced aside by a squad car roaring past, Klaxon blaring. I caught a quick glimpse of uniformed men grimly staring ahead, then they were past. We ran after them. Far down at the end of the dockage, the brake lights flashed, and I faintly heard the slide of tires on wet pavement. Figures boiled from the car and quickly set up a perimeter. Even with a stitch in my side and my lungs emptying themselves like bellows, I had to admire their proficiency. As we came closer to the site of the explosion, we passed men erratically stumbling in circles, pained expressions on their faces as they pumped cupped hands over their ears to equalize the pressure caused by the blast. A few ran with us to where a knot of men stood in front of a slip.

"What is it?" I panted. A man turned to face me, his face a mixture of shock and rage. I recognized Michael John. "What is it?" I repeated.

" 'Tis the end of it all, sure as I'm standing here," he said bitterly. "The bloody bastards! Damn their souls to hell!" I flinched at the vehemence in his voice but again demanded, "What the hell happened? What blew up?"

"The *Shadow V*," he grimly answered. "Lord Mountbatten himself and his party. Whatever hopes any held for Ireland went up with them."

I stood for a moment in shock, then began to try to push my way through the crowd. Grudgingly, they gave way. I was brought up short by a member of the *Garda Síochána*.

"Press!" I panted, searching frantically for my credentials. "The *Times*! Let me through!"

"Bloody hell, I will," he said grimly. "This here's cordoned off until after the Scene of Crimes men finish. And, if you're lucky, that may be by Christmas next."

"The explosion was large?"

"Aye. Not so large as to take down a mountain, but enough. Blew the poor ones halfway to Derry, it did."

"Any survivors?"

"Aye," he said. "A few. But best you get that information from the chief inspector. The figure," he added darkly, "might well change by then. You, there!" he shouted at a roughly dressed man trying to slip past the guard down to the docking gate. "And where in hell do you think you're off to?" He moved away, leaving me to stare at the blackened remains of an unimposing boat. The cabin was practically nonexistent: splotches of blood streaked the deck, fragmented glass lay over the fantail. Rescue workers lifted a body from the sea, but I couldn't tell if it was Mountbatten. With a sinking feeling, I realized the height was about right and turned away. I glanced down as I murmured an apology to the man next to me. A flash of silver caught my eye from the blackened boards of the landing. I bent to pick it up: a small piece of hammered silver.

"What do you have there?" a voice sharply asked. I looked up; a broad-shouldered man with a bulbous nose fleetingly reminding me of W. C. Fields suspiciously eyed me from behind the cordoned perimeter.

"Nothing," I said, slipping the piece of silver into my shirt pocket. "Dropped my pen, is all."

"Sorry," he said, hunching his shoulders forward in the tan overcoat. "You're the Yank from the press?" He pronounced the latter as if it left a foul taste in his mouth. I nodded, reaching for my credentials.

"Right," I said, flashing my card. "From the *Times*." He ignored it, his eyes coldly staring into mine.

"Let him through," he said to the uniformed officer between us. "Might as well deal with him now as later. Let me know when Scene of Crimes is through." The officer nodded and stepped aside to pass me through. I drew curious looks as I followed the broad-shouldered man down the pier to stop beside the *Shadow V*, still miraculously afloat. He silently stared down at the black water for a moment, then levelly said, "We do not have a lead, but we think this to be the work of the Provos."

I nodded. "But how do you know it's them? There are other terrorist groups. Unless you're Protestant, that is." His eyes flashed angrily at me. He deliberately pulled a cigarette from an inside pocket and took his time lighting it. He blew a cloud of dirty gray smoke my way.

"Now, you wouldn't be the type that would be giving me trouble, would you?" he said.

I shrugged and met his eye. "Depends on your answers, doesn't it?" He slowly nodded, drawing deeply upon his cigarette.

"Aye. No, I'm not Protestant, and the last time I dipped my knee was ten years ago at my nephew's first communion, and even then the roof timbers creaked in complaint."

"Sorry," I said, and grinned. I thrust out my hand. "Shall we start over? I'm Con Edwards. *Times*."

He shook it solemnly. "Inspector Joe Walsh. And maybe it would be better if we did begin again."

"Why the Provos?" I asked. At first, I thought he was ignoring me as he inspected the end of his cigarette. Then he spoke.

"Ah, what the hell! 'Tis only a matter of a few hours till it's official." He pointed a stumpy forefinger at me. "You'll not be printing this for at least another two hours, lad." I nodded. He sighed and turned to look out into the bay. "Two hours ago," he softly said, "we picked up two men in a routine road check at Granard in County Longford about a hundred and ten kilometers from here. In the trunk of the car, we found the fittings for making a radio-controlled bomb. The car was stolen from Sligo, but belonged to a shipping office that had kept odometer readings. The missing mileage adds up to the distance between Sligo and Mullaghmore and Granard."

"That's pretty good detective work on a moment's notice," I said. He glared at me, then sourly grinned, flipping his cigarette into the black water.

"Yes," he admitted. "It was. But there were two other explosions at Warrenpoint on a stretch of road by Carlingford Lough. Do you know the area?" I shook my head. "Well," he continued, " 'tis no matter. 'Tis on the other side of the country. The main point is that eighteen men were killed there. The first bomb was apparently detonated from across the lough and killed six. The second bomb exploded half an hour later and killed the others. At first, we thought the ones picked up in Granard had been involved in that bit of work, but they weren't."

"How did you know that?" I asked.

"Because we got a tip," he calmly said. "An anonymous call from Mullaghmore. Too short for us to get more than the town, but long enough to lay this nasty business in the lap of the Provos." He smiled a shark's smile. "It would appear there's an informer somewhere in the brotherhood."

A cold ball settled in my stomach. The informer was here in Mullaghmore and still weaving his spidery web filament by filament around us. My heart began to pound furiously. My breath seemed short. I drew deeply, turning toward the sea to cleanse my lungs as a familiar knell began in my mind.

FIFTEEN

The three of us huddled together in front of the fireplace, wishing the peat fire threw its heat farther into the cold of the cottage, whispering in the quiet of the night that reminded me of the quiet I used to hear before the first of the more violent monsoon storms in Indochina. The night seemed made for mourning: the cold, the loneliness, the despair from the awareness of what Mountbatten's death meant for a united Ireland. Curiously, though, I felt coldly aloof and separate from my surroundings; what Ed Logan and Ted Sinclair, my *Times* editor, called my "dispassionate reasoning." "When you get that feeling, that's when you write the best copy," Sinclair told me after my first Pulitzer when we were both pie-eyed in the middle of celebration.

Maeve reached for the bottle of poteen and tipped a healthy measure into her glass, slopping over the edge. She passed the bottle to Michael John, who silently followed suit. I refused. Everything appeared stark, bold, and brutal like a photograph by Candice Bergen: November, when the truth of winter is approaching.

"Paisley," Michael John said bitterly. "It must have been Paisley and his boys. Sure, and weren't they the mad ones when Mountbatten ignored their demands and hired the Catholics equally with their boys?" His face clouded with anger. He slammed his fist on the table, making the poteen bottle jump. He hurriedly steadied it. "Yes, I tell you it's Paisley! Who else?"

"What was the final count?" Maeve softly asked, the poteen slurring her consonants.

"They're still not sure," I said. I reached for another block of peat and settled it upon the fire. I pulled a small notebook from my pocket to refresh my memory. "There was Mountbatten, his fifteen-year-old grandson Nicholas Knatchbull, and a fifteen-year-old lad, Paul Maxwell, a local boy who liked boats and seemed a favorite of Mountbatten. It is doubtful if the Dowager Lady Brabourne will survive the night. Lord Brabourne is seriously injured, as is his wife, Mountbatten's daughter Patricia, and their son Timothy. But the prognosis is good, although there may be some lasting effects."

"Must you be so clinical? So dispassionate?" Maeve suddenly asked, her voice sharp and angry. She gestured at the notebook in my hand. "It's all just a story to you, isn't it? Just a story! That's all we are to gerrydancers such as yourself: bog-trotting Irishmen with droll wits and a glass of poteen in hand, singing sentimental, maudlin songs about lost freedom and blowing each other up between verses!" She began to cry, her lips loose and slack, her eyes bright pinpoints of frustration and hate.

"Easy, now, girl," Michael John said, awkwardly placing a huge hand over her knee. He gently shook it. " 'Tis the poteen making you talk like that, girl. Say nothing you'll later regret."

"Keep your hands to yourself, you gasconade." She pulled her leg from his grasp and thrust an accusing finger toward me. "Deny it if you can that you are working on a story."

I shook my head. "You're drunk, Maeve."

"Sure, and it's the truth he's speaking," Michael John said pleadingly. "*Muscha*—say no more." He gave me an anxious look. "The wake, you know. 'Tis the poteen."

"*In vino veritas*," I murmured. "I can't deny it; it's the truth. It's my job, what I do. It doesn't mean that I'm unsympathetic. I can appreciate what's happened. Yet I also know that what has happened is news, and that gives me further responsibilities. I'll mourn later."

"When it's fashionable," she sneered.

"Careful, girl! For Jaysus' sakes, you're getting too close from where there's no return," Michael John warned.

She tossed him a mocking look, then lurched to her feet, stumbling slightly from the effects of the poteen. She lifted high her glass in mock salute, quoting Synge. " 'Drink a health to the wonders of the western world, the pirates. preachers, *poteen*-makers, with the jobbing jockies, parching peelers, and the juries fill their stomachs selling judgments of the English law.' " Then, after a pause: "And, to those parchment-penning, privy-thinking panners proclaiming pro-Protestant propaganda as a panacea for Ireland's ills: the leavings of my bladder." With a violent twist of her wrist, she flung the poteen from her glass in my face. "There." She firmly slammed the glass on the table. "And thus ends my catechism." She took a step toward the hallway, stumbled, then caught herself, bracing herself with both arms against the opposite walls of the narrow hallway. She ducked her head under her arm to peer back at me. Her hair swung forward over her cheek like Veronica Lake's. "God-*damn* you!" she swore. The tears came then in heaving sobs. She stumbled down the hallway to the bedroom, slamming the door after her.

"It's the great pressure, lad," Michael John said. I mopped the poteen from my face. "Sure, and you know she didn't mean it. It's just that . . ." His voice trailed off as he fought for the words to reassure me. He drank from his glass, lowering it with a sigh and wiping his lips with the back of his hand. " 'Tis a dark day for Ireland. It's hard to understand. Not," he hastened to add apologetically, "that you wouldn't understand, just that . . . it's the end of a way." He looked beseechingly at me.

"I know," I said. "I understand. The fear she has comes from knowing that no one will ever understand the truth one knows. It's almost as if something alive inside has slowly withered and died."

Michael John stared into the fire, slowly nodding. "Aye. To the rest of the world we'll all be assassins now. And all because of that bastard Paisley! Sweet Jaysus! Is there nothing we can do?"

"Not much," I answered. "No ethical standard sanctions terrorism. Not even revolution. It's evil masquerading as good. More harm is done through the offices of good intentions than in the name of any despot seeking new lands to conquer. Maybe in time people will forget, but the problem with assassinating a hero is the hero becomes a martyr and those are never forgotten."

He covered his face with his hands. "Is there nothing we can do?" he moaned, his voice muffled, a cutting edge of despair in his words. I felt the envelope in my pocket in which I had placed the small bit of silver I had found on the Mountbatten dock. I frowned. The murky shadows of an idea not yet born began to shift through my idle brain.

"Maybe," I said. "Prove, if you can, that Mountbatten's murder was not the work of the IRA. It wasn't, you know," I added.

"I know. It was Paisley, wasn't it?" he muttered from behind his hands. He waited for my answer. "Wasn't it?" he repeated. My silence grew into words. Slowly, his hands slipped from his face. "By God," he said hoarsely. "What are you saying?"

I rose and walked to the seaward window and looked out onto the sea-fog, implacable beyond the window, moving landward, shifting, seeking its proper form. A coldness descended, making me suddenly shiver as if someone had walked across my grave. Visions from the past began to speak to me. I had my answer.

"I think," I thoughtfully said, "that I had better see MacCauley. Will you arrange it?" I turned away from the window and stared back at the bedroom, remembering Maeve's accusation and, with a pang, recognizing the truth she had spoken. I reached for my coat, shrugging into it. Michael John watched openmouthed as I gathered the car keys from the mantel.

"I must call in the follow-up to my story," I said to him. "You'll take care of notifying MacCauley?" He nodded.

The fog bank rolled in as I maneuvered the Cortina over the narrow road into Mullaghmore. I wondered how MacCauley was going to take Michael John's message. Marc Antony's funeral oration suddenly came to mind. I felt the gaze of dead IRA soldiers silently watching my every move.

I nudged the Cortina into a parking place next to the telephone booth beside The Gallows Tree and stepped out. The ancient sign over the pub door creaked eerily on rusty chains. A foghorn echoed from the docks. I shivered and entered the booth, closing the door behind me. I picked up the receiver and gave the operator the number, reversing the charges.

"Con Edwards," I said to the man at the other end. "I've got what you want."

SIXTEEN

Maeve was cross, suffering, I knew, from a monstrous hangover, as we approached the farmyard. Michael John was quiet but tense as he fidgeted on the seat of the Cortina beside me. Little had been said since we had left the cottage, which made me perfectly content, for I was trying to sort out my thoughts before I faced MacCauley.

The farmyard remained unchanged from our previous visit only a few days before. I felt, though, as if I were visiting it for the first time, knowing as I crossed the hard-packed earth that behind the door I would find the narrow hallway leading to the kitchen and Sarah patiently kneading dough with her red, work-roughened hands for the baking of the day's bread.

The door opened before we arrived, revealing the black-garbed Fallon leaning against the jamb. This time, however, he had no smile for us, no hint of recognition in his cold eyes, no words of welcome. He stepped aside, nodding at the hallway.

MacCauley waited for us at the kitchen table, a pot of coffee on the table in front of him, saucers and cups already waiting in front of chairs for us. His eyes were red-rimmed and weary, the lines deeply carved into his face above tight lips. He wordlessly gestured at the chairs and waited until we had seated ourselves before speaking.

" 'Tis a poor time for any of your *geabaireacht*, Maeve," he said, giving her a stern eye. She stirred uneasily, then defiantly raised her head. He shifted his attention to me. "And yourself. 'Tis no time I have for you either if the two of you are about to bait me again with Conor Larkin. But"—he affectionately nodded at Michael John—"this one says you know some-

thing about Mountbatten's murder. 'Tis that and that alone
that allows you to be here." His eyes narrowed warningly. "Be
quick. I'm holdin' off giving the order for Paisley and his UDA
bastards only because of you. The truth, now. Is it Conor
Larkin you're about, or is it Mountbatten? For sure and the
same, the two never met."

O'Bannion entered the kitchen from the hall and nodded
at me before moving to sit beside MacCauley. He pulled the
coffeepot toward him, poured a cup of coffee, then filled our
cups. MacCauley impatiently waited for him to finish. Maeve
reached with shaking hand for her coffee. She lifted hers to her
lips, sipped, winced, and sighed. Michael John spilled a portion
into his saucer, lifted it, and noisily slurped. I sipped slowly
from my cup, using it to gain time and collect my thoughts. I
steeled myself against the uneasiness threatening my stomach.

"I'm not really sure what I've got," I began. "Certainly not
proof, if that's what you're suggesting. I have a few ideas—
that's all. They may pertain to Conor Larkin's death—they
may not. I don't know. Either way, you'll get your chance at a
denial in the world press, which is really all you care about at
the moment, right?"

"We still have Drumm, remember?" O'Bannion mur
mured. "He's done well for us in the past. Besides, 'tis Paisley
we're blaming, not ourselves alone. Paisley is the one who'll
pay for yesterday's business. Him and the bastards who kiss
his arse."

"Drumm is a man who used to be a penny-a-worder with
a minor paper," I said, trying to sound contemptuous. It was
hard; I did not like having to sell an associate short in this
manner, but I could see no other way to make MacCauley feel
he needed me. "Maybe he still has influence on his old paper.
But how many *Telegraph*s are sold in Boston? New York? Los
Angeles? Sydney? London? It's a matter of economics: I have
the readers you need. Therefore, you need me."

MacCauley permitted himself a small smile, throwing his
hand up to stop O'Bannion from arguing. "Then," he said
softly, "I can presume you are about to speculate?"

"In a way," I said cautiously. "But I can think of many
words I would use instead of that one." He shrugged, a tiny
smile struggling to light the gray of his face.

"One word is as good as another. Besides, it's all immaterial anyway. Like Dickie says, it's Paisley." He closed his eyes and massaged the bridge of his nose. "You have heard, I presume, that TRANCO has suspended the Porcupine Banks Project until further notice?"

"I thought they would," I said. "It was a gamble anyway. Smart money doesn't go after long odds and have to put up with terrorists as well. One situation is enough headaches."

He nodded. "Yes. Very well. You're here, so we might as well hear you. Speak your piece."

"I don't know all the answers," I said, placing my cup in its saucer. "But I do know why it was not the IRA. That denial I can write with a few appropriate quotes from you, which should gain you a bit of time. But logic makes for dull reading, and what I write will not be an answer if proof is not soon forthcoming." I paused to see if MacCauley wished to speak, but he remained silent, impassively staring at me. I took another sip of coffee and continued.

"First, it makes absolutely no sense at all for the IRA to have killed Mountbatten. With him alive, an economic partnership existed between the two Irelands. Unification was only a matter of time—tomorrow, next week, a year maybe, but not much longer. I think you knew that, didn't you?" I paused again but received only a brief flicker of eyelids in acknowledgment. Taking heart, I continued. "Even with the highly developed siege mentality in Northern Ireland today, the majority of the people would not ignore any chances to honorably end the troubles without loss of face or a decrease in accustomed standards of living. That's why it couldn't have been Paisley and his boys who killed Mountbatten as well." MacCauley stiffened, his attention riveted upon my words. O'Bannion made an angry gesture, but MacCauley stopped him from interrupting me. I hurried on. "The Protestants have nothing to lose by such an agreement; the Catholics will only gain. So, we must look for other reasons. Who would benefit by keeping Ulster separate from the Republic? Anyone," I continued, answering my own question, "who had a vested interest with a large economic return. Of course," I added, "there is always the madman, but that bombing was too sophisticated an undertaking to be the work of a madman."

"A bomb is too sophisticated?" O'Bannion interjected. He laughed. "Children make them in Belfast out of liquid detergent and gasoline."

"But not," I said gently, "from cordite and set off by radio signal. Remember the blackened boards of the landing? Only cordite leaves a residue like that. And no one knew for certain the exact time when Mountbatten would be on board. In fact, he was late, for he stopped on the docks to visit with us"—I nodded at Maeve—"before he went to his boat. A bomb with a timer was too chancy. Control," I emphasized, gently striking the table with the edge of my hand, "control was needed. A radio directional device was the only answer."

"So far," MacCauley said, " 'tis a lot of playing with words. Get to the point, man."

"Somebody called the *Garda* claiming the Provos' involvement in the Mountbatten bombing plus the bombs that killed eighteen at Warrenpoint," I said, my voice ringing harshly in the kitchen. MacCauley and O'Bannion exchanged quick looks. I felt the eyes of Michael John and Maeve boring in as well.

"Warrenpoint?" MacCauley said. "You have that from the *Garda*?" I nodded. "Both?" I again nodded. "Sweet Jaysus," he swore, slumping back in his chair. "We're screwed."

"Not necessarily," I said. "What if I could give you a name?" The sudden silence sparked with an intensive force as all looked sharply at me. "Remember: I have no proof. But I can give you a name."

"Out with it," MacCauley said softly. "We can get the proof *if* we have the name." He turned to look at O'Bannion. "Call Fallon," he ordered. O'Bannion nodded and hurried away. He turned his attention back to me, hard eyes probing mine. "Well?"

"It looks," I said, carefully choosing my words, "as if Conor Larkin was right. There is an informer in your midst. I daresay he's been there for a long time." O'Bannion silently reentered the kitchen. Fallon followed like a silent shadow to stand by MacCauley's shoulder, patient Death dressed in black, waiting his master's bidding. Perspiration made my hands prickle. I had the feeling I had better not disappoint

MacCauley and remembered the ancient custom of dealing with messengers bearing ill tidings.

I turned to face Maeve. "I believe he was responsible for your arrest by the UDA and Brits as well. But I never had any reason to suspect him. I still don't. Except bits and pieces added together can only suggest him." A frown furrowed her eyes as she tried to remember. I turned back to MacCauley. "I never really put it together until last night," I said. I removed an envelope from an inside pocket and dumped out the small piece of silver I had found on the dock. "It was this bit of silver I found on the docks by Mountbatten's boat that made me begin to put it all together. Actually, it was a question that provoked an answer that asked another question that—" I caught a warning gleam in MacCauley's eye and hastily changed my speech. "Maybe it's nothing at all, but when I was interviewing the inspector, he mentioned he had received a call from Mullaghmore warning about two bombings that were about to happen two hours *before* the explosion. The caller didn't say where the bombings were to take place. Maybe it was coincidental, but when I tried to call TRANCO offices to inquire about Lord Mountbatten's plans, I received a busy signal. Mullaghmore is a small village. How many busy signals could there be at that time of day? Then I remembered who worked for TRANCO and the bits and pieces began to fall into place. Item: Who may have borne Maeve Nolan enough malice to turn informer upon her? Item: Who suddenly had a change in fortune? Item: Who knew we were in Dublin and could call in that business at the inn where we were staying? Item: Who could have had the contacts in Dublin to call out a search for us all the way to Clifden? Item: Who knew the location of Maeve and myself in Sligo to call in an assassination attempt? Item: Who knew we were going to be on the docks in Mullaghmore? Item—" But Maeve suddenly interrupted me.

"Liam Drumm!"

The name exploded among us with a fierce intensity. Then Maeve shakily laughed.

"But that's ridiculous, Con. Liam has been with us for years!"

"Is it?" I asked. "Perhaps. At first, I refused to believe it was Liam. I didn't want it to be Liam. We had been arrested together. But he escaped before we were **taken to** Castlereagh. Remember how the officer in charge stopped his men from trying to catch Liam when he slipped away? When I started to forget about Liam's arrest and focused on *how* he escaped, then things began to make sense. Who had the contacts with the British and the Protestants? Who had friends with the UDA? Who picked up pertinent information drinking with a British sergeant?" My throat suddenly felt dry. I paused to take a sip of coffee. I glanced at Maeve; she was gnawing her lower lip, uncertainty clouding her smooth brow. "Who," I continued, redirecting my attention to MacCauley, "could have been close enough to know your operations? How many operations have gone wrong the past few years?"

"A similar case could be made against O'Bannion. Even Fallon," MacCauley said. A faint smile twisted his lips. "Or me."

"True," I said, turning to Maeve. "But not many fit other criteria, do they, Maeve?" I spoke softly. "Who did you jilt after the banns were posted? Who didn't go back for you at Stormont when the riots broke out? Who told you, MacCauley, when I was being released from Castlereagh? And how did he know the exact time so Fallon could meet me outside? Who had a reason to tell Conor about the docks, knowing Conor would go there to his death? Who suddenly experienced a change of fortune, enough to afford shoes from Scotland? Shoes stamped with a silver *R*?" I pointed at the bit of silver resting on the table before us. "And who," I said gently, "has a habit of calling you 'my beauty' and why, Maeve, does that suddenly upset you, even now?"

The blood drained from her face, leaving her eyes large, dark pools filled with painful memories. "Liam Drumm," she whispered. "In the cellar. I was hooded. He was the first."

I gently placed my hand on her shoulder. "It's over, Maeve."

"Get Drumm," MacCauley said harshly to O'Bannion. "Bring him here. Alive. I want to talk to him." O'Bannion's eyes flickered to Fallon. "No," MacCauley said. "I have other work for Fallon." O'Bannion nodded and left, pausing long enough to give me an encouraging thumbs-up. MacCauley leaned back in the chair, staring at me. "It's very circumstantial, you know. Maeve could be mistaken. By her own admission, she was hooded. Under the circumstances . . ." His voice trailed off. I nodded.

"Yes," I said. "But there's just too many other coincidences."

"But why?" he said, slamming his hand upon the table in frustration. "Why?"

"Money, I think," I said. I leaned forward, folding my arms in front of me on the table. "There was something the inspector said yesterday at the docks that bothers me. The two men arrested in Granard were driving a car stolen from a shipping company. I'm willing to bet that that shipping company is Killian Shipping, which has offices in Belfast and Manchester. The name has probably changed since it merged with TRANCO, but I'm willing to bet that the car once belonged to that company."

"What are you saying?" MacCauley said.

"If I'm not mistaken, isn't Manchester one of the main ports from which arms and ammunition are smuggled to Ireland? And," I added, rising and carrying my cup of coffee to the window that looked out onto the farmyard, "doesn't NORAID also have an office in Manchester?" Maeve's head jerked around to watch me.

"NORAID?" MacCauley said. "And what would you be knowing about NORAID?" He looked meaningfully at Michael John.

"A bit," I said, staring at the barn. The ground in front was smooth and hard-packed. Weeds grew in other places but not in front of the barn. Yet the barn looked as if it had not been used in years. "What's in the barn?"

The room grew heavy in silence. I slowly turned to face MacCauley, leaving my coffee cup on the windowsill.

"Very good, Mr. Edwards," MacCauley said softly. "And how did you figure it out?"

I shook my head. "It wasn't very hard. Remember when we were here before with the good father and Dan's lament for the bygone days when the farm was well worked? I wondered why it was no longer worked and yet could support O'Malley and his nephew and wife. Especially since the nephew obviously did no hard labor; his hands were too soft. So. how was the farm paying its way?" I nodded toward the barn. "One way could be smuggling. What would be more natural than smuggling arms and ammunition and using the barn as an arms depot? Now, let's see if I can give you a scenario: NORAID smuggles arms into Sligo's port from Manchester through Killian Shipping. The Killians have long been sympathizers, haven't they? And who would suspect friends of Mountbatten? The arms are brought here and stored and slowly brought over the border. There's good money in smuggling arms. What would happen if an accord was reached between Northern Ireland and the Republic? The market dries up. Why not keep the market open? And what better way to do that than assassinate one of the world's best-loved heroes and blame it upon the Provos? The Provos would blame the Prods, and the fight would again be on as each accused the other of lying. A conservative company like TRANCO would undoubtedly pull out of a project that was highly speculative at best and leave things the way they were: unresolved conflict and an open market for the continued sale of weapons. Mountbatten also had to be killed because he was the inspector of the ships TRANCO was planning on leasing from Killian Shipping. NORAID didn't expect that. I believe the ships had been altered in some way, maybe with a false cargo flooring, to allow for the shipment of arms not only to Northern Ireland, but around the globe. Unfortunately, they didn't count on Mountbatten doing the inspecting *and* being the liaison in Mullaghmore. A man as experienced as Mountbatten with ships would have instantly spotted any alterations. They tried to kill Mountbatten on the docks, but Conor stopped them. Still, the incident postponed the inspection until the investigation was completed. They hoped that the alterations might be done before another attempt was made to inspect the ships, but Mountbatten was going to Manchester next week. That still wasn't enough time to get the ships ready. By killing Mountbatten, they eliminated the threat of exposure and kept a market open." I paused, shaking my head. "They even furnished the assassins with a car that could easily be traced back to Sligo. Then to make sure the *Garda Síochána* did not drag its feet, they furnished the *Garda* with enough information to warrant a check."

"Sweet St. Brigid," Michael John breathed, fists tightly clenched on the table in front of him.

MacCauley grimly nodded. "So. A conspiracy, and an informer."

"Yes," I said. "One who has been around for a long time. He has kept both sides from reaching any agreement for years by playing one side off against the other: the Protestants against the Catholics, the British alternately against both. It was very lucrative, especially with the NORAID connection and Killian Shipping. I think Conor was getting close to discovering Drumm was the informer. Drumm had to do something quickly because he knew Conor would kill him once he had evidence of Drumm's betrayal. Drumm pretended to discover the assassination plot on the Manchester docks and told Conor in an attempt to throw him off the trail. He knew Conor would go to Manchester; it was Conor's nature. He also knew Conor would have to go alone because you'd closed all IRA doors to him. Drumm could get rid of Mountbatten and Conor at the same time."

He flushed. "It was a good decision at the time," he said defensively. "One that I would make again."

"Tell that to Conor Larkin," I said. I waved my arm pointedly around the kitchen. "One last thing: where's Halloran?"

His face clouded for a moment in confusion, then slowly cleared as he realized the reason behind my question. "Of course," he breathed. "The receiver. Fallon?" He looked over his shoulder. Fallon nodded and quietly slipped from the kitchen. MacCauley looked at me. He turned his attention to Maeve. "Maeve," he began, speaking softly.

"Go to hell," she said, and walked from the kitchen. Michael John rose, gave MacCauley a withering look of scorn, and silently followed her.

"Mr. Edwards," he said. I held up my hand to stop him.

"I don't think I want to talk anymore with you for a while," I said. "You didn't give Conor the benefit of the doubt. You sold him out for the TRANCO deal because you thought he might ask too many embarrassing questions and queer the negotiations. Too bad. If you had listened to him, you might still have the TRANCO deal. Now you have nothing." I paused. 'You know, even Judas ended up with thirty pieces of silver.

What do you have?" I moved away from the table. "Now, I have to call in a story. Let me know when you have the ending."

I followed Maeve and Michael John from the house, pausing briefly to use the telephone. I felt dirty, used, and abused. All of this could have been avoided if MacCauley had listened to Conor Larkin months earlier. Or at least helped us when Maeve and I first came to him with our suspicions. I thought also about the friendship and trust that had been destroyed, and I wondered what was left now for Maeve, who had suffered the most. I climbed into the Cortina and drove in silence back to the cottage.

SEVENTEEN

Again, the fog bank moved in from the sea, blanketing the cottage in gray arms, sending us to huddle around the peat fire to keep off the chill. We helped the fire with liberal dollops of poteen, forgetting dinner, forgetting supper, in our desire to drive memory from our minds. Maeve drank sparingly, spending most of her time mesmerized by the flickering flames, answering only in monosyllables when spoken to, volunteering no conversation of her own. Michael John and I spoke in low tones, making small talk about innocuous subjects. But these were limited, and soon we contented ourselves with the poteen bottle.

They came for us near midnight, moving silently with the fog, and were in the house almost before we knew it, guns leveled, eyes hard and determined.

"Well," I said conversationally, straightening from my place beside the fire. "I was beginning to wonder when you'd arrive."

O'Bannion closed the door behind him and carefully moved into the room, a gaunt shadow, mercurial, with hollow cheeks, gray eyes cold and steady, mouth thin-lipped: the mouth of an executioner or a saint. The former, I thought, was more apropos. Drumm fanned out along the wall to his right, a police revolver clutched in his hand. His eyes glittered with hate and excitement. Halloran moved to his left, nervously waving a huge Colt .45 automatic back and forth between the three of us. His eyes were wide with apprehension as if he expected at any minute to have the pistol taken away by a disapproving adult and himself spanked for playing with dangerous toys. But it was O'Bannion that I determined to watch. He was the most dangerous of the three.

"You are alone, the three of you," he said. It was a statement and not a question, for I knew he would have checked the perimeter before entering the cottage. He had lasted far too long to be the careless sort. He was calm, dispassionate, and when killing us, I knew, would be as emotionless as swatting a bothersome fly.

"But you would know that, wouldn't you?" I asked. "Surely you checked."

"I did," he said. But I could tell from his eyes that I had made him nervous by calmly receiving him instead of issuing blustering threats, pleading, or exhibiting outraged innocence. "You do not seem very surprised."

"I'm not," I said. I clinched my thighs and calves hard to keep them from trembling and lifted my glass to sip the poteen in it, crazily thinking: Irish liquor for Dutch courage. International bravery? "There had to be someone within the Provisionals who could cover for Drumm with the officers. Someone who had intimate knowledge of the various operations and could pass word on to Drumm. He normally wouldn't have been given any details to keep the danger of a leak down to a minimum. Besides, as a liaison to the press, he would have no need to know anything until *after* any operation, and then only enough to be able to issue a denial if the Provos had been unsuccessful or an affirmation if triumphant. He held only the words, not the ideas. Someone, however, did. It could only be one of two people: either MacCauley or you. When the attempt was made to assassinate us in Sligo, I thought it was Mac-Cauley. I was sure of him when the second attempt was made in Mullaghmore. Yet, when I mentioned NORAID to him at the farmhouse, he seemed surprised that I knew anything about it. And, when I mentioned Drumm's name, I could see the doubt in his eyes. No, it couldn't have been MacCauley. Besides, he wouldn't have given us permission to continue looking if he had been the informer. And then there was the question of how the Protestants heard about the attempt we were going to make to free Maeve. How did they know enough to send the third car? That left only you, Dickie. You were the one who planted the bombs in the Volvos, weren't you?" He didn't say anything. "Ah, well. It really doesn't matter. It did throw me off considering Liam, though. It was only after I started wondering how people always seemed to find us despite everything we did. I didn't even suspect Liam in Dublin when your people tried to catch us at Maeve's friends' inn. But how could I suspect Liam? He stayed right there at the Gresham Hotel the whole time. It was easy, though, wasn't it, Dickie, for Liam to make a call to you from the hotel. It was you who arranged those attacks on our lives. Mind telling us why?"

He smiled, but no lights appeared in his eyes. My mouth suddenly went dry.

"A brave little jack-a-dandy, aren't you? A regular Paul Pry. But why not? 'Tis certain it'll go no farther than here but to the grave. So," he chuckled without warmth, anticipating his pun, "I'll gravely answer you. What?" he asked. "No sense of humor? I would have expected a man of words to appreciate any play with them. But perhaps you've something else upon your mind?" I didn't answer but forced myself to maintain eye contact.

"Shut up, O'Bannion," Drumm said. "You always had a big mouth. It's what got you in trouble in the first place."

"What got me into trouble, boy-o, was you," O'Bannion softly said. Drumm laughed.

"Yes, but then the money you've made from it has more than compensated you for any discomfort you may have suffered from your conscience. Remember, my beauty," he continued, addressing himself to Maeve, "that you weren't the only one gathered into the fold the day after Faulkner brought back internment a few years ago. O'Bannion, here, was one along with you. Only O'Bannion had an option you didn't: he, being one of the prize pigeons, was given a chance to 'come over.' It didn't take him long, did it, my buck-o, to make the shift. One jolt over the ol' tallywhacker, and O'Bannion here was babbling like a hobbledehoy. No wonder," he said to me, "that everyone thought it was you had made the scream. By the time they released you, O'Bannion here had found his way back to the litter. No one would have ever expected him to have been the informer."

"So you turned him in," I said. O'Bannion gave me a sharp look. I nodded. "Yes. It's true. That day in the coffee shop where he found us. Remember when you told us about O'Rourke and The Wild Duck? Who besides Maeve and I were there to get the information? You already had the soldiers waiting, didn't you?"

"Aye," Drumm said, eyes flashing angrily. "That I did, and why not? Tired I was of living hand-to-mouth, begging the Prods for something to cover other than flower shows and sewing circles and the odd murder when the crime boy was too deep in his cups to find the typewriter keys. The money was good and when I found Joe Killian, even better. That was easy. After TRANCO absorbed Killian Shipping, I started digging, looking for a story. That's when I uncovered the NORAID connection." His eyes darkened as he faced O'Bannion. "And 'tis an honest share you've been receiving all along, Dickie O'Bannion. Don't be coming up the martyr with me. Your hand's been out and palm up from the beginning!"

"The divil a work it's been, too!" O'Bannion hissed. "Toiling and dodging from dusk to dawn, fearing the peelers and the paddy-boys alike, wondering who the one would be to put a bullet behind each knee and one in my ear. But the worst of all, the worst of all, is the looking in the mirror and seeing a quisling looking back and walking the streets and having people stepping aside and tugging the bills of their scully caps out of respect and knowing yourself to be a dandy-dancer worthy only of their spit and contempt. And," he said through gritted teeth, "knowing yourself as a coward proven from which there's no redemption. No amount of money's worth that, Liam Drumm, for each pound burns the palm like one of Judas's thirty pieces, a scorching reminder of the unpardonable sin."

"Shouldn't we get on with it?" Halloran nervously asked, the hand with the automatic shaking as with ague. "For the love of God, man, but it's dangerous to be here so long. Kill them and let's be out with it!"

"Yes," Maeve said. "Why not? 'Tis a rank injustice done by a coward, and 'tis none better for it than yourself, Liam Drumm!" His eyes narrowed; his lips pulled back into a wolfish snarl.

"Ah, my beauty. You weren't so haughty at Castlereagh," he said maliciously. "I remember you then, all stretched out naked on that table in the basement. Do you remember begging and crying when your begging did no good?"

"You bastard!" she said thickly.

"Bastard? Me? No, it was justice. Justice for what you did. Or have you forgotten? The banns were posted, and we were to be wed. But then you met Conor-bloody-fucking-Larkin, and suddenly 'tis better things you want, a better man. Well, 'tis no better man he was; he died as hard as any man with a bullet in his guts."

"And Paisley?" I asked. "How does he fit in with this?" Drumm's face became smug. Maeve stiffened and stared at me. I knew she was remembering my words to MacCauley, but this was not the time to explain my lie.

"And what would a man of the cloth be having to do with the likes of us?"

"Oh, I think I can guess," I said. "It shouldn't be too hard. Let's see." Out of the corner of my eye, I caught Michael John slowly edging closer to Halloran. "How about fear?" Drumm's face went blank. "Yes, fear. If the Porcupine Banks Project proved successful, Paisley would be relegated to the background as nothing more than a barely competent minister. His ego wouldn't allow him to exist on that; he needs the fame, the adoration of the masses, the feeling of importance to exist. How long have you been working for Paisley, Liam?"

He started to answer, but the words froze in his mouth Michael John made an ugly sound in his throat and launched himself at Halloran. I threw myself backward over my chair, dragging Maeve to the floor with me. Michael John plucked the automatic from Halloran's hand and spun him around. Halloran screamed in terror. Bullets slammed into him as O'Bannion and Drumm fired simultaneously. His body jerked with each impact. I gathered myself to leap at O'Bannion, then sprawled flat as an automatic weapon fired from the window, spraying the floor between us with bullets.

"Don't!" a voice yelled. Drumm and O'Bannion whirled, weapons automatically rising. The door burst open behind them.

"Halt!" a voice demanded. They froze, weapons half-raised. I rose shakily to my feet, heaving a sigh of relief.

'That's cutting it a bit too close," I complained. Denis

Naismith flashed a wintry smile, eyes narrowly watching Drumm and O'Bannion.

"Terribly sorry to inconvenience you," he said. "But we had a ways to come. Bloody cottage sits out in the middle of nowhere. Lucky the fog came up or we might have been later. You didn't give me much time, you know. Had to make do with just Wilson." He nodded at the window. I looked: Wilson carefully inclined his head in greeting.

"Don't you think . . ." I said, pausing when saliva suddenly gushed into my parched mouth. I pointed at the pistols still held by Drumm and O'Bannion.

"Oh, yes," Naismith said. "Wilson! Watch them, now." He carefully advanced and plucked the pistols from their hands. "Hands behind," he commanded. They slowly placed their hands behind them. He pulled handcuffs from his belt and securely locked a pair around each man's wrists. "There. That should hold them. You may join us, Wilson."

"Con?"

I turned toward Maeve. She pointed a finger at Naismith and the now-empty window. Her eyes were troubled, pupils large, sclera showing stark white.

"You did . . . this?" I nodded. "Why the Brits? Why did you tell the Brits?"

"They were the only ones I could trust, Maeve," I slowly said. I looked at Michael John. He stared hard and angrily at me. Contemptuously, he let Halloran fall to the floor, then jammed the pistol in his belt and stepped across to the poteen jug.

"But . . . they're Brits," she said. I shook my head.

"Think, Maeve," I said. "We couldn't be sure about any of your people. Even MacCauley wasn't above suspicion. On short notice, who was I to go with? Who was I to trust? I had to go to the British because they were the only ones left."

"You could have told me. Or Michael John. We could have helped." Tears gleamed in her eyes.

"With whom?" I said again. "You people are too busy trying to kill each other. Who was I to trust?"

"What was that about Paisley?" she asked. "You told MacCauley that he had nothing to do with this. And Michael

John." She inclined her head. Michael John stared at me, his face mirroring his contempt.

"It was the truth," I said. I held up my hand as she opened her mouth to argue my words. "Drumm worked for Paisley, but he also worked for Killian and himself. Paisley wasn't in on the killing of Mountbatten; that was Drumm all the way. The minute the arms shipments stopped, his income stopped. Paisley didn't care about the arms at all. He simply fed on the hatred each had, making his way through the manipulations of others. In that way, Drumm worked for him. But"—I looked at Liam watching me like a viper—"he was playing both ends against the middle. The Provos against the Prods, and Paisley and his UDA against the Provos. The British were simply in the wrong place at the wrong time." Naismith gave me a frigid smile. "Most of them would just as soon be done with the partition question. No." I shook my head. "Paisley may be a lot of things, but he would not murder Mountbatten. Other people not as prominent, perhaps. But he could not risk being connected to the murder of someone as important as Mount-batten." A mask settled over her face. She turned away.

"What's going to happen to them?" she asked Naismith, pointedly ignoring me.

"They'll be taken back to Belfast and tried as conspirators in the Mountbatten bombing," he said.

"But this is the Republic," Maeve said. "The border is fifteen, twenty kilometers away. You have no jurisdiction here."

"But we have," a voice interrupted. We spun like one to face a thin-lipped Wilson standing slightly in front of Fallon and MacCauley.

"Sorry," Wilson said, his words clipped with anger. "I wasn't expecting them through the fog. Careless of me." Nai-smith shook his head and carefully placed his pistol on the table.

"Very good," MacCauley said quietly. He pushed Wilson none too gently to the side and stepped to the left to keep O'Bannion and Drumm in a clean line of fire. "Dickie." He nodded at O'Bannion.

"Sorry, Seamus," O'Bannion said, trying for a smile. MacCauley sadly shook his head.

"There were some good times, Dickie," he said. O'Bannion

nodded. His face seemed set and serene, eyes accepting the sentence that had just been passed.

"You will make it quick, won't you, Seamus? For those good times? I really don't know if I could stand any pain." He looked almost bashful as he ducked his head. "I didn't do well before, you know. I wouldn't want to soil myself."

"For the good times," MacCauley said, and shot him between the eyes as he spoke. O'Bannion's head jerked back from the punch of the bullet, the back of his head exploding. His body crashed to the floor, legs convulsing twice, then lay still, a child's crumpled doll.

"Sweet Jaysus!" moaned Drumm. He covered his eyes with his hands and fell to his knees. "Not me! Not me!" he cried. A large wet stain showed on the front of his trousers. The foul smell of coming death filled the room.

"Was that really necessary?" Naismith asked, his voice showing his irritation. "We had a use for him, you know."

"Oh, yes," MacCauley said. "The wild Irishman who murdered Mountbatten. The public trial, the moving from courtroom to courtroom like an organ-grinder's pet monkey. The English public would like that, wouldn't they? Probably even make the war popular again in Britain, wouldn't it? No, thank you. We have our own courts."

"So I can see," Naismith said dryly. He nodded at Drumm, still sobbing on the floor. "And him?"

"Maeve?" MacCauley said. She slowly faced him, face hard and unmoving as if carved from cliff rock. "What would you be doing with him?"

Maeve turned cold, emerald eyes upon Drumm. Terror slowly spread over Drumm's face as the implication of MacCauley's words registered.

"Mother of God!" he whispered. "You wouldn't be giving me to her!"

"Really," Naismith said nervously. "This is going a bit far, MacCauley. Even for you. Let me have him."

"Please," Drumm begged. "Please." He tried to grasp MacCauley about the knees, but MacCauley kicked him away. Maeve stepped forward and wordlessly lifted Naismith's pistol from the table. Slowly, she crossed behind the table and stood in front of Drumm. Tears ran in rivulets down Drumm's face, soaking into his collar. "Please! Please!" he moaned. "Money! I'll give you money! All of it! There's quite a bit left. Take the money! Take the money!" The last, delivered almost in a scream, made me wince.

"Maeve," I said quietly. She turned slightly to look at me. "Is he worth the dreams you'll have? There'll be a lifetime of living with it. Remember the kneecapping?"

"Dreams, I already have," she said bitterly. "Maybe this will lay them to rest. Besides, I think it gets easier. Isn't that what you were saying? It gets easier until the human disappears?"

"Think of Conor, then," I said desperately.

"I am," she said calmly, and shot Drumm in the groin.

EIGHTEEN

The fog was gone the Sabbath Day, but the morning sun remained hidden behind lead gray skies over the cemetery. Two weeks had passed since the business at Mullaghmore. MacCauley kept Naismith and Wilson captive for a couple of days while he debated releasing them. Finally, he turned them loose, bleary-eyed and unshaven, in Belfast, a bit resigned, knowing they had only a verbal report to file since Drumm and Halloran had disappeared. MacCauley stubbornly insisted it was more important now than before that the Provos appear secure. A bit of doggerel even began to circulate, crediting the Provos with Mountbatten's death after the Parachute Regiment shot and killed thirteen civilians on "Bloody Sunday":

> Thirteen gone but not forgotten,
> We got eighteen and Mountbatten.

A poor attempt to justify the carnage, but the synchronization of the Warrenpoint and Mullaghmore operations was skillfully managed into a massive publicity coup in the press and created an uneasy atmosphere promising an apocalyptic conflict between the Protestants and Provisionals in the next few months.

Maeve returned to London to finish working on the Conor Larkin assignment for television. I elected to stay close to Ireland for a while until the Mountbatten affair resolved itself. But I opted for London instead of Dublin as a home base; I needed distance to make me objective in this instance. Maeve had become withdrawn since Drumm's death. I had a feeling that in some way she considered me another Drumm, merging the thought of the two of us in a sort of endogamous union since I had gone outside the organization and brought in the British. In her eyes, that made me the equal of Drumm, a hated *gombeen* man, an informer. I tried to bring it out in the open once and got nothing for my efforts except a blank stare. Consequently, her note asking me to meet her at the cemetery by St. Brigid-On-The-Hill caught me by surprise.

Sea gulls furiously wheeled overhead as we walked toward Conor's grave. I had envisioned holding hands with Maeve beside the grave while we stood and shared the past with him. I was wrong. The distance between us began to grow uncomfortably large the closer we came to the grave.

"There really wasn't any choice," I said, breaking the silence. "I had no one else to turn to for help."

"I know that, Con," she said. I slipped my hand in hers. She gave it a tiny squeeze, a sisterly affection, and withdrew it. Although my intentions had been good, the Irish allow themselves to be ruled by memory and guided by centuries-old stories of betrayals. I became an outcast by going outside the pale and telling Special Branch about Drumm and O'Bannion.

"Maeve," I began, and stopped as she turned away from me, facing out to sea.

"Don't," she said. I remained silent, knowing she had more to say, not really wanting to hear it, but knowing also I had little choice. "I have to go back, Con. I hope you can understand that."

"It's over, Maeve," I said. "With the death of Mountbatten, the last hope died. There's nothing left but hate, and hate that has lasted too long to be anything other than a tradition that cannot be forgotten." She shook her head.

"No. It's just begun. The days of the old organization are nearly over. MacCauley doesn't realize it yet, but Mountbatten's death was the tolling of the bell for the movement. Now it will become more pacifist, and that is what will finally unite Ireland, Con. It may take months, even years, but eventually there won't be any MacCauleys left. Conor knew that, you know. That's why he left the IRA. He knew his time was over. That's really what he was doing on TRANCO's docks in Manchester: trying to put an end to an era. In a way, I think he wanted to end like he did. He knew there was no room for him in the future, but a legend is a bit difficult to put on a shelf. He belonged to another age."

"You're tilting at windmills, Maeve," I said.

"You used to see the windmills, too, Con," she countered.

"Yes, when I was much younger. But I'm not Conor. He was forever tilting at windmills. But instead of being thrown up among the stars like Cyrano, he was cast down to earth like Christian."

"I'm not too sure about that," she slowly said. "Perhaps we are the ones earthbound. At least, I would like to think that. Conor belongs among the stars; he was too vast, too large for Earth."

"What about us?" I asked quietly. She faced me, eyes large and soft in that triangular face, sad eyes.

"This I do not know," she said so softly I had to strain to hear. "I need more time." She paused, then gave me a tiny smile. "You know, in a way, we were all *gombeens*. All of us."

I listened to her words with a sinking heart, aware that a mere mortal such as I could little hope to win against the timeless memory of Conor Larkin, the modern Finn MacCool. Memory builds unfair monuments where the marble fossilizes flattery impossible for the living to parallel. I couldn't compete with a ghost and a memory.

She walked away from me, moving downhill toward Conor's grave among the rows of graves aligned in a rank and file like a brigade ready to march across the sea. I lifted my head to look beyond the cemetery as I had so many months before. . . .